A·W·O·L
LAST DAY ON EARTH

Books by Andrew Lane

AWOL: *Agent Without Licence*
AWOL 2: *Last Safe Moment*
AWOL 3: *Last Boy Standing*
AWOL 4: *Last Day on Earth*

Young Sherlock Holmes
Death Cloud
Red Leech
Black Ice
Fire Storm
Snake Bite
Knife Edge
Stone Cold
Night Break

Lost Worlds
Lost Worlds
Shadow Creatures

Crusoe
Dawn of Spies
Day of Ice
Night of Terror

A·W·⊕·L

LAST DAY ON EARTH

ANDREW LANE

First published in Great Britain in 2019 by
PICCADILLY PRESS
80–81 Wimpole St, London W1G 9RE
www.piccadillypress.co.uk

A CIP catalogue record for this book is available from the British Library.

ISBN: 978-1-84812-669-5
also available as an ebook

1

This book is typeset using Atomik ePublisher
Printed and bound in Great Britain by Clays Ltd, Elcograf S.p.A.

Piccadilly Press is an imprint of Bonnier Books UK
www.bonnierbooks.co.uk

Dedicated to the fine team at Bonnier Books who have taken my words and turned them into something amazing, and something of which I am immensely proud: my editor Emma Matthewson; my copy editors Talya Baker and Anna Bowles; my publicist Tina Mories; Nick Stearn and Stuart Bache for the art; and Emily Cox and Roisin O'Shea in Marketing. Thanks, everyone.

CHAPTER ONE

'So, have you thought about what you want to do when you leave school?' said Ms Gestner.

She leaned forward, putting her elbows on the desk and resting her chin on her clasped hands, smiling reassuringly. The pose was probably supposed to look casual, but to Kieron it just felt like she was invading his personal space, so he slid his chair back slightly, hoping she wouldn't notice, or mind.

'Not really,' he said cautiously. In fact, he tried desperately to think about his future as little as he could. His mum had started asking him the same question. Telling her or Ms Gestner that his preferred career path at the moment was joining MI6 and becoming the handler and tech support for an undercover agent out in the field would sound like out-and-out fantasy. It was, however, what he seemed to be best at, based on what had happened to him over the past year. Not the kind of thing you could put on a CV though.

'Because –' her gaze flickered to the sheet of paper on the desk between them – 'I mean, your grades aren't *brilliant*. I know you've had to take some time off school and I know you're working from home at the moment because of . . . things . . .'

Thing like bullying, he thought bitterly. *Things like people calling me names, and putting dead rats in my locker 'Because emos like dead stuff.'*

'. . . But I have to say, though, that your work has improved dramatically since you stopped coming in.'

That's because I have a piece of high-tech kit that enables me to find the answer to any question within seconds, he thought. The ARCC kit that he'd been using on behalf of the British secret agents he'd met a year ago, Bex and Bradley, was really helpful for writing essays and doing maths tests. Maybe it was technically cheating, but surely it wasn't any worse than using Google or Wikipedia to find the answer to a question, and everyone did that. Even though the ARCC kit could access various secret databases and knowledge sources unavailable on the general Internet.

'We do need to try and get your grades up if you want to do anything, you know, *meaningful* with your life.' Ms Gestner shook her head slightly, without lifting it off her supporting hands. The effect was really weird, as though her head was wobbling from side to side like those silly plastic dogs some people had in the back of their cars. Kieron had to bite the inside of his cheek to stop himself from laughing.

'By *meaningful*, you mean not serving fast food or working the till in a garage on the night shift?' he said.

'You're better than that, Kieron. Some of the kids here, honestly, yes, that's all I can see them doing, but you're different. You could do great things, if only you could

2

concentrate and pull yourself together. And, you know, tidy yourself up a bit. That goth look won't help your chances.'

'Emo, not goth,' Kieron murmured.

Ms Gestner went on as if she hadn't heard. Which was probably true. 'Did you get that link I sent you – the one for the personality test that matched your personality type with the jobs that best suit you?'

'Yes.'

'Great! What did it say?'

'It told me I should be a landscape gardener.'

She frowned. 'Yes, it does that a lot, I've been told. I'm going to have to put in a complaint.' She glanced down at the sheet of paper again. 'Normally I'd be trying to push someone like you towards higher education, but I'm not sure that's the best fit in this case.' She switched her gaze back to Kieron. 'I know you're quite . . . sensitive,' she said in what she probably thought was a sympathetic, understanding voice. 'Maybe living alone in a hall of residence would be difficult for you. Then again, there are universities here in Newcastle. You could still live at home and go to lectures and tutorials every day.' She waited for a response, but Kieron didn't know what to say, so she continued, 'Media studies, maybe? Or something more technical? Game design? I know you kids love your games.'

He shrugged. 'Actually, I was talking to Sam. Sam Rosenfeld. He and I thought we might be able to set up a computer-repair company.'

Yes, his brain said while he was speaking, like the scrolling headline subtitles you saw on TV news channels, *but that*

3

was if we couldn't get jobs with MI6 – or maybe it could even be our cover story if we did!

'We're both really good at fixing computers, and tablets, and mobile phones,' he went on, doing his best to ignore the voice in his head. He could hear himself speeding up and getting louder as his mind realised it was in comfortable territory. 'And most technical problems are really simple, like replacing a cracked screen, or updating device drivers, or doing a virus check. People don't realise that.'

'There, you see!' Ms Gestner leaned back and clapped her hands together. 'You *do* know what you want to do! Maybe I'd be your first customer. I see those "upgrade" messages on the screen sometimes and I haven't got a clue what they mean.' She glanced around. 'I've got some packs somewhere on how you can set up your own company. You'll need a bank account, of course, and somewhere to work out of – a little unit on an industrial estate, maybe. A logo is really important, and you'll need an Internet presence so people can find you. Oh, and you'll need to be able to drive, because you'll probably have to collect people's PCs and deliver them back again, or visit people at their own homes or offices. Let me gather some stuff and I'll put it in your pigeonhole later.'

Kieron began to panic. He could feel his heart begin to race, and there was a fluttering in his chest, as if something with wings was trapped in there and trying to get out. He hated it when things went too fast for him. 'Thanks,' he said. 'I'll check it out. Er – is there anything else?'

'No. Thanks for coming in.' She smiled at him, but she

looked uncertain. 'Kieron – can I ask: how long have you been wearing glasses? It's just that I don't remember seeing them before. And is that a . . . a hearing aid?'

For a second he froze. In fact, he didn't need glasses at all, and his hearing was perfect, but it had become second nature to him to wear the special ARCC glasses and the wireless earpiece. It wasn't that he expected to be on call all the time to support Bex in some undercover secret-agent adventure; it was just that he felt like a stronger person with them than without. The glasses were a barrier he could hide behind, and he thought the earpiece made him look more tech-savvy and important, as if he had a career and lots of money, and people who might call him at any moment. Together they were like a mask he could wear to face the world. He was grown-up enough to know that this was just the last vestige of the dressing-up phase that all kids go through, but he also knew that it was *real*. The glasses and earpiece weren't fake; they connected him with a real world of adventure and excitement – a world where he could make a difference.

'It's . . . like a sociology project,' he said lamely. 'I'm trying to see if people get treated differently when they have an obvious impediment, like bad eyesight or a problem with their hearing.'

'Oh,' she said. 'Well, good. Let me know how it goes.'

'I will,' he said, and turned away before she could ask any more difficult questions.

Sam was outside the door to Mrs Gestner's office. The corridor was busy – the bell for the end of school had rung while Kieron had been talking with her.

'How did that go?' he asked.

'What's the phrase the politicians use on the news? It went "as well as could be expected".'

Sam nodded. 'Landscape gardener then?'

'No, actually I told her about the plan to start our own IT repair company. She's totally on board.'

'It's my turn tomorrow morning. I'll probably get the same spiel. Still, if she can help, then we shouldn't turn her down.'

Kieron opened his mouth to respond, but before he could say anything he felt someone shove him between the shoulder blades. He stumbled forward, and would have fallen if Sam hadn't caught him. He turned, ready to lash out, but the kid with the close-cropped blond hair who'd pushed him was already continuing on down the corridor.

'Why don't you two get a room?' the kid said over his shoulder, still walking.

'Stupid emos,' a girl muttered to her friend as they passed by. 'I hate them.'

'That's OK,' Sam called to her. 'We'll still pray to our Dark Satanic Lord to look after your souls.'

The girls just wrinkled their noses and walked away.

'I see things haven't changed much,' Kieron said as Sam pushed him back upright.

'Oh, it's got worse, if anything. And the teachers still haven't worked out that the bullies do whatever they do quietly, while their backs are turned, but if we respond then the bullies make lots of noise and make out they've been hurt, and it looks like we were the ones who kicked off.'

''Twas ever thus,' Kieron said.

Sam looked at him blankly. 'What?'

'I dunno. I just read it somewhere.' He sighed. 'Where do you want to go?'

'Coffee?'

'You mean some kind of huge ice-based drink with two shots of espresso somewhere at the bottom, filled with caramel syrup and topped with whipped cream?'

Sam nodded. 'And sprinkles. You up for it?'

'Absolutely.'

They got the bus into the city centre to the cafe that had become their new favourite haunt. Part of that was guilt, because they'd been passingly responsible for the bomb that had gone off nearby a few weeks back, but part of it was because Kieron had started a relationship with Beth, one of the baristas who worked there. He wasn't sure what kind of relationship it was – so far they'd just wandered around a bookshop, seen a movie together and held hands once or twice for a few moments – but it was definitely something.

Beth was clearing tables when they got to the cafe, but she smiled at Kieron in a way that made him feel like his insides were melting.

'I wish someone would smile at me like that,' Sam muttered.

'What happened to that girl you were seeing?'

Sam looked away. 'Yeah, turned out that rugby players were more her type. The last time I tried to play rugby I ended up face down in the mud with someone's boot in the

7

small of my back pushing me down. I nearly drowned.'
He frowned. 'Or suffocated. I dunno with mud. It could
be either.'

'Or both. You go and bag a table. I'll get the order in.'

Kieron gave their order to the barista at the counter, then
collected the drinks and brought them over to the table. Sam
nodded his approval. 'Sprinkles. That's good.' He took a
chunk of whipped cream and sprinkles off the top of his drink
and transferred it to his mouth with the long spoon that only
specialist coffee places seemed to buy. 'That *is* good. Seen
anything of Bex and Bradley since we got back from Norway?'

Kieron let the words roll around his brain for a few
moments. *Since we got back from Norway.* And before
that, Venice. And before that, America. Who would have
guessed a year ago that he would be so well travelled in such
a short time, and would have had so many adventures? And
would have risked his life so many times?

Fingers brushed the back of his neck. He looked around,
startled. Beth was just walking away from the table with
a tray of crockery precariously held in one hand and the
other hand suspiciously free. He smiled at her again, and
she smiled back.

'They've been keeping quiet,' he said. 'They do this, after a
mission. They just hunker down and recover from what went
on. I guess they have to submit reports and stuff as well.'

'Bradley's taken Courtney out on a couple of dates,'
Sam sniffed. 'From what she's told Mum, she likes him a
lot. I just hope he's not going to hurt her. She's got a habit
of picking the wrong bloke.'

'Bradley's one of the good guys,' Kieron said firmly. 'And from what I've seen, he's really fond of her too. I'm sure he'll be good to her.'

'He'd better,' Sam said darkly.

'I thought you didn't really get on with your sisters.'

'Doesn't matter. They're family. Nobody messes with family.'

Kieron was about to tease his friend for being old-fashioned when something across the cafe caught his attention. Not some*thing* – some*one*. Someone he recognised. 'Oh hell,' he muttered.

'What is it?' Sam asked.

Kieron winced, and looked away. 'It's my mum,' he said. 'And she's with a man.'

'Wow!' Sam turned to look. 'Where?'

'*Don't draw attention to us!*' Kieron hissed, keeping his head down and turning away. 'Maybe it's her new boss,' he muttered hopefully. 'Yes, that must be it. He's her boss, and they've come out for a coffee so he can do her staff evaluation in private, or something.'

'I don't think so. They've got their heads close together.' Sam sounded like he was enjoying himself. 'That's a good sign. Well, good for her. Bad for you, I guess. He's very distinguished – got a touch of grey hair at his temples. And he's quite smart as well. No jeans, no T-shirt and no obvious tattoos. Chinos and a decent jacket. Good shoes as well – not trainers. He's got some class. You're going to have to up your game, mate.'

'Just stop it!' Kieron pleaded, slumping further down

in his chair and wishing he was dead. Or somewhere else. Or both.

Sam continued relentlessly. 'She's smiling at him. She's obviously made an effort – make-up and nails too, it looks like. She might have had her hair done as well. Ooh!'

'What?' Kieron asked, eyes closed. He didn't want to know, but he *had* to know. Dark fascination dragged him on.

'He's just reached out and put his hand over hers, and she's not pulling away. Or slapping him, which is what happened to me the last time I tried to put my hand on a girl's. Well, to be fair, it wasn't her hand, it was her waist, but the important thing is that I got slapped. Well, not slapped exactly– she kneed me in the groin. But her message was clear.'

'Can we just go?' Kieron pleaded.

'No, this is far too much fun.'

'Has she seen you yet? Or me?'

'No, she's too busy gazing into his eyes. And he's gazing into her eyes as well. That's probably a good thing. It would be awkward if she was gazing deeply into his eyes and he was looking at someone else.'

'You're just torturing me now.'

Sam snickered. 'Too right, mate.' He made a sudden surprised sound. 'Ooh! I wasn't expecting that!'

Kieron groaned. How much worse could this get? 'What's he done? Don't tell me he's proposed? He has, hasn't he? He's whipped a ring out and he's proposing!'

'No – it's worse than that. Your girlfriend's stopped by that table, and she's talking to them.' He laughed. 'That's

10

brilliant – your girlfriend and your mum, talking, and neither of them knows who the other one is. And your mum's got her new boyfriend with her, and she doesn't know *you*'re here! This is priceless!'

Kieron wished that a gateway to damnation would open up beneath him and swallow him up. Surely the eternal fires of hell would be a comfort compared to the agony he was going through.

'OK, she's moved away. She was just checking to see if they needed their table cleared.'

'Phew!' Kieron felt his tensed muscles relax.

'Whoops,' Sam said.

'What?'

'Your mum's just seen us.'

Kieron rearranged his face into a smile that probably looked as fixed and unreal as the Joker's smile in *Batman*, and turned his head to look.

His mum and her – boyfriend? – were sitting in a booth by the wall. It did seem like she'd made an effort to look nice, but the effect was ruined by the fact she'd gone pale on seeing Sam and Kieron. Sam waved. Kieron's mum waved back, but weakly.

Her lips moved. She was still looking at him in surprise – maybe even shock – but her words were probably directed at the man sitting opposite her. Kieron wasn't sure, but he thought she said, 'Oh my God, that's my son over there!'

The look of shock on her face vanished, replaced by a smile too wide to be genuine. She beckoned Kieron over.

'Wish me luck,' Kieron muttered to Sam as he stood up.

'If you're not back in three weeks,' Sam muttered back, 'I'm sending in the Marines.'

Kieron picked his way past several tables. He could feel his feet dragging; he really didn't want to have this conversation. Not if the man was who he thought he was. Not an employer, or a work colleague. A boyfriend. Or, at the very least, a date.

His mum stood up as he got there and gave him a quick kiss on the cheek. 'Kieron, what are you doing here? I thought you were meant to be going into school for a careers chat?'

'I finished the meeting. Sam and I thought we'd come here for a coffee.'

She sighed. 'Coffee. It wasn't that long ago that all you wanted to drink was milkshakes.'

Kieron glanced back at the two massive, cream-and-sprinkle-topped, syrup-filled drinks in front of Sam. 'They might just as well be milkshakes,' he said. 'They're just as sweet. But what about you? I thought you were at work. I mean, if this is a work meeting then I'll leave you to it.' He was pretty sure it wasn't, but he had to try.

'Actually,' his mum said, 'since I'm on flexitime I thought I'd take the afternoon off.' He saw her swallow nervously. 'Kieron, this is Tyler.'

Kieron turned to the man in the other chair, who stood up and extended a hand. 'Hi,' he said. His voice was deep, and his tone warm and friendly. 'I've heard a lot about you, Kieron.'

He was taller than Kieron, with huge hands. Kieron tried to squeeze as hard as he could, but he had a feeling that Tyler could have broken his fingers if he'd wanted to.

'Whatever you've heard, it's not true,' he said.

Tyler laughed as he sat back down. 'Actually, your mum's very proud of you. She's only got good things to say about you.'

'So . . .' Kieron said, then forced the words out, 'how do you two know each other?'

Tyler looked at Kieron's mum, who was still standing up as well, letting her answer.

'We met – erm, online,' she said.

'Online?' Kieron had to stifle a laugh. 'Mum, you can hardly check your emails without crashing your laptop.'

'Actually,' she said primly, 'I'm better at computers than you think. But yes. I've been –' she swallowed again, and continued in a quieter voice – 'on an online dating site. Tyler saw my details and got in touch a few weeks ago. He invited me out for a coffee, and I said yes.'

Kieron opened his mouth to say something, although he wasn't sure what, but before he could work it out Tyler stood up and interrupted, saying, 'I'll just head to the bathroom. Back in a few minutes.' He moved past Kieron, towards the door beside the counter.

'That was very tactful,' Kieron observed.

'He is tactful. And very nice.' His mum looked embarrassed. 'Look, I should have told you,' she said, 'warned you in advance. It's just that . . . I didn't know how you'd react. I mean, I know you're not that fond of your father, but he *is* your father, and I'm not looking to replace him or anything . . . It's just that I realised I was lonely, and I needed a man in my life. Another man,

I mean. You're nearly a man.' She closed her eyes. 'I'm babbling, aren't I?'

'Wonderfully.' Kieron gave her a quick hug. 'Mum, it's your life and you can do whatever you want with it. And Tyler seems nice. I hope he makes you happy.'

She smiled in relief. 'Thank you. That means a lot.'

'Just keep the noise down when he comes round to the house.'

Kieron's mum punched him softly in the shoulder. 'Hey, don't be cheeky.'

'What does Tyler do?'

'He's a chef. He's actually the head chef in a hotel restaurant in the centre of town. He told me he trained under Marco Pierre White, and he's worked on several big cruise ships.' She sounded proud. 'Apparently, on the cruise ships they have a refrigerated storage cabin the size of this place just for their grapefruits! Imagine!'

'That's brilliant.' Kieron was about to say he was going back to his and Sam's table when he felt the warmth of a hand touch his. It wasn't his mum. He turned his head and saw Beth standing beside him, smiling.

'Hi!' Beth said brightly. 'You must be Kieron's mum!'

'Yes.' Kieron's mum looked confused.

'I'm Beth. Kieron probably hasn't mentioned me – you know what men are like. We're kind of seeing each other. I just thought I'd introduce myself, because I know he wasn't going to do it for me.' She turned towards Kieron and kissed him briefly on the cheek. 'Call me, babe,' she said, then smiled at him, smiled at his mum, and walked away.

'Something you want to tell me?' Kieron's mum said, staring after Beth with a surprised expression.

'Absolutely nothing at all,' Kieron said. He glanced over to his table, where Sam was giving him a big thumbs up. 'I'm thinking we're going to be having a long talk tonight, aren't we?'

'Oh yes.' She suddenly ruffled his hair. 'But we're both going to have a glass of wine in our hands.'

'Actually, can I have amaretto? It tastes like marzipan.'

'No. Just wine. And just one glass.'

'Fair enough. See you later,' Kieron said. 'Have fun. Don't stay out too late.' Before his mum could come back with a retort he'd started to walk back across the cafe, aware that Tyler was just emerging from the bathroom.

'That was embarrassing for so many reasons,' Sam said as Kieron re-joined him.

'You and I need to get our own flat as soon as possible,' Kieron told him. 'My place is starting to get a bit too small.'

'Agreed. Well, with your landscape gardener's salary, you'll be able to afford it.'

Kieron noticed that his mum and Tyler had stood up and were putting their coats on. He was sorry he'd made them so uncomfortable, but he was also relieved. This was his cafe, his territory. Well, his and Sam's. And Beth's.

This was getting complicated. Was adult life like this all the time? If so, he didn't like it.

His mum waved goodbye as she and Tyler reached the door, and he waved back. Tyler nodded at him in a friendly way.

15

'Shall we stay here and have enough coffee to make us twitch, or shall we wander across town and see what's going on at the flat?' Sam asked.

'I hate it when I've had too much caffeine. Let's go see Bex and Bradley.'

The apartment wasn't that far away; still in the centre of Newcastle but in a side street away from the noise and crowds. Like the last place the two agents had rented – which had been destroyed by a bomb contained in a drone – the building was a converted warehouse with crumbling brickwork, dating back a couple of hundred years. Kieron sometimes thought he could smell the lingering remnants of tobacco floating through the air. Inside, however, all the apartments were modern and open plan, like the kind you saw on American TV.

A woman was leaving just as the two boys arrived. She smiled briefly at them as they passed her in the corridor.

Bex and Bradley were sitting in the living area, Bex on the sofa and Bradley in an easy chair, when Kieron and Sam entered the flat. Bex sprang to her feet as they came in. Bradley tried to do the same, but Bex waved him back. He slumped into the chair again with a sigh of relief. The glasses and Bluetooth earpiece that formed his part of the ARCC kit sat on the arm of the chair beside his elbow.

Kieron took his ARCC glasses and earpiece off and put them on the low coffee table in front of the sofa, then he and Sam sat down at the dining table.

'Guys, we haven't seen you for a while. Are you OK?'

'We're fine,' Kieron said, worried. 'Who was that? One of your bosses from MI6? Does she know about us?'

'That was my doctor,' Bradley replied. 'I don't know if you remember, but Bex arranged for her to come around before we all went off to Venice. The poor woman's been trying to get me back on my feet since . . .' He trailed off, waving a hand vaguely, but Bex filled in for him.

'Since he got beaten up by those fascist bloody thugs from Blood and Soil.'

'I thought you were getting better,' Sam said, frowning in concern.

'He was,' Bex said, 'but Venice set him back.'

'Well, being chased by men with guns, then being shoved, soaking wet, into a rackety old van and then a helicopter, and flown up to the Arctic will do that to you.' He looked at Bex and shrugged. 'Only saying, that's all. I'm meant to be the one who sits in an air-conditioned location with a nice cool drink while you risk your life. It's not working out that way. I want danger money.'

'Actually,' Bex said, 'any money would be welcome at the moment.' She glanced at Kieron and Sam. 'This place isn't exactly cheap, and we didn't have a customer for the Venice mission. That was just us trying to find out who wanted to kill us.'

Bradley nodded. 'Which is good business practice, by the way. Always avoid getting killed, if you can. Then you're open to take on any job that comes up.'

'But no jobs are coming up?' Kieron ventured. 'That's the problem, isn't it?'

Bex sat down on the wide, padded arm of the sofa. 'We're not sure why, but MI6 have stopped sending us work. We think it might be because the agent Blood and Soil have got inside the organisation is trying to cut us off – isolate us and render us vulnerable so that they can take action against us.'

'But you know who it is, don't you?' Sam said.

'Avalon Richardson.' Bex paused, biting her lip. 'She's a mid-grade MI6 analyst. I met her a couple of times, when Bradley and I were first recruited as freelance contractors. She was our handler for a while, before she got promoted. I would never have pegged her for a double agent or a traitor. She always seemed so . . . normal. Like a librarian.'

'Oh, I've dated some librarians,' Bradley said. 'Don't underestimate them. Hidden depths, and all that.'

'Moving on,' Bex said swiftly, 'getting enough evidence to identify the traitor who wants us dead is one thing; getting enough evidence to convict her is another.'

Kieron frowned. 'But I thought the Norwegian police passed her name on to MI6. Isn't that enough for them to suspend her and start an investigation, especially if you and Bradley put in a complaint about her?'

'There are probably a lot of Avalon Richardsons in the world,' Bradley said. 'As far as MI6 are concerned, any one of them could have hired the Norwegian girls. And anyway, someone hacked the Italian police records. The name "Avalon Richardson" vanished, replaced with "Rebecca Wilson".'

Kieron and Sam both looked at Bex, shocked.

'She put your name in instead of hers?' Sam breathed. 'Oh, that's cold. Really cold.'

'I removed it straight away,' Bradley went on, 'but there was no point putting her name back in. Good as I am, I would have left traces. It would have looked as if someone was trying to frame Avalon Richardson, which is the last thing we want.'

'So,' Bex continued, 'we're stuck. We were just talking about what to do next when the doctor arrived.'

'Talking of which,' Kieron said, heading over to sit down on the other end of the sofa to Bex, 'how are you?'

Bradley shrugged. 'Tired and battered, but there's no obvious physical damage. The concussion has gone now. The trouble is –' and he looked away from Kieron, embarrassed – 'look, to be honest, I've apparently been left with an inability to wear or use the ARCC kit for more than a few minutes at a time. The doctor isn't sure whether it's something neurological or psychological or whether it's permanent or will wear off. She's suggested having a brain scan done, but that would have to be private rather than on the NHS, and we can't afford it at the moment.'

'You didn't tell her what the ARCC kit does, did you?' Sam asked.

Bex shook her head. 'No. We said it was a virtual-reality gaming system we were developing . . .'

'So you need work, but MI6 won't give you any, and even if they did you wouldn't be able to do it anyway,' Kieron summarised. 'That's not a good position to be in.'

'Any and all suggestions welcomed,' Bex sighed. 'With the exception of you boys replacing Bradley. As we've said before, we can't risk your lives like that.'

Sam looked from one to the other. 'There's always landscape gardening,' he pointed out.

Bradley opened his mouth to say something sarcastic, but a *bing* from his ARCC earpiece interrupted him. He reached for the glasses. Sam stepped forward, but Bradley waved him away. 'I'm OK for a little while,' he said. 'The headaches only kick in after about three minutes.' He slipped the glasses on and the earpiece in. Kieron watched as his hands moved through the air, manipulating menus, screens and buttons that were visible only to him, projected into his eyes by the hidden technology in the glasses. 'Ah,' he said after a few seconds. Then, 'Oh.'

'What is it?' Bex asked, standing up in concern.

'It's a secure email from MI6. They want us to come in for a face-to-face meeting.' He took the glasses off and stared at Bex. His expression was serious. 'And the email is from Avalon Richardson.'

CHAPTER TWO

Next day, Bex and Bradley hired a nondescript car and headed off to the meeting with Avalon Richardson. It was being held in a location between Reading and London, just off the M4 motorway. According to Google Maps it was just a patch of open ground, covering several square miles, with no buildings or roads. *Odd*, Bex thought. She'd expected the meeting to be in the MI6 headquarters on the banks of the Thames at Vauxhall, made famous by the James Bond films that MI6 agents simultaneously loved and hated.

'What do you think this meeting is about?' Bradley asked during one of their frequent breaks.

'I'm not sure.' She shrugged. 'The email didn't give away many details. On the surface it's probably going to be a review of the work we've done recently and a discussion about where we go next. Underneath that, I reckon it's going to be Avalon trying to find out how much we know about her and her links to Blood and Soil.'

Bradley frowned. 'Is there any chance she's found out about Kieron and Sam?'

Bex considered for a few moments. 'I don't think so,' she answered eventually. 'If MI6 knew we've been using two teenagers with no security clearance for top-secret work, they'd have fired us straight away. Even if they didn't prosecute us under the Official Secrets Act or just make us quietly vanish. No, I think we're clear on that score.' She sighed. 'I really just think this is a fishing expedition on Avalon's part.'

'It could be another attempt to get us out of the way,' Bradley pointed out. 'Bombing our apartment didn't work, so maybe she's luring us to some out-of-the-way location so she can have us quietly killed. Or even not-so-quietly, given how isolated it is.'

'Again, I don't think so. MI6 seemed to buy it when we told them the police thought it was a gas leak at the flat – I mean, that was actually true. But any more attempts on our lives and Avalon's bosses are going to get suspicious, which she won't want. She'll be thinking that if we *do* suspect her, we've got information – and will have briefed people to send it in if we turn up dead.'

'Did we do that?' Bradley asked. 'I don't remember doing that. Although it actually sounds like a good idea.'

'Well, in a sense, we did. Kieron and Sam won't let it rest if we don't come back. They'll get word covertly to Avalon's bosses, and name her. No, the more I think about it, the more sure I am that she won't risk direct action.'

At the next stop, near Oxford, Bradley asked, 'Are we going to explain about my . . . you know, problems? I mean, if I can't do the work, then they're not going to employ us any more, but if they *do* employ us then I can't do the work. It's a vicious circle, as Kieron pointed out.'

Bex took a sip of her coffee. Thinking about what might happen if Bradley didn't recover made her panicky every time. She wasn't normally the nervous type, but then she could usually see a way out of bad situations. But with Bradley like this, it was all so uncertain. She didn't *want* a new partner, but she might have to consider it. It wasn't like they could swap places – she was the one with all the undercover training and experience. In the meantime, she had to keep Bradley's spirits up. If he *was* going to recover, then he'd need all the positive energy he could muster. So . . .

'No,' she said, with as much firmness as she could manage, 'we keep quiet about your condition. Hopefully you'll recover before long, and we'll be able to work like we used to. Until then . . .'

When she didn't go on, he finished her sentence. 'We use the uncleared teenagers and hope nobody realises, and nothing bad happens to them.'

'Yes. It's a plan. I'm not saying it's a *good* plan, but it's a plan.'

Bradley was silent for a while, then said, 'Do you think it's all in my mind, Bex? Not being able to use the ARCC kit. I mean, the doctor can't find any physical problems. Maybe . . .' He hesitated. 'Maybe I'm just, you know, scared. Maybe my brain won't let me use the kit because it thinks the job is too dangerous for me. Maybe I've burned out. Agents do – one minute they're on the MI6 roster and the next they've been taken off as if they never existed.'

She shook her head firmly, if only as a way of trying to convince herself. 'I don't believe that for a second, and if you weren't so affected by this then you wouldn't believe it either. There *is* a physical problem at the bottom of it all, and we're going to find out what it is.'

'If it kills us,' he said.

'Well, hopefully it won't be necessary to go that far.'

The last leg of the journey took them along the M4. Just before Reading the route planner on Bradley's phone directed them to take a junction that didn't actually exist. As they approached the place they were supposed to turn off, Bradley said, 'What do we do? I mean, there's been no signs for any junction. We can't just come off on the hard shoulder – can we?'

Bex was just about to answer when they saw a sign showing a side road coming off the motorway. 'Service Road Only' it said, in red letters.

'That just means some kind of construction site. Building a new road or something,' she pointed out.

'Yes . . .' Bradley sounded intrigued. 'But that sign's dusty and rain-streaked. It's been there for years.' He pointed off to his left, where the side road curved away from the motorway. 'And look – there's lights on poles along there. Since when did a service road leading to a construction site have proper lights? Usually they're temporary things on masts powered by a generator.'

'Let's find out.' Bex slowed down, turned the wheel and took the car down the service road. She'd expected it to be bumpy, but it was properly tarmacked.

She followed the road over a bank of earth, putting them out of sight of the motorway.

A minute or so later, they found themselves approaching a checkpoint with a barrier. A uniformed security guard waved them to a stop while a second one stood nearby, watching. Bex couldn't help noticing the diagonal straps across their chests. They were both well-built, muscular, with close-cropped hair and faded blue eyes. Special Forces operatives on secondment to MI6, probably.

'I bet they've got semi-automatic weapons behind their backs,' she said as she gradually braked.

'I'm not taking that bet,' Bradley said.

The first security guard moved closer, while his companion stayed put, one hand held behind his back so he could bring his weapon into play if Bex or Bradley made the slightest suspicious move. 'Are you lost, ma'am?' he asked after Bex had wound her window down.

'We have a meeting,' Bex said. She gestured past the barrier. 'Somewhere that way.'

The guard nodded, unsurprised. Presumably this happened a fair amount. 'Names?'

'Rebecca Wilson and Bradley Marshall.'

He must have had the list of expected visitors already memorised, because he just said, 'That's fine. Are you OK if I do a retinal scan?'

'No problems,' she said.

As the guard unclipped a small device from his belt, Bradley muttered, 'What would happen if it *wasn't* OK with us?'

'Shut up,' she hissed.

The guard held up a small device like a mobile phone. 'Please stare into the lens,' he said. Bex obeyed. A bright flash obscured her vision for a moment. As it was fading into a green patch, then a smaller red patch, she heard the guard say, 'Identity confirmed. Now you, sir.'

'If I must,' Bradley said, lowering the window on his side.

Another flash, and: 'Your identity is confirmed as well. Thank you. Please keep driving for a mile, then park in the area indicated. Someone will be there to meet you.'

The barrier rose, and Bex slowly drove onwards, smiling at the guard as the car passed him by. He didn't smile back. From what Bex knew of Special Forces operatives, he would have that same uninterested expression on his face if he was shooting someone. Even just off the M4 motorway.

The road led in a gradual curve across the countryside. Wild grasses grew to head height on either side, seedpods bobbing on top of the long stems like tiny heads, shielding from view whatever was beyond them. After a few minutes the road widened out into a car park. Maybe twenty cars were there, along with two coaches – all relatively common, relatively anonymous brands of vehicle.

'It's not like the movies, where secret agents drive Aston Martins, Lotus Esprits and Ferraris,' Bradley lamented. 'Ours is the best car here, and it's a rented Skoda!'

Bex found a convenient spot and parked. As they got out, she noticed in the distance a set of buildings – two storeys, with tiled roofs. They looked just like houses, as if a modern estate had been plonked down in the middle of nowhere.

A soldier in camouflage gear emerged from the grasses beside them, his weapon in full view. The pretence was gone now – they were in a secret establishment, with the guards to prove it.

The soldier indicated a path that led through the grasses towards the housing estate. 'Please follow the marked route.'

'Did I mention,' Bradley muttered as they entered what was almost a tunnel of grass, with the seedpods on top seeming to bend towards them, 'that I get hay fever?'

'Only several thousand times since I met you. Try not to sneeze. You might set one of the guards off, and I don't mean with an asthma attack.'

Two more soldiers stood at the end of the path, but Bex was more interested in the buildings. Yes, they were houses, but now she and Bradley were closer she could see they were empty inside, with holes where the windows would have been. There was no variation – every house had been painted the same colour. Some of them had children's toys and play equipment scattered in the small front gardens, where the grass had been cut short, but they looked like they'd never been used. The whole place had an eerie, unreal atmosphere, like a film set.

'You hear about villages out on Salisbury Plain that were taken over by the Army during World War Two for training, and the inhabitants relocated,' Bradley murmured. 'Is this one of them?'

'It looks like something similar,' Bex said, 'but the buildings are too new for it to be an old village. And there's no sign that anyone ever lived here. No, this place was built specially.'

'What for?' he asked.

'I'm not sure,' she said.

One of the soldiers gestured towards the empty buildings. 'Number forty-seven, Lapwing Crescent,' he said. 'Go down Sparrow, then right into Falcon and left into Lapwing. She's waiting for you.' He stepped towards them and held out two yellow laminated cards on yellow lanyards. 'Wear these. They'll tell everyone you're off limits.'

'Off limits to what?' Bradley asked as he took the lanyards, but the soldier just stepped back.

Cars were parked along the main road into the village, but they looked like they'd been bought at a breaker's yard and towed to where they now rested. Several of them had flat tyres, and one was missing a door.

'Burn marks on the tarmac,' Bradley observed as they walked along the pleasantly named Sparrow Road. He handed Bex her yellow card and lanyard.

'But no burnt-out cars,' Bex replied, slipping the lanyard over her neck. In fact, the cars that were there had mostly been placed over the burnt areas. 'This must be a riot training area for MI6. Agents working undercover in some countries – usually the Eastern European ones – get caught up in riots sometimes. They probably train here so they know what it feels like to actually be in the middle of one. It's not a pleasant experience, having police using water cannons against you, and petrol bombs going off. If you've never been through it, then you might freeze, but if you've had the training then you can think more rationally about ways out.'

'So they fake riots. With what, Army regiments providing the fake rioters and fake police?'

'Pretty much,' Bex said, trying to imagine the street filled with rioters throwing rocks, bricks and petrol bombs, and soldiers trying to force them back. She'd never been in that kind of situation herself, and she never wanted to be.

They came to the junction and turned right into Falcon Road. The street was as empty as the one before, and the air was just as still, just as silent, but to Bex it felt like an *expectant* silence, as if something was about to happen. Like the moment between an orchestra conductor raising his baton to start an overture and bringing it down to trigger the musicians. She checked over her shoulder. She couldn't see anyone watching them, but she had a feeling they were being observed nevertheless. Probably security cameras everywhere. 'It would be fun for them,' she added. 'Infantrymen always like a good punch-up.'

She glanced at the houses as they passed. Some of them had doors and some didn't, but the ones that were there looked like they'd received a lot of abuse over the years. Most of them had heel marks where they'd been kicked in, or dents in the wood, and some of them were hanging off one hinge.

Some of the walls had red streaks on them. For a second she thought it was blood, then she realised there was a more likely answer.

'Ah – lipstick rounds,' she said.

'What?' Bradley glanced at her, confused.

She nodded towards the marks. 'Lipstick rounds. Bullets made out of the same material as lipsticks. They can't kill you, because they disintegrate if they hit you straight on, but they hurt, and they leave a mark. Obviously they don't want to use proper ammunition here. Too dangerous.'

'Except that I can see bullet holes,' Bradley said. 'Look over there at number 12, and there at number 16. They've been filled in with mortar, but they're there. Some of these cars have got bullet holes in the doors. And that one – the windscreen has a hole through it. They must use live rounds sometimes.' He tapped the yellow card hanging around his neck 'I'm glad we've got these. I'm guessing they give us free passage. Anyone wearing one of these is safe from the riot.'

They turned again, left this time, into Lapwing Crescent. Again there was nobody around. It was like the end of the world had occurred and nobody had told them.

'It's like a zombie computer game,' Bradley murmured.

'I'll take your word for it,' Bex replied. She wasn't a gamer, but suddenly she couldn't shake the mental image of dead bodies suddenly appearing in the shadowed doorways and stumbling towards them, arms outstretched. 'You couldn't have just kept that thought inside, could you?' she added. 'You had to say it.'

Number 47 was located about halfway around the crescent. They hesitated in the gateway, waiting to see if anything happened, if anyone appeared, but all was silent. Not necessarily peaceful – the sense of imminent danger pervaded everything – but quiet.

'Here goes,' Bex said, and walked into the shadows of the dead house.

The hallway was illuminated by a bare bulb hanging from the ceiling, and the walls were streaked with the red slashes of lipstick rounds. Ahead of her she saw a kitchen area; to her left, stairs leading upwards; to her right, a doorway. And behind her, Bradley.

She went right, into what she assumed was a living room.

Avalon Richardson sat in the centre of the room, behind a large oak desk that looked massively out of place in that small suburban house. She wore a sharp business suit, and her hair was piled up in an elaborate hairdo. She was older than Bex remembered, and less mousy. She looked every inch the professional MI6 officer, right down to the top-of-the-range laptop on the desk in front of her. A yellow badge hung from her neck on a lanyard. Two men in dark suits stood behind her, also wearing yellow badges. *They* looked every inch the professional MI6 bodyguards. Bex knew that fifteen seconds after leaving the room she wouldn't be able to remember their faces. But they would remember hers, and Bradley's.

'Thank you for making the journey, Rebecca,' Avalon Richardson said calmly. 'Please, come in. And you, Bradley. I'm Avalon.'

Bex noticed there were no seats in the room apart from the one Avalon sat in. This, then, was what the military called 'an interview without coffee'. She and Bradley were meant to feel uncomfortable.

'I apologise for my hair,' Avalon said, 'but there's an event I've got to be at tonight, and it's posh. Never mind.' She smiled, and glanced from Bex to Bradley and back. 'So – I thought it was time we got together and compared notes on your work for the SIS Technology-Enhanced Remote Reinforcement unit. How are things going? How are you finding your work?'

'Wonderful,' Bex answered. 'We've been kept busy, but the jobs have been interesting.'

'And you've done very well,' Avalon said. She consulted something on the screen in front of her. 'The Mumbai mission went off in an unexpected direction, but you coped admirably, and bringing Todd Zanderbergen down provided Her Majesty's Government with a lot of points on the international stage. It's always good to have leverage with our American cousins, and they were very embarrassed by Zanderbergen's unauthorised activities.'

'That's good to know,' Bex said neutrally.

'When you were in India,' Avalon continued casually, 'did you get involved with any other groups? We know, for instance, that a billionaire entrepreneur named Anoup Patel had people in the area as well. We're very interested in his activities.'

Bex remembered Anoup Patel clearly, but she wasn't going to admit it. He was a philanthropist who was trying to rid the world of weapons of mass destruction by collecting them himself, but working with him had been nothing to do with MI6, and completely at odds with what Blood and Soil wanted. 'Was it his people who took the briefcase I was meant to be watching?' she asked, hoping her face didn't give anything away.

'No,' Avalon said. 'What about any . . . other groups?'

Bex shook her head. 'Not that I remember.'

Bex thought she could hear a noise outside the house, although she wasn't sure what it was. Voices, perhaps.

Avalon's eyes narrowed slightly, an indication that she didn't believe the answer she'd been given. 'We received intelligence that a . . . fascist group were in Mumbai at the same time. Did you see any of them?'

Bex shook her head, trying to look innocent. 'No. Maybe they were there on holiday.'

Avalon looked at her screen again. 'And the Zanderbergen mission, in America. Did you take anyone else with you?'

'Just me,' Bex lied. She felt a shiver run through her. Avalon obviously had some inkling that Kieron and Sam had been involved, but not enough to confront Bex directly. 'I remember there were a couple of English kids staying in the same hotel,' she went on, as if the thought had only just occurred to her. 'Maybe you're thinking of them.'

'Hmmm. And what about Italy? What can you tell me about that mission?'

It was a trick question. Italy hadn't been a mission – it had been an attempt to stop the people who had been employed to kill her and Bradley. Employed by the woman sitting across the table.

Bex put on an expression of exaggerated confusion. 'There was no Italian mission. I think you must have given that to a different team.' Time to go on the attack, just a little bit. 'It must be so hard, keeping all those missions straight in your mind,' she went on with mock-sympathy. 'I don't know how you do it. It's not surprising they get mixed up sometimes.'

A smile flickered across Avalon's face, but there was no humour in it. Bex had seen the same kind of smile on crocodiles in the Florida Everglades as they drifted away from the banks towards her small, fragile boat. 'Oh, I don't get confused,' she said. 'Not ever.' She turned her penetrating gaze on Bradley. 'You've been very quiet, Bradley. How did that explosion in your apartment affect you psychologically?'

Before Bradley could answer, an electronic beeping sound from outside filled the air. Some kind of warning, perhaps? Bex glanced at the window, then at Avalon.

'Don't worry about that,' Avalon said with a dismissive wave of her hand. 'It's just one of the riot exercises starting up. We have some trainees who are being run through the experience to toughen them up. So, Bradley, your reaction to the explosion? Did it affect you badly?'

Bex felt Bradley shrug. 'It's just one of those things, isn't it? Old buildings are prone to gas leaks. I'm just glad that nobody was killed. Thank God we weren't there.'

Good answer, Bex thought.

'You don't think it was a deliberate attempt on your lives?' Avalon pressed.

'I doubt it,' Bradley said calmly. 'I mean, there was another explosion in Newcastle city centre, wasn't there? I guess there must have been some problem with the gas supply. And who knew where we were living?' He paused, then said, 'I mean, if there was some kind of terrorist threat then you would have received intelligence reports about it, wouldn't you? And you would have warned us.'

Careful. Don't push her too hard, Bex thought. She tried to project the warning telepathically though the air towards Bradley. She didn't know whether he'd picked it up or not, but he didn't say anything further.

'Perhaps we ought to get you both checked out by an MI6 doctor,' Avalon said, her expression one of exaggerated concern.

'No need,' Bex said. 'We've both been examined by an independent doctor. And don't worry, we paid for it ourselves. You won't get the bill.'

Avalon smiled thinly. 'Well, make sure you provide us with the address of the place you're living now, just for our records. Are you still in Newcastle?'

'I'll send you an email with the address,' Bex said, ignoring the question. She thought could hear shouting from outside the bare shell of the house. Shouting, and the chanting of slogans, except that she couldn't make out what was being said. And she thought she could smell smoke.

'Fine. Well, that's about all. I just wanted to touch base, make sure that you were both all right and happy.' Her face creased into a slight frown, as if she had only just remembered something trivial. 'Oh yes – while you're here, perhaps we should check over your ARCC equipment. My technicians are upstairs. They can give it a quick once-over, see if there are any little tweaks they can make to improve its efficiency.' She held out a hand expectantly. 'It won't take long.'

Bex had no intention of handing the ARCC glasses or the earpieces over to Avalon Richardson. If they were taken out of her and Bradley's sight, then the very least that would happen was that a tracking device would be hidden inside, and probably a bug as well that would send any information seen or heard by the glasses directly to Avalon. Worse: her pet technicians might be able to get into the cloud storage system the ARCC kit used, and access the files from their recent missions, and that would be a disaster. There were a lot of things there that Bex did not want Avalon to see. And if all of that wasn't enough, Bex and Bradley had designed and built that equipment themselves. The last thing they wanted was MI6 ripping off their hard work.

'Oh,' she said with exaggerated surprise, 'I'm sorry, but we didn't bring the kit with us. If we're not on a mission we keep it in secure storage, just so it doesn't get accidentally broken. If you'd said you wanted to check it over then obviously we'd have put it in the car, but we assumed you wouldn't want any covert recording devices on a top-secret MI6 site.'

'So you left it all behind?' Avalon's voice was suddenly cold.

'Yes.'

'In Newcastle?'

'Near where we're living now,' Bex said, hoping it sounded like she was being helpful without actually giving away the fact they *were* actually still in Newcastle.

'That's a shame.' Avalon looked at Bex, then Bradley, and the expression on her face was suddenly emotionless and calculating. A shiver ran down Bex's spine as she realised that Avalon was almost certainly debating whether to believe her or whether to have her bodyguards search them. And if they were searched, the kit would be found. Despite what she'd told Avalon, Bex always made sure that she had her glasses and earpiece with her. Bradley would normally carry his part of the kit with him, except that his state of health meant that Kieron currently had it, back in – yes – Newcastle.

'A shame,' Avalon said eventually. 'Well, we'll just have to make another appointment so it can be checked over.' She smiled. 'Thank you so much for coming in. I hate to hurry you out, but as I said, I have an appointment tonight. My helicopter is out back, waiting for me. So nice to see you both.'

Avalon looked down at her laptop screen. It was about as clear a dismissal as Bex had ever received.

'Thank you for your time,' she replied quietly, then turned to go. Bradley glanced at her, raised an eyebrow, and then followed her out into the hall.

Another of Avalon's black-suited bodyguards stood by the front door. He opened it for them to leave, and Bex suddenly saw what was happening outside. A crowd of men wearing balaclavas, or scarves around their faces, were running past the front garden of the house. The noise of yelling and cursing filled the air.

'Will we be OK going out there?' Bradley asked nervously as the bodyguard gestured them towards the door.

'Perfectly.' He reached up to tug at his yellow badge. 'These things will protect you. It's like being invisible. You can just walk through the crowd and it'll part in front of you and close up again behind you. You're invulnerable.'

'Presumably the rocks and the petrol bombs just bounce off us,' Bradley said, and smiled. The bodyguard didn't react.

'That's very reassuring. Thanks,' Bex said.

She and Bradley exited the house and started walking down the path towards the garden gate. The crowd of fake rioters was still running past. There must have been hundreds of them, all shouting slogans and insults. It was hard not to get spooked. Bex tried to pretend that it was all happening on a TV screen in front of her. A very big, high-definition TV screen.

A sudden explosion off to her left made her jerk her head around and stare down the street. A cloud of vapour suddenly hid the fake rioters from sight. Smoke grenades? Tear gas? Whatever it was, she was glad that she and Bradley were headed in the other direction.

With some trepidation, Bex stepped out from the relative safety of the garden and onto the pavement. The fake rioters running past her didn't even seem to notice her. The bodyguard had been right: the yellow cards and lanyards worked like some kind of protective amulet. They might just as well have been invisible.

Bradley joined her. 'This is weird,' he said. Bex almost couldn't hear him over the shouting of the crowd; she had to read his lips.

'Just walk calmly back to where we left the car,' she shouted.

Men and women ran past her, their faces – where they could be seen – distorted with rage. Most of them held sticks, stones and bricks that they waved angrily. Good actors, Bex thought – if they were acting. Maybe they just loved taking part in organised riots. They all managed to pass Bex and Bradley by without touching them, or even looking at them, like a shoal of fish detouring around a rock in the middle of a stream, or a flock of birds – sparrows or lapwings, perhaps – separating to avoid a predatory falcon. She realised then just how deliberate the naming of the roads was, and smiled bitterly. Someone had a strange sense of humour.

Bex and Bradley got to the junction of Lapwing Crescent and Falcon Road. As they turned the corner, Bex heard another explosion; nearer this time. The sides of the houses ahead of them lit up orange and red. She turned to look behind her. Someone must have thrown a petrol bomb: fire had spread out across the street between the rioters and where she assumed the soldiers were, around the curve of the crescent. Some rioters were running up to the edge of the flames and throwing stuff over the top, and towards the soldiers on the other side.

'Very realistic!' Bradley yelled.

'Too realistic for my liking!' she shouted back. 'It's a wonder nobody gets hurt!'

A passing rioter wearing a motorcycle helmet accidentally brushed her with his shoulder as he ran past. Bex turned to watch him, but something suddenly jerked her forward, almost making her fall. It took a moment to realise that

39

the first incident had been a distraction to allow someone else, passing by, to grab her badge and pull it hard. The lanyard snapped, the ends whipping against her cheeks as they were yanked away. She felt Bradley grab hold of her arm, steadying her, and she saw a flash of yellow moving away from her. It vanished as the thief merged with the crowd.

'Come close to me!' Bradley shouted. He tried to pull her nearer, so she would be protected by *his* badge, but even as she moved towards him she saw a hand snatch the laminated yellow card and pull it from his neck. He staggered to one side, tugged by the force.

Bex glanced around wildly. Both badges had gone, vanished into the morass of rioters. Avalon Richardson wanted them vulnerable, and in the middle of an increasingly dangerous situation. That had been her plan from the start!

A crackle of gunfire made her turn her head even as Bradley grabbed her arm to stop her being pulled away by the rioters. Down Falcon Road – the direction they had originally come from, before the meeting, and the direction they needed to go to get to their car – she saw a contingent of soldiers in mottled green camouflage approaching in a line. They all wore gas masks, making them look like some invading alien army, and the rioters were running away from them. The soldiers held semi-automatic rifles, which they aimed above the rioters' heads. As Bex watched, frozen with the uncertainty of what to do next, the soldiers fired again. A veil of blue smoke swirled around them; the remnant of the gunpowder that propelled the rounds.

'Lipstick rounds or real bullets?' Bradley shouted into her ear.

Bex glanced around desperately. Soldiers filled the branch of Falcon Road down which they needed to go to get to their car. The rioters occupied Lapwing Crescent, presumably facing up against another contingent of soldiers on the other side. The only way to go was down the *other* part of Falcon Road – away from their car, not towards it. She tugged at Bradley's sleeve to tell him where they were going and turned to move.

More smoke drifted across that part of the road, hiding its length, but even as she took her first step, pulling Bradley with her, an armoured riot van emerged like a whale surfacing from a cloudy sea. A protective grille covered its windscreen and it had a turret on top from which she guessed the local commander would be issuing orders.

Three directions available, and all of them blocked.

Bex froze, her brain desperately cycling through the three options and finding no way through.

Something the size and shape of a tin of beans came hurtling through the smoke. It passed over the top of the armoured van and hit the road, bouncing a few times before landing maybe twenty feet away from Bex and Bradley. It sat there for a moment, then suddenly exploded into a mass of milky white vapour that expanded towards them, hiding the armoured van from sight.

Bex opened her mouth, intending to ask if Bradley had any ideas, because she was fresh out, but before she could make a noise something seemed to rasp the back of her throat. Her nose began to tickle, then itch, and then almost immediately it was as if someone had poured vinegar inside it. She doubled up, coughing, trying to get it out of her lungs.

'Tear gas!' Bradley shouted in her ear. 'We need help!'

Bex tried to say '*From where?*', but the tear gas had made her throat close up. She could hardly breathe.

Was this it? Was this the end?

CHAPTER THREE

Kieron and Sam were at their local leisure centre when everything went wrong.

They had decided that if they were going to spend any more time helping Bex and Bradley then they needed to get fit. Also, if they wanted to seriously try to get a job in intelligence when they got older, then physical fitness was probably a good thing. There were highly fit secret agents, and there were tech nerds supporting them, but a highly fit tech nerd? That was a good thing to have on your CV. Very deployable.

'Can I help you?' the girl on the reception desk asked as they nervously approached. Human interaction wasn't something that either of them liked.

'We want to go to some kind of get-fit class,' Kieron said when it became clear that Sam wasn't going to say anything.

'OK,' the girl said. 'We've got a fully equipped fitness centre, but you'll have to have an assessment before you can use any of the kit – to stop you hurting yourselves.' She slid two leaflets across the counter. 'This will tell you the times of the assessments. Fill out the form on the back and hand them in, and we'll get you access cards.'

'That's fine,' Kieron said. 'Thanks.' He had a feeling he recognised the girl. Maybe she'd been at his school, but in a higher year than him. He didn't want to remind her that she knew him. She was already looking at him and Sam as if she was wondering if their black hair dye would wash off in the swimming pool, leaving a scummy stain around the edge. He didn't want to see her lip curl as all the memories of the stupid things Kieron had done, and the way that he'd been bullied and laughed at by pretty much everyone, flooded back to her.

'I fancy some chips,' Sam said as they turned away. 'They do great chips in the cafeteria here. With cheese melted on top. That and a frozen drink would go down great right now. And the cafeteria overlooks the swimming pool, so we can watch all the idiots mucking around and showing off.'

As they headed up the stairs towards the cafeteria and the viewing balcony, Kieron said, 'I've never really understood why they sell burgers and chips in a place that's supposed to be making people healthier. Shouldn't they be providing salads? Fruit, maybe?'

'They tried that,' Sam pointed out. 'Nobody ordered the salads or the fruit. It all had to be thrown away. Everyone complained about the absence of greasy fast food. People are strange that way.' He glanced at Kieron. 'If you want fruit or salad, make a complaint.'

'Maybe later.'

While they were sitting waiting for their food to arrive, the ARCC kit bleeped.

'It's Bex,' Kieron said to Sam as he pressed the Link button on the glasses. 'Probably giving us an update on the meeting with her boss.'

Once he had his own glasses on, a picture of what Bex was seeing through hers appeared as a semi-transparent overlay on Kieron's field of vision. It looked like Bex was in the process of pulling the glasses out of her pocket – the picture was dark for a moment, and then blurred as she swung the glasses up. He felt a momentary flash of vertigo, but it quickly faded. He'd done this enough over the past few months that he was used to it. As the picture stabilised, and the technology in the glasses compensated for the sudden change in brightness and contrast, he heard her voice in his ear saying, 'Kieron? Can you hear me?'

'Yes. Is the –'

'Listen,' she interrupted, just as he realised with horror that he was looking at a scene of chaos, with people throwing bricks and stones, the flickering orange-and-yellow glare of flames illuminating everything. 'We need help, urgently.'

'What do you want me to do?' Kieron took a deep breath, getting ready for whatever came next. He realised that Sam had straightened up in his seat and was paying attention.

'We're in some kind of agent-training place. There's a fake riot going on, but it's turned real. We need urgent help to get out.'

'OK. Wait a moment.' Kieron manipulated virtual menus and buttons projected into his eyes that only he could see, scrolling through the options and selecting what he needed by making small gestures with his fingers that the sensors in the glasses picked up.

'Right. The GPS chip in your glasses says you're in Berkshire, near the M4. The standard maps just have fields and woods where you are. I'm switching to the classified maps. Yes, I've got you. The secret MI6 database of training locations has something there. It's called the Burnt Hill Environmental Training Area. It's been used since the fifties to get agents used to high-risk environments.'

Through his earpiece, he heard something explode, and the sound of Bradley swearing.

'The history lesson is much appreciated,' Bex said, 'but we do need that map.'

'I'm calling one up right now. OK, I've got you. Yeah, it's an entire town that doesn't exist on the standard maps. You're at the junction of three streets.'

'And they're all blocked off by fake rioters and the Army,' she said. 'Is there any way out? We need to get back to the car park.'

Kieron selected the centre of the map with the tip of a finger and moved it around, before zooming in with a two-fingered gesture. 'Can you see a house on a corner with an alleyway alongside it, running between it and the next building? Probably to your right.'

'Ye-es,' she said.

'Can you get to that alley?'

'One way or another,' she said grimly.

Kieron switched the view in his glasses to show what Bex saw, keeping the map minimised in one corner of his vision in case he needed it again – which he almost certainly would.

'What's happening?' Sam asked.

'I'll tell you in a minute.'

He watched as the point of view of Bex's glasses swung around to focus on a house nearby. There was indeed an alleyway running along the side, between it and the next house – probably a way of getting to the gardens at the back. The view surged forward as Bex ran towards the house. A brick flashed past her face, making Kieron flinch reflexively, and the picture suddenly jerked. All Kieron could hear was shouting and random explosions. A woman's face suddenly appeared from Bex's left-hand side. Everything from her eyes downwards was covered by a scarf with a grinning skull-face motif on it, while her eyes themselves were wide and scary. She held a metal pipe in her right hand. She raised the pipe threateningly, preparing to bring it down on Bex's head.

Kieron watched as Bex punched the rioter in the nose. The woman fell backwards, blood staining the skull-kerchief. The metal pipe clattered to the floor. Bex bent down and picked it up.

Bex's head swivelled around as she looked for Bradley. Kieron saw that Bradley had his arm around the neck of another rioter. As Kieron watched, the rioter slumped to the ground, unconscious, and Bradley let him go.

Bex's arm appeared in the picture. She grabbed Bradley and pulled him with her. Her head turned back as if to see where they were going.

It seemed to Kieron that his two friends were running

through hell. Bodies lay on the ground, writhing and choking, while smoke kept on drifting past and obscuring the scene. Everything was lit by flames. He could see soldiers in the distance, approaching with their weapons raised. They wore gas masks. It was like something from a first-person shooter computer game, set in some kind of post-apocalyptic environment, but this was England, this was now, and his friends were there.

'This is carrying realism too far,' he said.

'Tell me about it,' Bex muttered.

Shockingly, shots echoed between the buildings. Some of the rioters that Bex and Bradley were pushing past flinched or ducked, while others ran.

Kieron could hear the pounding of Bex's shoes on the road as she and Bradley sprinted away from the crowd of rioters. The picture in the ARCC glasses bounced up and down. The alleyway grew large in the picture, and then they were inside it, in shadow, and Kieron felt himself relax.

'Two portions of cheesy chips!' a voice said. Kieron jerked his head sideways, surprised. He hadn't known anyone was there. The serving lady from the cafe stood beside him, holding two plates.

'Thanks,' Sam said. 'If you could just put them down on the table, please.'

The woman seemed to be staring at Kieron. 'Is he all right?'

'Don't worry about him. It's Tourette's syndrome. He's on medication though.'

Kieron felt as if he ought to be defending himself, but

what was happening in Burnt Hill village was more urgent. He let himself get pulled back into that world again, even though the smell of the melted cheese wafting past his nose along with the smoke he could see from the fires formed a surreal juxtaposition.

Bex's gaze was directed out at the road, where three of the rioters stood together, arguing. One of them pointed over to the alleyway.

'They *are* targeting us!' Bex muttered. 'Up until now I'd hoped it was just a mistake, but –'

'You'd better get going,' Kieron said as the pair started walking towards the mouth of the alley. 'You'll end up in the back gardens. Go right to the far end. There's a pathway there that leads all the way along the back of the gardens, parallel to the road. Turn right and head that way.'

Kieron watched as Bex did what he'd suggested, moving along the side of the house, but rather than head down the edge of the garden she moved into it, pulling Bradley with her to French windows. As Bex's head turned Kieron could briefly see inside the building, where bare walls and a bare concrete floor made a mockery of the relative realism outside.

'What are you doing?' Kieron asked. 'They're right behind you!'

'I know. We can't make it to the car with them following us. They might call for reinforcements, or have our path blocked off by their friends. I have to deal with them.' She turned her head briefly to look at Bradley. Over Bradley's shoulder Kieron could see a small grassy rectangle of garden, with a shed at the end. Grass grew through the wheels of an overturned plastic kid's bike. The bright orange and green seemed strangely out of place.

'I'll take the first one, you take the second,' she said urgently. 'Then whoever's quickest gets to take out the third one.'

'Oh joy,' Bradley said. The grimness of his expression belied the levity of his words.

Just as Bex swung her head back, Kieron saw Bradley bend down to pick something up from the lawn.

Running footsteps echoed down the alley. A man in jeans and a denim jacket appeared. Just as he saw Bex and tried to skid to a halt, she swung the metal pipe at him. The rioter ducked desperately, and the pipe hit the wall, sending shards of brick flying. Bex backed away, and the man lunged towards her. He held a kind of knife in his hand – Kieron recognised it from computer games, and from the hard kids at school who hung around the bike sheds, smoking. It was a balisong – although people called them 'butterfly knives' – where the handle could split into two hinged halves that rotated to cover the blade. The hard kids used to do tricks with them, flipping the hinged bits back and forth across their knuckles, and suddenly exposing the blade.

Kieron was fleetingly aware that a second figure had slipped past the first one, heading for Bradley.

The knife flashed up towards Bex's face, but she brought the metal pipe up into the man's wrist. He screamed and dropped the weapon. His arm seemed to Kieron to be bent at an odd angle.

Bex jabbed him in the face with the end of the pipe and he fell backwards.

She glanced sideways briefly to check on Bradley. He was fighting the second rioter. His opponent had a longer knife, the kind the media like to call a 'zombie knife', while Bradley had a garden rake. It didn't seem to Kieron like a fair competition.

Something moved in the corner of the glasses' field of view. Bex moved her head backwards just as the end of a concrete post flashed past her. The third rioter stood at the corner of the house, holding what looked like a stave he'd pulled off a park fence. His face was contorted into a vicious snarl. As he yanked the concrete stave up for another attempt at bashing Bex's brains out, she stepped forward, swinging her pipe around so she could hold it at both ends horizontally in front of her. Her assailant was having problems manoeuvring the heavy stave, and before he could swing it around and down again Bex stepped forward and jerked her bar straight up, into his chin.

His head snapped back and he staggered away into the alley. Kieron thought he saw the man falling in a heap, but Bex was turning to look at Bradley again.

The result was: garden rake 1, zombie knife 0. Bradley's attacker lay clumsily over the abandoned bike. It seemed like a very uncomfortable position, but Kieron assumed that he was unconscious, so he probably didn't care.

'We need to run,' Bex said breathlessly. 'Kieron, what's the quickest route to the car park?'

'Actually,' he said, 'I've got a better idea.' With a couple of quick flicks of his fingers he overlaid the houses with the blueprints of the village as a kind of glowing wireframe diagram. The edges of the houses, the boundaries of the gardens and the tops and bottoms of the fences between them were all marked in green and blue – but underneath, as he had hoped, red lines showed what was buried underground. Not water pipes, sewage pipes or electrical cables, as there would have been in a real village, but access tunnels, CCTV wiring and even entire subterranean rooms.

'Can you see a round metal plate on the ground near the house?' he asked urgently. He saw something strangely like a submarine's conning tower leading down from the plate into the network of tunnels and rooms beneath, and hoped it was as clear to her as to him.

'Yes. You want us to go down into the sewers?'

'Not sewers. It's a tunnel, probably part of a network for the trainers to get from place to place without getting involved in the riot. Nobody will expect you to go down there!'

'*I* wasn't expecting to go down there,' Bex muttered. 'Good work.'

Kieron watched as she pulled the manhole cover away. 'OK,' she said, 'there's a metal ladder bolted to what looks like old brickwork. Bradley, you go first. I'll follow and pull the cover back so nobody knows where we've gone.'

Within a few moments they were both climbing down a shaft in the darkness of the world beneath Burnt Hill village. Kieron switched to an infra-red view to compensate for the darkness – but recoiled with a horrified 'Urgh!' when Bex reached the bottom of the ladder and turned around.

'What?' Bex said urgently. 'What is it?'

'Er, nothing,' he muttered. 'Sorry. It was something at my end, not yours.'

Actually, it wasn't. What he'd seen, the moment he switched to infra-red vision, was a phalanx of rats retreating down the tunnel. Some of them looked to be the size of small dogs, but that was probably just a trick of the sensors, which showed everything in shades of red and white. The rats kept turning around as they ran and showing their teeth, like black needles against the glowing heat of their mouths.

'Are you sure it's nothing? Only I can hear rustling up ahead.'

'Just the noise of air moving through the tunnel; keep going straight ahead,' he went on, trying to make his voice sound normal and unworried. 'Keep a hand on the wall. You're heading towards the car park.'

'Bradley,' Bex said, squeezing past him, 'Kieron's going to guide me. You grab hold of my belt so we don't get separated in the darkness.'

'Are you sure that rustling is just air?' Bradley asked. 'Only it sounds more like –'

'Just air!' Kieron insisted. 'Keep moving!'

The viewpoint of Bex's ARCC glasses moved along the tunnel. Now it really was like a computer game, Kieron thought nervously. The infra-red sensors only showed him heat sources, and with the rats having run ahead far enough that he couldn't see them, all that was registering was the glow of Bex's hand as she ran it along the wall. Everything else was darkness. Kieron ran through the available options on the ARCC kit, looking for a different way of displaying the scene. He discovered that there was something called a 'Low Light Intensifier', so he switched to that instead. And wished he hadn't.

'Oh my God!' he exclaimed involuntarily, as the red-and-white picture shifted to shades of green, revealing thousands of cockroaches scuttling along the brick tunnel walls, only just managing to avoid Bex's moving fingers. Trying to control the sick feeling in his stomach, Kieron realised that he hadn't seen them on the infra-red sensor because, obviously, they didn't have warm blood. They were as cold as the tunnel walls. He wasn't sure where the meagre light that was feeding the low-light sensor was coming from – maybe narrow ventilation ducts in the roof of the tunnel, or maybe luminescent fungi for all he knew – but he wished he hadn't shifted to that view. But now he knew it was there, he couldn't shift away. The constant scurrying of the cockroaches was too horribly hypnotic.

'What?' Bex asked ominously. 'More stuff happening at your end?'

'Ye-es,' he said, knowing how unconvincing he sounded. 'It's a little bit fraught here right now. Just keep on moving forward.' He had to bite down on a squeal as a cockroach that looked like it was the size of a Yu-Gi-Oh! card ran up the wall just a millimetre or so in front of Bex's fingers, its long antennae trailing to either side. She obviously wasn't convinced by his reassurance, because she glanced around wildly, even though she couldn't see anything, and

Kieron felt a sick chill run through him as he saw that the entire tunnel roof above her was a seething mass of insects as well.

'You're just about to enter a room,' he said, breathing steadily to calm himself down. 'You'll lose the wall, but just keep walking straight forward. I'll guide you.'

Moments later Bex and Bradley walked into a large room whose boundaries were marked by glowing red lines on Kieron's glasses, although on the low-light display it just looked like a large dark space, a cave maybe. As they crossed it – Bex instinctively holding her hands in front of her in case she walked into something – Kieron saw chairs and the edge of a table come into view.

'Argh!' Bex gasped, and waved her hand in front of her face.

'What is it?' Bradley asked from behind her.

'Cobweb,' she said. 'Don't worry.'

'There are spiders down here?' Bradley queried. His voice sounded edgy. 'How big? Only I wouldn't have signed up for this mission if I'd known there were spiders involved.'

'I can't see any spiders,' Kieron said truthfully. He could only see cockroaches. Thousands of cockroaches. Maybe they'd eaten all the spiders. But as long as Bradley didn't ask about cockroaches, everything would be fine.

Bex and Bradley had made it about halfway across the underground room when Kieron thought he saw something moving ahead of them. The trouble was that the low-light sensor made it difficult to see anything at distance if there was no light source at all– which there wasn't in the middle of the room. He touched a virtual button on the screen of his glasses to switch the sensor to infra-red. Shades of green and black gave way to glaring red, white and blue.

Something sat in the middle of the floor, maybe fifteen feet away from Bex, and she was getting closer to it by the moment. For a heartbeat Kieron thought it was a cushion, abandoned by some previous occupant of the room, but then it opened its mouth.

It was a rat – the biggest Kieron had ever seen. The biggest down there by far. King of the rats. It had obviously decided to turn around and make a stand against these invaders of its dark kingdom.

Bex was maybe five steps away.

And she couldn't see it.

Kieron thought he could tell, from the way the image wobbled back and forth, which of Bex's feet was on the ground at any moment. Judging his moment carefully, waiting until her left foot was just coming into contact with the ground,' he said calmly, 'Stick your right foot out now, like you're drop-kicking a rugby ball.'

Bex didn't ask why. She just swung her right leg forward. Kieron saw her foot appear at the bottom of the image, travelling in a perfect arc. It hit the rat just as the creature was about to spring forward. Instead its head snapped back, and it flew like a missile into the distance.

'What the hell was that?' Bex gasped.

'I'll tell you later.'

In the stark colours of the infra-red sensor, Kieron saw a wave of smaller rats converge on their injured king. As it vanished beneath them Kieron switched back to low light.

'A lot later,' he added.

As Bex passed the mass of struggling rats she must have known something was there, because she swerved slightly to avoid them. Kieron switched his attention to what was ahead. His two friends were almost across the room now, and the glowing green lines of the schematic display indicated that there was a doorway ahead.

'Careful,' Kieron warned. 'The tunnel starts up again just ahead. You're heading right for it. Don't deviate.'

Bex went straight into the tunnel without hesitation and kept moving. 'Still OK, Bradley?' she queried, head turning reflexively to look over her shoulder even though as far as she was concerned everything was darkness. By contrast, Kieron was treated to a close-up of Bradley's face. The agent looked scared. Maybe the physical problems he'd had over the past few months since being beaten up and tortured by Blood and Soil had taken their toll mentally. Maybe he just really didn't like the idea of spiders. Maybe he just really didn't like being out in the field and exposed. Whatever it was, he looked like he was close to cracking.

Which was why Kieron decided not to mention the massive cockroach on top of his head. As he watched, horrified, the cockroach's long antennae drooped forward and brushed against Bradley's forehead. Bradley frowned, and swept his hand back across his hair, knocking the cockroach off.

'I hate cobwebs,' he muttered, just as Bex turned her attention back to what was in front of her, and Kieron lost the image.

Now that things seemed to be running smoothly – insects excepted – Kieron reached out a hand to where he thought his frozen drink might be.

'If you're reaching for your drink, it's three inches to your right,' Sam said from somewhere in front of him. 'If you're doing something with the glasses, then I can't help.'

Kieron's fingertips touched the freezing-cold cardboard cup. He picked it up and took a drink from it. The coldness slaked his thirst and the sugar gave him an immediate energy boost. 'Thanks, mate,' he said.

'What?' Bex queried.

'Nothing. I was talking to Sam. But there's a side tunnel coming up ahead, to your right. You need to go right on my mark.'

'Turning right, Bradley,' Bex warned her partner. 'Be ready.'

'Turn in three . . . two . . . one . . . Now!' Kieron said.

On cue, Bex turned right. Presumably Bradley followed her, because neither of them said anything and Kieron couldn't hear the sound of the man running into the corner brickwork.

As there were no obvious obstructions ahead, he zoomed in on the schematic so he could see what was coming up. 'Another ladder, bolted to the left-hand side of the tunnel. It leads right up to where I think the car park is.'

'Brilliant!' He could hear the relief in Bex's voice. 'Not sure how much more of this I can do.'

'OK, stop. Turn left. Reach out your hand. The ladder is just there.'

He saw Bex's hand clutch at the faint outline of the ladder, as revealed by the low-light sensor. 'Bradley,' she said, 'keep one hand on my belt, then when I'm far enough above you just reach forward and grab the rung. I'll see you at the top.'

Kieron watched nervously as she started climbing. He could see a ghostly image of the brickwork behind the ladder; more like the memory of a wall than an actual wall. The image in the glasses grew brighter as Bex climbed – maybe light was squeezing around the edges of the iron cover above her and illuminating the scene.

'Got it,' Bradley called from behind. 'I'm coming up.'

Bex kept moving upwards, but as Kieron watched, something odd seemed to be happening. He could see her hands clearly, and the rungs of the ladder, but the brickwork behind seemed to be growing fainter, and getting further away.

And then, as the grating of metal on brick sounded through the ARCC kit's microphones, he realised the terrible truth.

The ladder was pulling away from the wall. The bolts that secured it towards the top must have rusted with age, or the brickwork around them had crumbled.

'The ladder's coming off the wall!' he cried.

Bex's reached her right hand up as high as it could go, passing several rungs. She looked upwards.

'I can't see anything! How close am I to the top?'

Kieron could see a dim, sketchy outline a few inches above her grasping fingers. 'Just a little bit further!'

More grating of metal on brick, louder now.

'Bex,' Bradley called, 'something's happening, and it's not good!'

'I know. Trying to solve it now!'

Bex sped up, lunging up the shaft. Her fingers pressed against the cover as her feet pushed down hard against the rungs, even as they continued to pull away from the wall. A ring of intense white light appeared above her like the moment of an eclipse. To Bradley it probably looked as if she'd suddenly developed an angelic halo. Kieron hoped the sudden glare didn't distract him into losing his grip.

'Reach up and grab my belt again!' she called as she slid the cover to one side. 'I'll support you!'

As Kieron watched, unable to take a breath, Bex sprang upwards, half-emerging from the manhole and into bright sunlight. She thrust her elbows out sideways, bracing herself against Bradley's weight.

Which suddenly almost dragged her back into the manhole. Her elbows slammed onto the ground and her shoulders nearly vanished back into the darkness. For a seemingly endless moment Kieron thought she was going to fall backwards, but then Bradley's right hand appeared and grabbed the side of the manhole. His left hand followed. With whatever purchase he had left on the rungs of the failing ladder, Bradley pushed himself and Bex out of the hole and onto the surrounding grass and dirt. Kieron heard a screech of metal against brick, followed by a clattering as the ladder finally gave way. There was a final, distant, *bang!*

Bex stared up at the blue sky and the passing clouds. Kieron had to do the same; his view was slaved to hers. He could tell by the way the view shook that she was breathing heavily, and he thought she might be trembling. Eventually she turned her head to look at Bradley, who had rolled to one side. Cobwebs and dust had turned him grey.

'You can be honest now,' he groaned. 'There were spiders, weren't there?'

She exhaled long and loud, then said, 'We can't afford to hang around. They'll assume we're trying to make it back to the car. They'll try to cut us off.'

'Who?' Bradley asked. 'Just out of interest. Is the whole of MI6 after us?'

'No, just the bits that Avalon Richardson controls. Her and a handful of others. Most of the people in the riot didn't know or care who we were. Only the person who took our badges, and maybe three or four others, will be searching for us. Come on.'

They got to their feet and looked around. Bex spotted the car park first, just a little way away. Nobody appeared to be standing near their car. They walked quickly across open ground, unlocked it and got in.

Bex started the car and turned it to head for the tarmac road that led back to the secret and yet obvious entrance and exit off the M4. Kieron could tell that she wanted to press the accelerator to the floor and speed as fast as she could, but she restrained herself. The car moved at a sedate five miles per hour along the curving road towards the barrier.

Where one of the sentries was speaking into a walkie-talkie.

'I think Avalon's alerted them,' she said. 'We could be in trouble. They're armed and we're not. Not that we'd shoot them anyway; they're just following her orders. She's probably told them that we've taken something secret, and they need to hold us until she or her people get here.' She paused. 'Kieron, is there anything you can do?'

'I've got an idea,' he replied cautiously. Quickly he called up several other screens – one showing the view from a nearby motorway camera and one that allowed him to hack into a traffic-management and route-planning system used by many major trucking firms. He selected a passing articulated lorry and pulled its licence plate from the digital recognition system, then fed that into the route-planning software. As he had hoped, that particular lorry was getting real-time traffic updates from the Internet-based system. Rapidly he told it that there had been an accident directly ahead, and the driver should urgently divert onto the side road that would be coming up immediately on his left. All he could do now was hope that the driver was alert enough to see the warning and the redirection and yet not alert enough to question them.

Ponderously, the lorry began to swerve left.

Kieron switched back to the view from Bex's ARCC glasses. The car was maybe a hundred yards away from the barrier, which was down. The guard still had his radio pressed to his ear.

'Kieron . . .' she said warningly.

'I know. Wait for it.'

Suddenly, over the top of the slight rise that lay between the barrier and the M4, the articulated lorry hove into view like a dinosaur emerging from a swamp. The driver wasn't speeding, but he wasn't expecting a barrier across the road either. His face contorted into an exaggerated mask of shock and he tried to brake, but it was too late. As the armed guards leaped for safety the lorry smashed through the barrier and swerved to one side.

Leaving Bex to calmly drive through in the opposite direction. Shards of plastic and bits of metal crunched beneath her wheels. By the time the guards had got to their feet she was over the rise and heading back onto the M4.

'Good work, kid,' she said. 'We're heading home.'

'Yeah,' Bradley added. 'Really good work.'

With relief, Kieron swept the glasses from his face. It took a moment or two for his eyes to adjust to the light levels in the cafe and to focus on what was really around him. When he could finally see straight, he realised that everyone at the surrounding tables was staring at him.

'Computer game,' he said, tapping the glasses. 'I won.'

At least five people, including Sam, applauded.

Kieron bowed, feeling his face getting warm with embarrassment, but within a few moments everyone apart from Sam had turned away and got back to whatever they had been doing before he had distracted them. He was just turning his attention back to Sam when the lenses on the ARCC glasses began to flash red, overwhelming his vision and making him suddenly nauseous. He had to put his hands flat on the table to stop himself falling over.

'What's wrong?' Sam asked, concerned.

Kieron's hands were raised to whip the ARCC glasses off his head when the flashing stopped. Instead he was looking at a blue screen – the same colour as the 'blue screen of death' that he sometimes got when his PC crashed at home. In the exact centre he read the words:

CONNECTION LOST. UNABLE TO ESTABLISH LINK TO SECONDARY ARCC EQUIPMENT. PLEASE CHECK LINK.

'I think we've got a problem,' he said, feeling a mounting sense of dread rising in his chest. 'And so have Bex and Bradley.'

CHAPTER FOUR

'Kieron? *Kieron?*'

No answer. Bex fought against the temptation to slam her hands on the steering wheel of the hire car.

'What's the problem?' Bradley asked.

Bex looked over at him. He still had dust and cobwebs on his jacket and his hair, from the underground tunnel, and the stress of their exit from the secret military base had left him pale. She thought she could detect a slight tremor in the hand that he had rested on his knee. He really wasn't up to sustained agent work – he was an agent handler, more used to sipping latte and eating croissants while providing her with information and support. In the past few weeks he'd had to go well outside his comfort zone.

'The ARCC link has gone down,' she said, switching her attention back to the road. She glanced at the rear-view mirror, looking for any sign that they were being followed. The number plates on the cars were all different to a few minutes ago: she had deliberately varied her speed and changed lanes a couple of times so that anyone trying to stay behind them would have had to match her movements, making themselves obvious. Most drivers picked a speed and a lane and stayed with it. Spotting someone who wasn't behaving like everyone else – that was one of the main tricks of undercover work.

'That shouldn't happen,' Bradley said, sounding concerned. 'I checked the power on both sets of glasses earlier, and they were fully charged. They couldn't have lost power that quickly. And it's not like a mobile phone, where you can lose coverage if you get out of range of a transmitter. We designed the ARCC kit to piggyback off military satellites, and there are always at least five of them visible in the sky anywhere in the world.'

'Solar flares?'

'No. Those satellites are hardened against high levels of radiation.' He frowned. 'I suppose it's theoretically possible that we're being jammed, but the frequency the kit works on shifts around randomly to avoid that very problem.'

'I hate to mention it, but could Avalon Richardson have done something? Uploaded a virus, maybe, or hacked the code?'

'Nah. I hate to blow my own trumpet, but the code is encrypted and unhackable. She couldn't get into it.' He paused for a moment, obviously thinking. 'Maybe Kieron's just dropped the glasses into his fizzy drink.'

'Maybe he's dropped them on the floor and accidentally stepped on them.' Bex frowned. 'If he's broken them, he's going to be in so much trouble.'

'The frames are built from a Kevlar-titanium composite,' Bradley said reassuringly, 'and the lenses are made out of a transparent metallic compound called strontium vanadate rather than glass. To break the ARCC kit, you'd have to be really deliberate about it.'

'Fair enough.' Bex relaxed, but only slightly. There was still the worry about *why* the kit had stopped working. 'Broken wire inside? Dry solder joint?'

'Military-spec materials and construction.' She felt, rather than saw, Bradley shake his head. 'You could put the glasses in the washing machine and leave it running for an hour and they'd still work when they came out.'

'And they'd be freshly scented with lavender,' Bex pointed out. 'Don't think I didn't notice you've changed the fabric conditioner we use.'

'I bet James Bond never has to wash his own clothes,' Bradley muttered.

Out of habit, Bex checked her mirror again, then indicated right and, a few seconds later, accelerated across to the outside lane of the motorway. She checked her mirror again to see if anyone behind her sped up in response, but nobody did. It looked like they'd got away safely.

Assuming Avalon Richardson's team didn't put an electronic tracker underneath the car while it was parked, a small, uncomfortable voice inside her head piped up.

'We should check the car for bugs,' she said.

'Interesting segue there, from fabric conditioner to bugs,' Bradley said. 'I do wonder about the way your mind works sometimes.' Before Bex could respond, he reached into his jacket and pulled out a small black box the same size and shape as a mobile phone. 'This thing can check for any transmitters or active electronics. Next set of services we get to, I suggest you pull in and I'll check beneath the car while you get two large salted caramel lattes to go. I didn't really have time to check when we left the car park. Things were a bit rushed, and I didn't want to hold us up.'

'Good thinking. Yes, I could do with a coffee. And a toilet break.' Even as she was speaking, her mind was considering the malfunctioning ARCC equipment. 'I've never known the kit to just go down like this,' she said. 'It's disturbing. I mean, I know we can switch it off when we want to, but I get used to just having it there, always in the background.'

'You haven't *actually* switched it off by accident, have you?' Bradley asked. 'I mean, while you were scratching your head or something?'

Bex took a hand off the steering wheel and pulled the glasses off her head, then passed them across to Bradley. 'Do you want to check?'

Taking them, he said, 'Good idea. I'll run a system diagnostic as well.' He went quiet for a moment as he examined the glasses, turning them over in his hands and running his finger along the arms. 'OK, it's switched on. That eliminates one possible cause of the problem.' He reached into his jacket and pulled out a small leather case. Bex had seen it before – it contained the tools he needed to carry out any maintenance on either of the two pairs of ARCC glasses. Opening it, he selected something like a small screwdriver, with a shaft no thicker than a piece of wire, and carefully manoeuvred it into an almost invisible hole that Bex had noticed some time ago, located right in the middle of the bridge that joined the lenses together, on the inside surface where nobody could see it. The only reason Bex had spotted it before was that a bit of fluff had got caught there.

'Right, I've set a system check running.' Bradley put the glasses on. Bex couldn't help noticing that he hesitated just fractionally before he did so. Clearly there was still some kind of psychological issue there. He couldn't even *wear* them without getting nervous, let alone *use* them. 'Because these glasses can't project information onto the lenses the way Kieron's ones do –'

Kieron's glasses? she thought with a twinge. If Bradley was thinking of the glasses that were meant to be his as *Kieron's* then it sounded like he'd mentally given up. And where did that leave their team?

'– the chip inside can give a verbal readout of the top-level status of the system. Give me a minute while it tells me what's going on.'

A sign ahead of them indicated that the nearest services were one mile ahead. Bex checked her mirror again, then indicated and changed lanes, first to the middle lane and then again to the inside lane.

'Well,' Bradley said after a few moments, 'the chip is talking to me, which means that firstly the chip itself is working, and secondly the miniature loudspeakers in the arms are working as well.' He paused for a moment. 'OK, all of the top-level diagnostics are coming over as being fine. Obviously the diagnostic can't go into a huge amount of detail verbally, but it's not reporting any error codes. It's just not getting any signal from Kieron's glasses. I think the fault actually is at his end.'

'Is it possible that he can hear us and see what our glasses are seeing but we just can't hear him?' Bex asked.

'I don't see how that could happen,' Bradley said, sounding cautious, 'but there's an easy way to find out.' He paused, then said in a louder voice, 'Kieron, if you can hear this then please call my mobile. I know you've got the number.'

The half-mile warning for the services flashed past. Bex got ready to take the slip road off the motorway, while waiting to hear the Bradley's ringtone. Nothing happened.

'Just my luck if it rang right now,' he said, 'and it turned out to be my mum. But no, either Kieron's unable to call for some reason, or he can't hear us just like we can't hear him.'

'We'll call him when we've stopped,' Bex said, steering the car left off the motorway and slowing down as they approached the car park and the large, hangar-like structure that contained the services. The car park was about half full, and she drove past several empty spaces before she found one she liked – with an additional empty space on either side, minimising the places where people could hide, and a third space in front which meant she could pull away quickly if there was any trouble, rather than having to reverse out. She wasn't anticipating any problems, not here and not now, but it was the way her mind worked. Always make sure you have a clear exit and plenty of space.

She parked and switched the engine off. Bradley unclipped his seat belt and opened the door. He took the ARCC glasses off and slipped them into his shirt pocket before climbing out of the car. He held his little scanner device up so that Bex could see it. 'I'll check around the car. You call Kieron.'

'I'm not going to set that thing off if I call?' she asked.

He shook his head. 'It automatically detects mobile phone protocols and ignores them.' He looked around. 'It's a good filter to have: I imagine most of the people here are on their phones a lot of the time.'

As Bradley crouched down and began to move around the side of the car, presumably holding his scanner underneath it where someone might have attached a bug magnetically to the car's body, Bex pulled her mobile from her jacket pocket. It was the generic pay-as-you-go one she'd bought in Venice a few weeks before – known in the spy trade as a 'burner'. That was another rule of secret-agent work: never use your own phone, or a phone that could give away anything about your real identity. The number for Kieron's own pay-as-you-go mobile, bought at the same time, was programmed in there, but under the name 'Ryan Drewe'. His friend Sam was in there as 'Craig Drewe' and Bradley was listed as 'Tom Drewe', along with a bunch of other made-up people. It would give the impression that she had a wide circle of friends and family if anyone ever took the phone off her and looked through its data.

She called 'Ryan Drewe', hoping that Kieron still had his own phone on him. She'd told him and Sam to keep their burners on them at all times, charged up and switched on, but she knew what kind of memory teenagers had. Or, rather, she was learning every day. In the event that Kieron didn't answer then she would call his real mobile, but then she'd have to throw her own burner away, because she would have corrupted it with real-world information that someone could use to trace Kieron.

Bradley suddenly stood up in front of the car's bonnet as the phone started to ring. He held his scanner up. 'Nothing,' he said, his voice muffled by the car windows. 'We're clean.'

'Go and grab two coffees, and a couple of Danish pastries,' Bex called. Bradley waved his agreement, and headed off to the main building.

'Hello?' It was Kieron's voice speaking in her ear, but not with the clarity of the ARCC kit. This was a crackly, muffled, compressed phone line. He sounded wary.

'Kieron? It's Bex.'

'Can we use real names?' he asked. 'I wasn't sure what the rules were.'

'As long as there's no data left electronically on the phone, it's OK. Just, if you ever leave a message, call me Chloe.'

'OK.' He paused, then said, 'What happened to the ARCC kit? The communications went down at my end. I wasn't sure if you could hear me or not, but I couldn't see or hear you. I was worried that . . . that something might have happened.'

'No, we lost communications as well. What about pulling in data? Can you still do that? Can you access the Internet, and classified databases?'

'No. The glasses are – well, just glasses. They can't *do* anything.'

'OK, don't worry. Bradley and I are working on it. We're heading back now, so we'll see you in a few hours.'

'There's an error message,' he said.

'Tell me what it says, and I'll relay it to Bradley.'

A moment's pause, then Kieron said, 'There's words on the bottom of the virtual screen that's projected in the middle of my field of vision. They say: "*Connection lost. Unable to establish link to secondary ARCC. Please check link.*"'

Bex thought about the error message. It confirmed what she and Bradley had pretty much already decided: the problem wasn't with the glasses, it was with the communication link between them.

'Bex?' Kieron's voice again.

'Yeah? Sorry, I was thinking.'

'Is this serious?'

She hesitated before answering. She didn't want to worry Kieron, but she'd promised herself a while back that she would never lie to him. 'It might be,' she said eventually. 'We need to know more about what's causing the problem.'

'It's just that –' Kieron's voice broke off momentarily, and when it came back he sounded excited. 'The message has vanished! It looks like the glasses are rebooting! Give me a second . . . Yeah, there's a different message telling me that the link's been re-established!'

'OK.' Bex felt a knot inside her chest start to loosen. 'Let's not start celebrating too early. Don't use them until I say you can. I'll let Bradley know what's happened.' She considered for a moment. 'It's looking more and more like there's a problem with sending information between our glasses. The glasses themselves may not be the problem.

If you need to talk to us, call on your burner until we get this sorted.'

'Will do. Look, I've never asked, but how exactly does the ARCC kit transfer information around? I mean, I know it's done via satellite, but not normal communications satellites, surely? That might get intercepted.'

'No, you're right, that wouldn't be secure at all. Bradley and I designed it so the information is passed through a dedicated British military navigation satellite system code-named PEREGRINE. There are seventy-six satellites in an orbital constellation, just like the American GPS system and the Russian GLONASS.'

'So how did you manage to get access to a British military satellite system?' Kieron sounded impressed.

Bex smiled, remembering. 'Bradley and I went to work for the company that made the satellites, when we left university. We realised that if we could put a small extra package on each satellite then we could reroute coded messages back and forth anywhere in the world, and nobody would realise anything was happening. The signal is spread-spectrum, so it can't be traced easily, and most of the processing is done within the glasses themselves, with links out through the Internet cloud to various databases. Bradley wrote the software and I designed the hardware, then we briefed MI6 on what the kit could do. They liked the idea, and paid the company to put a little black box and an extra antenna on each satellite. We built ten sets of linked ARCC glasses, and we lease them to MI6. Everyone is happy, and Great Britain is safer as a result. Everyone wins. Well, except the bad guys.'

'So there *are* other agents like you? You've kinda referred to them before, but you've never actually confirmed it.'

Bex nodded, even though Kieron couldn't see the gesture. 'Nine other teams. We don't know who they are and they don't know who we are. Each team is freelance, recruited by MI6, each team reports directly *to* MI6, and each team uses two pairs of ARCC glasses – one like yours and one like mine. One agent handler working somewhere safe; one agent out in the field, probably not safe.'

'But you and Bradley invented it.'

'Me and Bradley invented it,' she confirmed, 'but inventing it wasn't enough. We had to use it. That's the fun part.'

'And you weren't worried about MI6 just grabbing one of the other sets of glasses and taking them apart to see how they worked, so they could make more? That's the sort of thing they do, isn't it?'

Bex laughed. 'No, there's hardware and software booby traps in the ARCC kit – lots of them – and MI6 know that. Try and take the glasses apart and they'll fry the chip and wipe all the memory completely. It's unhackable and unexploitable.'

'I'm impressed,' Kieron said, and he sounded like he meant it. 'But if the problem isn't with the glasses but the satellites – the top-secret military satellites – then doesn't that mean there's a bigger problem?'

'It does.'

'And aren't those other nine teams at risk?'

'They are,' she said grimly. 'All across the world, there are nine other freelance undercover secret agents who suddenly lost all their support, and nine other handlers who couldn't talk to their agents. That's not a good thing to happen. It looks like everything's working again now, but we can't be sure there won't be another outage. We have to find out what's gone wrong.'

'Shouldn't you, like, *tell* them that something's gone wrong?'

Bex sighed. 'In an ideal world, yes, but we don't know who they are. We don't know who MI6 issued the ARCC glasses to. Only the MI6 bosses know that, and frankly, Bradley and I don't know who to trust there.' She took a deep breath. 'Also, if we admit that there's a problem with the ARCC kit, then MI6 might just walk away, and that would leave Bradley and me without a job. We really need to sort this problem out ourselves, if we can.'

'Bex, I don't –'

'Look,' she interrupted, not wanting to prolong the argument, 'we need to set off again. I'll call you when we're about an hour away from Newcastle, OK?'

'OK.' He sounded disappointed. 'Be careful.'

'You too, kid.'

As Bex stowed her phone away, she realised that Bradley was approaching her with coffees and a brown paper bag that presumably had their Danish pastries in.

'You're looking relieved,' he said, 'but you're also looking grim. What's going on?'

Standing outside their hire car with their coffees on the still-warm bonnet, Bex quickly briefed Bradley on what Kieron had told her.

'OK,' he said, holding his pastry up and examining it closely, 'things could be worse. I mean, they could be better, but they could be worse. At best this was a one-time thing, it'll never happen again and we can move on with our lives. At worst, it'll come back for longer and longer periods of time until the SIS-TERR capability is unusable, in which case we stop getting paid.'

'And other agents like me are at risk,' Bex pointed out.

'Yes, that as well.' He licked the icing on the Danish experimentally. 'Mmm, cinnamon. Lovely.' He took a bite.

'So what do we do about it?' Bex grabbed her coffee and took a swig.

Bradley frowned. He was silent for a long time, then he said, 'Look, Bex, I'll be honest with you. Given that I've obviously still got some kind of psychological block about using the kit, and given that neither of us wants to put Kieron's life at risk any more than we already have, I'm very tempted to just leave the kit, walk away and invent something else that we can make money from.' He held a hand up as she started to interrupt. 'No, let me finish. That's what I *want* to do, but I know the way your mind works. You love the undercover work of course – we both know that – but you also feel responsible for those other nine teams. You don't want them to be left hanging. You also don't want to let MI6 down, although heaven knows someone inside MI6 is quite happy to let *us* down, and hard. So, we have to sort out this mess.' He took a quick gulp from his own coffee. Knowing he wasn't yet finished, Bex waited. She knew that Bradley's mind worked like any computer programmer's:

he broke problems down into simple steps and solved each step one at a time, with occasional diversions off sideways if he suddenly had some wildly creative idea. She had to be patient. 'So we go back to Newcastle,' he went on, 'and I put the two sets of glasses together and connect them to my laptop to see if I can diagnose any underlying problems. If I don't, well . . .' He took a bite of his Danish and chewed it for a few moments before swallowing. '. . . in that case we're going to have to break into the control centre for the top-secret PEREGRINE satellite system and work out what's going wrong there.'

'But we don't know where the PEREGRINE satellites are controlled from,' Bex pointed out calmly.

'Correct. But MI6 do, so first we're going to have to break into MI6 and find out where in the world the control station is located.'

Bex nodded. 'Simple. Shall we do all that this afternoon, or can we get home and grab some dinner first?'

Bradley smiled. 'I didn't say it was going to be easy. I just said that's what we're going to have to do.'

'And you're sure you're up to it?'

He shrugged. 'I'm going to have to be, aren't I?'

They finished their coffees and pastries in silence and got back in the car.

As they pulled away from the services and re-joined the motorway, Bex became preoccupied with trying to work out how to get inside MI6 and access their computers. This wasn't like sneaking into a tech company or a university, both of which she'd done before. This was a whole order of magnitude harder.

Her mind turned to a quote she'd read somewhere. Maybe it was the ancient Chinese military philosopher Sun Tzu, or maybe it was the much more recent Prussian military strategist Carl von Clausewitz. It might even have been Michael Jackson for all she knew; Bex had a bad memory for quotes and names. It was something about choosing the ground on which you were going to fight, rather than letting the enemy choose it.

OK, MI6 had huge amounts of security to stop anyone from breaking into their headquarters and their outstations. The trick, then, would be not to break into *them*, but break into somewhere else. Somewhere easier.

That didn't actually make any sense.

But there was a germ of an idea there. A seed. She just needed to leave it alone and give it time to grow. The subconscious mind was great at problem-solving, but you couldn't hurry it and it didn't like to be stared at while it was thinking. She wasn't like Bradley: she tended to come to conclusions without knowing at the time how she'd got there. It was only afterwards that she could work out the steps her subconscious had taken – sometimes very quickly, sometimes not.

Automatically she checked her mirrors again, sped up and changed lanes.

'Everything OK?' Bradley asked. 'You've been very quiet.'

'I've been thinking.'

Behind her, a black BMW sped up and changed lanes to match her.

Bradley noticed the sudden tension in her posture. 'Problem?'

'Not sure.' She overtook the car that had been in front of her, then moved back into the central lane and slowed down slightly, making sure she left enough space between her and the car that she thought might be following her for it to slot into – but no more than that.

Most cars, if they'd pulled out to a faster lane, would overtake all the cars in front of them and only then decelerate and move back into a slower lane, confident they were in the lead. It was a subconscious thing. Most drivers hated to be stuck looking at someone else's boot. The fact that this black BMW was staying very carefully behind her, but not letting her get too far ahead, suggested very strongly that it was following her.

She indicated left, then slid into the inner lane running alongside the hard shoulder of the motorway.

The black BMW slid in behind her and slowed down to match.

Bex half smiled to herself, remembering a time in New Mexico just a few months ago when she'd been in a similar situation. Today she wasn't feeling so forgiving.

A sign flashed past indicating a slip road a mile ahead. She maintained a safe speed in the inner lane. The driver behind her, if they were indeed following her, wouldn't know whether she was going to stay on the motorway or come off on the slip road. She could exploit that uncertainty.

The half-mile marker sign came and went. Bex took a deep breath. She wasn't sure how the other driver would react to her next manoeuvre, but she was ready.

As her car passed the III, II, I markers counting down to the slip road, she flicked her indicator on as if she was going to take the exit.

The black BMW kept driving straight, not indicating. Maybe she was wrong.

She turned the steering wheel a little bit so that her car veered slightly towards the exit.

The car behind her veered as well. The driver still wasn't signalling – some drivers didn't – but they were definitely coming off the motorway.

Bex slammed her indicator upwards, indicating right instead of left, and turned the wheel hard so that her car veered back onto the motorway just in time.

She'd hoped that the driver behind her would keep going up the slip road, but they veered back onto the road too.

'We're being followed,' she said grimly to Bradley.

'Avalon Richardson's people, or someone else?'

'Difficult to tell from where I'm sitting, but they know that we know now. The cat's out of the bag.'

The black BMW suddenly swung out into the central lane and sped up, causing a white van behind them to brake suddenly and beep its horn.

'They're trying to overtake us,' Bex snarled.

'Well, don't let them,' Bradley replied.

'Good thinking, genius. Why don't you just sit there and lick the crumbs of Danish out of your beard while I handle the driving?' She swung the wheel abruptly, bringing them out in front of the BMW; bumpers almost touching.

Instead of slowing down, the BMW accelerated again, out into the outside lane. Before Bex could do the same it sped up even faster, coming alongside them.

'I think they're going to try a hard stop!'

'Is that as bad as it sounds?' Bradley said, sounding panicked.

'Well, they can't follow us to where we're going, so they're going to take us prisoner.'

'Or kill us!' Bradley half screamed.

Bex glanced sideways. The windows of the BMW were made of darkened glass. All she could see of the driver was an indistinct shape, but just as she was about to turn her head away the rear passenger-side window slid down and something poked out of the gap. For a moment she thought it was a gun, but it was too bulky, too much like something from a science-fiction movie.

'What the –?' she cried.

Bradley glanced past her as the BMW accelerated. The person in the back, hidden behind the blocky device, was aiming it apparently at the bonnet of their car. The front of the device, like a gun barrel but as wide as those extra-large coffee cups Kieron got from his barista girlfriend, gaped like the mouth of some bizarre animal.

'They're going to shoot the tyre out!'

'No,' Bradley corrected, 'they're going to stop the engine. That thing shoots a pulse of electromagnetic energy. It's meant to scramble the engine management system on the car. All our power will cut out and we'll slow to a halt.'

'Are you *sure*?'

'Yeah. I've seen the specifications online.'

'That's when they'll take us.' She saw the person in the back settle the weapon against their shoulder, preparing to fire. Or whatever you called it.

Bex slammed her foot on the brake.

Her car skidded, the tyres squealing against the asphalt of the motorway. The BMW shot ahead as its driver failed to anticipate her manoeuvre. The gunman in the back activated the weapon, but the BMW was too far in front for them to hit Bex's engine. She thought she saw a flash of blue light just as the white van whose driver had beeped the BMW earlier accelerated past her car on the *inside*, the other side to the BMW. Maybe the driver had gotten annoyed that they were blocking the central and outside lanes; maybe they were worried about the game the two cars were playing. Whatever the reason, the white van pulled ahead of Bex's car just as the weapon fired.

The van suddenly slewed sideways. Bex glanced at the driver, who was staring at her dashboard with a panicked expression. She swerved towards the hard shoulder, slowing down fast, and as Bex passed her by she saw in her rear-view mirror that none of the BMW's lights appeared to be working.

'I don't think they'll be able to try that again for a while,' Bradley said. 'The power drain on that thing is incredible. Unless they've got a spare battery pack for it they'll have to recharge it from the engine, and that'll take some driving.'

'Fair enough,' Bex cautioned, 'but I'm worried they're going to try something else.'

At first the BMW had been hanging back, the team inside

presumably waiting to see what happened to their engine, but they had obviously decided that they needed to try again. The car accelerated hard to pass Bradley and Bex. She tried to steer sideways, blocking them off, but she was too late. The car sped past them, then cut hard into the lane in front of them.

A weapon appeared from the same window as before. This weapon was different though – the barrel was longer, like a rifle, but flared like a fire extinguisher. Bex caught a glimpse of whoever was holding it, just black hair and part of an ear.

'Any guesses?' she asked, checking her mirrors to see if she had space to swerve left or right. There was just about enough space, although there was a car coming up behind her fast, and she was worried that it might suddenly decide to overtake. That ruled out swerving right.

'Only that it'll be non-lethal again. They want to stop us, not kill us.'

'The problem is –' Bex started to say, but the strange barrel of the new weapon suddenly jerked, and a stream of grey liquid shot out. Bex slammed the steering wheel to the left, moving their car rapidly out of the way of the liquid, whatever it was. Acid? Sticky, fast-hardening goo, like the stuff that had been used against Kieron in Albuquerque a few months ago? Whatever it was, she didn't think she'd like it all over her car.

As they slid into the inside lane, the car behind, a yellow Lamborghini, accelerated to take their place. The grey liquid splattered against the windscreen of the Lamborghini. It hardened instantly into a thick, fuzzy, grey shield. The driver of the sports car switched their windscreen wipers on, but all they did was spread the stuff further across the glass without actually clearing a space. The Lamborghini slowed down, its driver obviously panicking about being unable to see. Bex pushed her foot down hard on the accelerator, speeding up past the BMW. As she checked to see what the BMW was going to do next she noticed in her rear-view mirror that the Lamborghini was slowing even more, and moving onto the hard shoulder. Smart move.

'Flocculent,' Bradley said.

'Is that your word of the week?' She glanced sideways as she zoomed past the BMW, but the passenger-side rear window had been raised again and she couldn't see inside.

'It means "resembling tufts of wool".'

'I'll remember that in case it ever turns up in a crossword.' She swerved suddenly right so that she was in the middle lane of the motorway again, and directly in front of the BMW. 'I'm sick of this,' she added. 'Time to fight back.'

'All for that. Flocculent, yeah, the stuff that second weapon fired was flocculent. The moment it hit that Lamborghini's windscreen it dried and turned into a kind of woolly paste. It's designed to blind drivers so they have to stop.'

'Well, that's two car-stopping weapons they've tried so far. I wonder what else they got for Christmas.' She jerked the steering wheel left again, taking them suddenly into the inside lane, still ahead of the BMW. Before their pursuers could react she slammed her brakes on. She and Bradley slammed into their seat belts as their car abruptly skidded, tyres squealing. The BMW, taken by surprise, passed by on their right. She could see the driver's head: just a dark shape through the smoked glass. She thought they turned to look at her as they went by.

As the BMW overtook them, Bex nudged the steering wheel right. Their car drifted towards the BMW's back wing.

'You're going to crash into them!' Bradley shouted.

'Just a little bit,' she muttered.

The front bumper of the hire car just touched the rear bumper of the BMW. Bex turned the steering wheel hard right, pushing against the BMW, then hard left, steering rapidly away from it. The BMW began to wobble as the driver tried to regain control, but whichever way they turned the steering wheel, it just seemed to make things worse. The BMW was shaking and juddering as the driver completely lost it. They must have floored the brake pedal, because suddenly the BMW was behind Bex and Bradley, disappearing in a cloud of smoke from its tyres. Other cars, their drivers already spooked by the on-going battle, swerved around it.

'That,' Bradley said, sounding like he'd been winded by the seat belt, 'was a neat manoeuvre. Please don't do it again.'

'Did I ever mention that MI6 sent me on a defensive driving course?' Bex asked, still watching the chaos behind them in her rear-view mirror.

'That was not, by any definition, "defensive",' Bradley observed.

CHAPTER FIVE

The ARCC link went down twice more while Bex and Bradley were driving back from London to Newcastle, but by the time they arrived back at the apartment Kieron thought he'd got some kind of handle on what was happening.

'It's five minutes in every hour,' he said as the door opened and Bex came through.

'What's five minutes in every hour?' Bex asked.

'It's the period of time when he acts like a normal human being,' Sam called from the kitchen, where he'd gone to make a Pot Noodle.

'Shut up,' Kieron called back, then turned to where Bex and Bradley were now standing. They looked dusty. 'Five minutes in every hour is how long the ARCC link goes down for.'

'Interesting.' Bradley crossed to the sofa and threw himself onto it with a huge grin.

'Do you want a cup of tea?' Sam yelled. 'I'm boiling the kettle.'

'A glass of red wine would be better,' Bex said, ruffling Kieron's hair as she passed him by and then sitting down in a comfortable chair, 'but tea would be perfectly acceptable.'

Bradley sniffed. 'Is that curry I can smell? Have you got a takeaway? That's very thoughtful of you.'

'Or, heaven forefend, are you teenagers actually cooking?' Bex asked, smiling. 'That would be a shock.'

Sam appeared in the kitchen doorway holding a large mug from which small spirals of steam rose up. 'It's a Pot Noodle. A tandoori chicken Pot Noodle.'

Bradley closed his eyes and sighed. 'I despair for the youth of today. Have you guys never even *heard* of real food?'

Sam frowned down at his mug. 'This *is* proper food.'

'We'll find somewhere online that delivers,' Bex said, waving a hand at Bradley. 'I'm more interested in this "five minutes every hour" thing. What could be causing it?'

Bradley pulled himself upright and reached over to where Kieron had left the ARCC glasses on the arm of the sofa. Kieron noticed that the other set – the ones Bex and Bradley had taken with them – were stuffed in the pocket of Bradley's shirt. 'I'll run a diagnostic on this pair, just like I did on the others, but I'm not expecting to find anything wrong. I'm pretty sure the issue is with the PEREGRINE satellite system.'

'Yeah.' Kieron glanced over at Sam, who was blowing on his Pot Noodle. 'We've been worried about that. If there's a problem with an entire military satellite network, doesn't that mean that World War Three might be about to start? I mean, that's the first thing Russia, or China, or North Korea would do, isn't it? Jam all the military satellites?'

Bradley's attention was largely fixed on the ARCC glasses,

where he was fiddling with a piece of wire that he'd poked into a small hole in the frame between the lenses, but he was still paying attention to the conversation. 'You're right,' he said. 'That probably would be the first sign of a large-scale conflict, but I doubt that's what's happening here.' He smiled, still focused on the glasses. 'They used to say that the captains of nuclear submarines were told that if they surfaced but couldn't hear the Shipping Forecast on the radio then they should assume war had been declared.'

'What's the Shipping Forecast?' Kieron asked, puzzled.

'What's radio?' Sam asked at the same time.

Bradley shook his head sadly. 'Moving on, there are seventy-six PEREGRINE satellites in inclined circular orbits around the Earth. Those orbits "precess", which means they rotate around, so the satellites pass over different parts of the planet, although eventually the orbits will start to repeat themselves.' He looked at Kieron and Sam's blank faces, and sighed. 'Imagine the Earth, then imagine seventy-six circles way above the Earth and surrounding it like a net, and then imagine that the net itself is gradually turning. The idea is that there should always be at least ten of them visible in the sky from anywhere on the Earth's surface at any one time. Operating a decent satellite navigation system isn't like satellite communications where you just need to see just one satellite so you can upload or download a message. You need at least four satellites in sight, each one broadcasting its own position, so you can triangulate your *own* position.' He frowned. 'Well, technically not "triangulate" if there's you and four satellites. "Pentagulate"? Is that even a word?' He shook his head. 'Anyway, the PEREGRINE "constellation", as they call it, is fully populated, so there are no holes. But, if some of the satellites are malfunctioning, then gaps start appearing in the coverage. So we're looking at a technical problem with the satellites rather than a problem with the ARCC glasses.'

'But,' Bex said quietly, 'if satellites were failing randomly, then you'd expect several gaps in coverage as they passed overhead. Surely, if there's only one gap – and that's what you said, isn't it, Kieron; just one gap every hour? – then that implies that the satellites are failing *in order*, one after the other.'

Bradley put the glasses back down on the arm of the chair and stared at her. 'That's worrying,' he said. 'Actually, that's *very* worrying. It means that, somehow, the PEREGRINE satellites are being affected by some outside force that's accessing them from a ground station. As each one passes over, it's being affected.' He thought for a moment. 'Maybe a virus in an upload, but the uploads are encrypted, and whoever was uploading the virus would have to break that encryption. More likely someone in one of the actual PEREGRINE control stations is sending up false commands to make the satellites do things they're not supposed to.'

'So it's an inside job?' Kieron asked, feeling a chill run through him. It was bad enough thinking that some other nation was sabotaging British military satellites, but for someone actually *in* the military to be doing it . . .

Bex nodded. 'It's looking that way, isn't it?'

Bradley tapped the glasses. 'These are fine, by the way.

It's definitely PEREGRINE that's the problem.' He glanced over at Sam. 'Where's that tea?'

'Oh, sorry.' Sam vanished back into the kitchen.

'What are these PEREGRINE ground stations?' Kieron asked.

'They're just what they sound like. Places with computers and antennas pointing upwards where instructions can be sent up to the satellites. Normally you'd have a main ground station and a couple of backups, just in case the main one goes down, or in case you need access to a satellite right away but it's not in sight of the main station.'

'And where are they?'

Bradley grimaced. 'That's the problem – they're top secret. We don't know. They could be anywhere in the world.'

Kieron nodded towards the ARCC glasses. 'That's OK. We just use those to find the information out. They can access any database, anywhere.'

Bradley coughed. 'Except the top-secret UK databases that have been deliberately left out,' he said. 'The whole point of the ARCC kit and the SIS-TERR capability is that it gives agents information they can use when they're under cover. There's no sensible reason why an agent would need to know highly sensitive information about the way MI6 or the Ministry of Defence work. Those databases are blocked. No access.'

Kieron thought for a moment. 'OK, but the main one would be in England, surely? I mean, it makes sense that the others are somewhere else in the world, but the main one would *have* to be in England.'

Bex shook her head. 'Not necessarily. Remember, it's a military system, meant to provide navigation and communications in time of war. If the UK is attacked, then the ground station might well be taken out. For that reason you might want to put it abroad – Gibraltar or somewhere else we control. Or hidden in an embassy abroad.'

'So . . .' Kieron closed his eyes, trying to sort his way through the mass of information that had just been thrown at him. It was like a science lesson back at school. 'I understand that when you thought there was a problem with the ARCC kit itself you didn't want to talk to MI6, but now you know the problem is with the satellites, why not just tell them and let *them* sort it out?'

Bex looked at Bradley, then back to Kieron. 'Because we know there's a traitor in MI6, and they might be trying to get at us through the PEREGRINE satellites. To put us out of action. Avalon Richardson will just use this to put more pressure on us to transfer the system to her, and we're not going to do that. I think we're going to have to sort this one out ourselves.'

'Again,' Sam said, re-entering the room with two cups of tea. 'I'd say it was just like old times, except that "old times" was only few weeks ago.' He crossed the room and handed the mugs over to Bex and Bradley. 'OK. First, how are we going to find the main ground station, and second, how are we going to get in there?'

'I've been thinking about that.' Bex took a sip of her tea. 'Ooh, that's nice. Sorry – yes. The ground station will be largely automated, so that's not necessarily a problem.

Finding out where it is . . . That's a problem, because the information on its location is top secret. We have to find someone who *does* know and get them to tell us.'

'Just like that?' Kieron asked. 'You make it sound so simple.'

'Not simple,' Bex said, smiling, 'I mean, when is anything in our lives simple? But I've got a plan. Stay with me on this one. Ideally, we'd break into MI6 and find the information ourselves, but that's just so impossible it takes the word "impossible" to a whole different level. So what we do is –' she paused for impact – 'we fake a room at MI6 that Bradley and I both know, we find someone who works there on the night shift, we knock them out without them realising and bring them to the fake room, we wake them up again, we tell them they must have fallen asleep, and then we chat to them about the PEREGRINE satellite system and get them to tell us where the ground station is based.'

Kieron looked over at Sam. Sam looked back at him.

'Do you want to tell them all the problems with that plan?' Sam asked.

'It's not really a *plan*, is it?' Kieron replied. 'I mean, it's just a string of unlikely things all put in a row.'

'Yeah, very funny.' Bradley looked at each of the boys in turn. 'Do you have a better plan?'

'I dunno,' Sam said. 'Give us half an hour.'

Yet by the time they'd ordered a takeaway from the local Thai restaurant and Bradley and Sam had gone to collect it, none of them had thought of anything better. It looked as if they were stuck with this plan whether they liked it or not.

'OK,' said Bradley around a mouthful of *pad thai*. 'We need a room in MI6 that we're familiar with, and where someone works who knows about top-secret satellite communications.'

'The ops room in the Edinburgh MI6 outstation.' Bex had a forkful of massaman curry in her hand, and waved it about for emphasis. 'We've both been there, which means we know how it's set out. And the people who work there have access to all the communications equipment and systems that MI6 use.'

Bradley nodded. 'Even better. I've got photographs on it on my phone. We can use them to recreate it perfectly.'

Kieron watched, amused, as Bex gave Bradley a hard stare. 'You have photographs of a top-secret MI6 operations control room? Have you never even *heard* of security? The Official Secrets Act? Those things?'

Bradley shrugged defensively. 'It was a party. Remember, you were there? The main comms guy was retiring, so he'd got some bottles of warm white wine and some nibbles, and we all had a session after the bosses had left. I took some selfies, but the background of the selfies is the ops control room, seen from various different angles. Good, eh?'

'Selfies.' Bex raised a hand to her forehead and closed her eyes momentarily. 'We were supposed to hand mobiles in at the main gate. They get put in a lead box, remember? You're supposed to collect them on your way out.'

Bradley winced. 'Yeah, that day I had two different

mobiles on me. The old one had a cracked screen, but I hadn't moved everything across to the new phone. I handed one in but I forgot about the other one.'

'Sometimes I despair of you.' She shrugged. 'Still, it's a good thing you've got those photographs.'

A thought occurred to Kieron. 'Can I ask a question?'

'Can we stop you?' Bex and Bradley asked together.

'Why don't we just program a virtual-reality simulation of this ops control room into the ARCC glasses?' He looked from one to the other. 'That way we don't have to build a complete recreation, we just make sure the person we kidnap is wearing the ARCC glasses when they wake up. I'm guessing we can adjust the glasses so that rather than showing see-through virtual screens they can show a completely solid image?'

'We're not using the word "kidnap",' Bex said quickly. 'We're just borrowing the person without them knowing.' She glanced at Bradley. 'But – interesting. Opinions?'

'It won't work,' he said decisively, shaking his head. 'There's several risks. Firstly, we'd have to choose a worker there who actually wears glasses. That's not necessarily a problem, but secondly, what happens if they decide to take the glasses off, or accidentally knock them off, and suddenly find themselves sitting on a chair here in our flat rather than being at work in their control room? Thirdly, the ARCC glasses aren't all-enclosing, like real gaming goggles. Whoever we choose would be able to see stuff around the edges that isn't part of the simulation. And fourthly, we'd have to put *ourselves* in the simulation so we can talk to them, and our simulations wouldn't be anywhere near as lifelike as we are. It's a problem with virtual reality – they call it the "uncanny valley". The nearer a simulated person gets to a real person, the scarier they look. It's something about skin tone, and the way the eyes don't blink properly. Also, the skin and the hair are almost too perfect.'

'Let's take a look at those selfies then,' Bex said, waving a hand at Bradley.

They downloaded the images onto the ARCC system and connected it up to the plasma TV screen in the apartment so they could all see them. In all there were twenty images of Bradley taken in the same room. The room itself was large, with maps pinned to the walls and several rows of monitors and desks facing a massive screen that seemed to take up most of a wall. Most of the monitors had padded headphones clipped to them. There were no windows. Every image also had several other people in the background, eating, drinking and talking, and each image had a bit of wall and some furniture in it. In some of the images Kieron saw Bex. She was standing by a wall, alone, with a glass of wine in her hand.

Bradley pointed to a man who appeared in several of the jigsaw-piece images. He was about the same age as Bradley and Bex, and he had a ginger beard, and long hair pulled back into a ponytail. 'That's the guy I think we should target,' he said. 'I seem to remember he was the night manager for the ops centre. He lives alone, or at least he did when these photographs were taken. I remember him as being a bit of a weirdo. Very intense, if you know what I mean. His name is Scott. I think. Or Lee. He'll be on the staff list anyway.'

'Right,' Bex said. 'I'll check out this Scott, or Lee. You do your magic with the simulation.'

As Kieron and Sam watched, Bradley used the ARCC software to stitch all the images together into a kind of collage, a jigsaw puzzle that covered most of the room in a massive panoramic picture.

'What I can do now,' Bradley said, waving his hands around as he accessed controls on the virtual screens that only he could see, 'is pull this combined image into a high-tech simulation-creator, get it to take the people out, and *then* get it to create a simulated environment that we can use as a reference to build what is effectively a fake theatrical set for our little performance.' A few minutes later the panoramic image on the plasma TV screen flickered and vanished, to be replaced with a single picture of the same location, but seen from one particular point of view – looking directly at the wall-wide screen. It was almost too perfect to be believable.

Bradley turned his head slightly, and the image shifted to match.

'Right,' he said, 'this is what I'm looking at right now.'

Bex glanced up from her laptop.

'As far as I can remember, it's just like the real thing,' Bradley went on, 'except that the simulation doesn't have any coffee stains on the carpet or screwed-up empty snack packets near the bin where someone threw them and missed.'

'So what now?' Sam asked. 'We actually *build* this?'

'What happens now,' Bex said, 'is that we convert that simulation into a set of blueprints which we give to a company – probably one that makes sets for theatres and movies – and we get them to build it for us. They can find all the right furniture to match the stuff in the images, and put it all in the right place.'

'We'll have to hire a warehouse or an industrial unit with a big space in the middle,' Bradley pointed out. He turned his head to look at Bex, and the picture on the TV screen slewed alarmingly.

'This is all going to cost money,' Bex pointed out. 'It's probably going to take a week or so to construct, and that's if they're not working on something else already and we have to wait.'

'Well, we'll just have to earn it back again.'

Bex looked over at Sam. 'Like you said, it's just like old times.'

It was getting late, so they agreed to split up and get back together the next morning. Sam and Kieron walked back to his flat, and then Sam headed for home alone while Kieron nervously went inside.

His mum wasn't in. That was good. Actually, that wasn't good, as he liked talking with her, but he'd been worried that she might have invited her new boyfriend round. That would have been awkward. But no, they were probably out somewhere. On a date.

A date. Kieron shuddered. Grown-ups shouldn't go on dates. That kind of thing should be reserved for teenagers. Grown-ups should just have nights out.

That thought made him pull out his mobile – his real mobile, not the burner that Bex had given him in Italy – and send a text to Beth just to check that she was OK. Fifteen seconds later a text arrived back.

Im good. U OK? CU soon? ☺

He smiled. Teenagers dating was a *good* thing. He wasn't sure if this was actually dating, but it was probably heading that way. He hoped.

The next morning Sam called for him, and together they headed to the cafe where they'd agreed to meet Bex and Bradley for breakfast. It wasn't the cafe where Beth worked. Kieron would have voted for that, but Bex had been firm about the fact that they had work to do and she didn't want him distracted.

Bex and Bradley were already there, looking at printouts they must have brought with them.

'We've got the entire life history of Scott Bailson here,' Bex said, waving them over. 'His name *is* Scott. Bradley was right; he's a perfect choice. I've managed to access his personnel file, and it turns out he's had a fair amount of time off with migraines and viruses. He's a bit of a hypochondriac, if you ask me, but that means if he suddenly passes out in his flat and then wakes up at what looks like work it'll be relatively easy to convince him that he's had another "episode" of whatever it is that he suffers from.'

'And I've got a list of local companies who make film and TV sets,' Bradley added, tapping his pile. 'Turns out the north of England is great for that kind of thing. We've selected the best three, and we're going to talk to them today and get quotes.'

'How exactly are you going to knock this guy out without him realising?' Kieron asked, puzzled. 'I mean, if you just punch him, or hit him on the back of the head, he'll know something's up. I certainly would.'

Sam put a hand up, as if he was at school. 'Ooh, I know! What about that neural net mesh thing we had in Albuquerque that wraps around someone's head and gives out signals to send their brain to sleep?'

'Two problems with that,' Kieron pointed out. 'Firstly, he'll realise that his head has been wrapped in a metal mesh in the few seconds before the signal sends him to sleep, and secondly – and more importantly – *we made that up*. It isn't real. It was just a story we invented so I could get into the Goldfinch Institute undercover.'

'Oh yeah,' Sam said, frowning. 'Yeah, I remember now. I thought that thing was too good to be true.'

Bex held up a hand. 'We've thought about sedatives,' she said, 'but getting the dose right can be problematic, as can slipping them into his food or drink. We also thought about doing it the old-fashioned way, with Bradley distracting him while I come up behind him and put pressure on a nerve junction in his neck in a kind of martial arts thing so he passes out. The problem with that is, he's likely to remember being grabbed from behind and his neck being pinched.'

'So there's lots of options you can't use,' Sam pointed out. 'What *can* you do? Anything?'

'Have you ever heard of "flicker vertigo"?' Bradley asked.

Kieron glanced over at Sam, who shook his head. Kieron did the same. 'Sounds cool though,' he said.

'You know that some people can get epileptic fits if they're exposed to flashing lights?' Bradley went on.

'That's why TV programmes and movies have to have a warning if there are any flashing lights in them.' Sam looked over at Kieron. 'Remember Lee Jansen at school? He got triggered once at the school prom by the lights on the dance floor. Poor guy fell over and started twitching.' He looked back at Bradley. 'Is this Scott bloke epileptic then?'

'No, but researchers have found that ordinary people, non-epileptics, can be sent into a trance or a state of sleep by lights that flash at a particular frequency. Helicopter pilots sometimes get it if the sun is shining through the rotors, and pilots of light aircraft if they're flying a propeller-driven plane and the sun is directly ahead of them, low on the horizon. MI6 did some work on flicker vertigo in case they could use it to render people safely unconscious. We're going to use the same principle to knock Scott out when he comes out of work. He'll be tired then, and he'll be more vulnerable.'

Sam frowned. 'Wasn't there something with a *Pokémon* episode, back in the day? I'm sure I heard something about that.'

'Like we'd know,' Bex scoffed.

'Well,' Bradley said, 'actually . . .'

Sam typed rapidly into his mobile and nodded. 'Yeah, apparently an episode of *Pokémon* they showed in Japan back in 1997. That's, like, years before me or Kieron was born.' He was speaking as he was reading the screen. 'There's a scene in it where Pikachu has to use his lightning attack to blow up some missiles, but he and Ash are actually *inside* a Pokéball transmitter at the time, so the animators couldn't use the normal effect that they would have done in the real world. They decided to have the TV screen strobing red and blue for the explosions, but lots of kids in Japan started having problems when that went out on TV. Some of them had blurred vision or felt sick; some actually passed out. Apparently about seven hundred kids had to be hospitalised. That episode's never been repeated, or released on DVD or Blu-ray. So, yeah, flashing lights *do* have an effect on people.'

Bex glanced at Bradley. 'Did *you* understand what he said?'

Bradley winced. 'The episode was called "Electric Soldier Porygon",' he said quietly. 'It's the thirty-eighth episode of the first season. I've actually got a pirate copy.' He looked over at Bex, and shrugged. 'I was a bit of a geek when I was a kid. I loved *Pokémon*.'

Kieron gazed at Bradley with an increased level of respect. Bradley caught the look, and blushed.

'Anyway, the great thing is,' Bex pointed out, 'that he's on the night shift, so he leaves at dawn, when the streets are quiet. We should be able to get him easily without anyone noticing.'

Kieron noticed that Sam was looking over at him with a sceptical expression. Kieron shook his head slightly. Best not to argue with Bex or Bradley. They had much more experience in this kind of thing than the two boys did.

The next few days passed in something of a blur for Kieron. He was still being home-schooled, supposedly, so there wasn't a problem with him missing lessons. The problem was with him not being at home working on the assignments that his teachers kept sending through, and whenever he was outside Bex and Bradley's apartment he was terrified that someone would see him, recognise him and report him to the headmaster. Or his mum. He wasn't sure which would be worse.

Bex and Bradley had decided to go together to do all the administrative stuff necessary to rent an empty warehouse space for a month or two and then to hire a company to build a fake MI6 office inside. If just one of them went, they had decided, it might look a little odd, and if one of them turned up with a teenager then it might look even odder. Two adults in smart clothes, however – that looked professional. Kieron's job was to provide them with support via the ARCC equipment in those periods when the PEREGRINE satellite network was working. Sam's job was to provide Kieron with energy drinks, and to make snarky comments.

Hiring the warehouse was a relatively quick and painless process, the only slight problem being that it needed to be in Edinburgh rather than Newcastle. Obviously, as Bex pointed out, if they were going to knock out and 'borrow' an MI6 operative, the last thing they wanted to do was drive for over two hours to question him, then knock him out again and drive for over two hours back again to return him home. Fortunately there was a lot of warehouse space lying unused in the Edinburgh area, and Bex and Bradley managed to get a very good deal on a three-month rental. Hiring a local company to make a recreation of an MI6 office turned out to be slightly trickier. Bex and Bradley drove up to Edinburgh specifically to talk to the companies, but two of them turned it down straight away because of how short a time they were being given, even though the blueprints were ready.

'We might have to look for a couple more options,' Kieron heard Bex say quietly to Bradley as they stood in the foyer of the third company.

'The trouble is,' Bradley replied, equally quietly, 'that these were the best choices. Any other option won't be as good.'

Back in Newcastle, Kieron watched as they were led across a large hangar-like construction space. Right in the centre sat what looked to him like a spacecraft. An honest-to-God spacecraft.

'Can you ask the bloke who's escorting you what that is?' he asked.

'What's the spacecraft for?' Bex asked a few moments later.

The young technician who was leading them across the hangar space turned his head. 'It's a prop for a new science–fiction series on one of the streaming networks,' he said. 'Dunno what it's called. We just make the thing. We've had to put it together to check that everything fits, but it comes apart for transport, then gets reassembled in their studio.'

'Can't they just use CGI?' Kieron asked. 'I mean, computer-generated images?'

'Can't they just do that with computers?' Bex parroted.

'Apparently the director wants stuff done for real, as much as possible,' the technician replied. 'He wants actors in spacesuits hanging onto the sides of the spacecraft while there's explosions going on. You doing something like this?'

'More or less,' Bradley said.

Bex and Bradley were taken into a workshop area on the far side, where a burly man in a T-shirt and jeans was looking at plans spread out on a table. Bex explained to him exactly what it was they wanted him to build, and how long he'd have to do it, while Bradley showed him the blueprints and the simulation on his laptop screen. The man stood there for a while, thinking, while Bex and Bradley watched. Eventually he nodded.

'We can do it,' he said finally. 'We've just finished work on that big spaceship you saw outside, and we've got another fortnight before the next project is ready to go, but I'm confused. It's a sealed set, with four walls and a roof. If it's for a film or a TV series, where are you going to put the cameras? Or if it's for a play, where are the audience going to be? I mean, I guess we could make it so you could take any of the walls out and film through the gap, but you haven't asked for that.'

None of the other two companies had asked that question. They'd just said politely that they didn't have time to do the job and they'd escorted Bex and Bradley out.

'Good point,' Bradley said. Kieron spotted him in the corner of the ARCC glasses as he glanced across at Bex.

'Drones,' Kieron said quickly. 'Drone cameras, used for realism.'

'We're filming with drone cameras,' Bex said smoothly. 'The actors will be positioned around the set, moving normally, and the drones will follow them around. It's meant to be hyper-realistic.'

The T-shirted man nodded. 'Yeah, I can understand that. Those steadycams that cameramen carry around take up a load of space, and you can sometimes see actors having to move out of the way so that the cameras can get past them. Drones are definitely the way to go. Let me make a quick calculation on the number of carpenters, plasterers and electricians I'll need, and then I'll email you a quote.'

'Ask him about the chairs and tables and computer screens,' Kieron reminded Bex. 'It's called "set dressing" in the trade.'

'What about set dressing?' Bex repeated as if the idea had only just occurred to her. 'Are you able to get tables and chairs and computer stuff?'

The man nodded. 'Easily. We're in touch with a lot of second-hand furniture places. Just tell us what kind of chairs and tables you want and we'll get hold of them. Computers are easy as well. Just give us a make and model and we'll source them.'

The meeting broke up shortly after that, and the junior technician escorted Bex and Bradley back past the fake spacecraft.

'I am definitely watching that series,' Kieron said over the ARCC link.

Outside, alone in the open air, Bex turned to Bradley. In Kieron's vision, Bradley's face looked huge.

'I think,' Bex said, 'that we're in business.'

'Just the kidnapping to go,' Bradley said.

'It's not a kidnap,' Bex hissed. 'We're just borrowing someone without his permission!'

It took the contractors that Bex and Bradley had hired four days to build the fake office. On the morning of the fifth day Kieron's mobile woke him up. He groaned, pulled abruptly out of a dream in which he and the President of the USA were, strangely, solving crimes in a cowboy town, and reached for the phone. Blearily he noticed the time. 05.30.

'Hmm?'

'Kieron?' It was Bex. 'Time to get up. We're waiting downstairs in the car.'

He dressed quickly and headed for the hall. As he opened his door he heard the bathroom lock *snick* open. His mum! He froze for a moment, then quickly scooted back to bed and pulled the duvet over himself. He waited, hardly breathing, as the bathroom door opened. Was his mum going to go straight back to her room? Straight back to sleep? What happened if his phone went off again right now – Bex wanting to know what the delay was? He pulled it out of his pocket and quickly muted it.

The door of his room *creak*ed open. He lay there, imagining his mum standing in the doorway, looking at him. Checking that he was OK.

Just as long as she didn't come over and pull the duvet away from his face so she could gently stroke his cheek. She did that sometimes, when she thought he was fast asleep. He never said anything, because he didn't want her to get embarrassed and stop. But if she did that now, she would see that he was fully dressed.

Eventually, after so long that his pent-up breath was burning in his chest, Kieron heard the door *creak* again, and his mum moved off down the hall to her room. He counted to one hundred, then climbed back out of bed and moved to the door again. He opened it just enough for him to be able to slip through the gap but not enough for the hinge to squeak, glancing down the hall first to check that his mum's door was closed. It was.

Fifteen seconds later he was outside the house.

Bex and Bradley had parked down the road, outside a row of shops, so that the sound of their engine didn't wake anyone up. As he slipped into the back, nudging a sleeping Sam, he said, 'Sorry – my mum woke up. I had to wait until she was out of the way.'

'No problem,' Bradley said from the front passenger seat. 'Are you kids ready for an adventure?'

'Not really,' Kieron said honestly. Sam just snored.

CHAPTER SIX

'I'm getting flashbacks, and not good ones,' Bradley said, looking up at the metal exterior of the warehouse and then at the other deserted buildings around it. He glanced at Bex, catching her eye, then nodded towards Kieron and Sam. 'The first time I met these two was in a place not dissimilar to this.'

'I remember,' Kieron said. 'It was pretty horrible.'

'Hey,' Sam bristled. 'You didn't get beaten up or tied to a chair. We did.'

'Kids, no bickering,' Bex said. 'Remember, this is *our* place.' She moved towards a lockbox on the warehouse wall, located between the main door and the roll-up shutter that allowed vehicles access to the inside. She'd been to the warehouse several times over the past week while arranging the rental details and checking its suitability, and she knew the code to type into the box's keypad by heart. It opened; she took the key from inside and used it to unlock the main door.

Darkness filled the cavernous interior, but a chunky red push-button switch on a post set into the concrete floor just inside the doorway turned on the lights. Sudden illumination burst from the floodlights that were attached high up on the walls, and on the girders that supported the roof.

'This place smells of fertiliser,' Kieron said, moving inside and sniffing. 'Don't terrorists make bombs out of fertiliser? Are you sure this isn't a terrorist base?'

'It is not a terrorist base. Apparently the previous occupants ran a garden centre and used this place to store their excess stuff,' Bex said absently, but her attention was taken up more by what was in the centre of the space: a large wooden box, about the size of their entire apartment, the outside of which was covered in rough wooden planks, exposed nails and projecting beams. A doorway could be seen in the middle of one of the sides. Cables and pipes snaked across the floor from somewhere over the far side of the warehouse and ran up the sides of the box to its top.

'Nice,' Sam said. 'Money well spent.'

'Don't be rude,' Bex replied. 'The real magic is inside, not outside.'

She turned to look at Bradley, wondering what his opinion was, but saw he was smiling.

'What's so funny?' she asked, curious.

'It just reminded me of something, that's all. Not that industrial place I was kept prisoner in. Something else.'

'What?'

'I went to a technology conference once, a few years back, in the Ministry of Defence main building in Whitehall. I think you were in Thailand at the time. There was an evening reception afterwards, held in what we were told was Henry VIII's original wine cellar, dating back five hundred years.

It had been rediscovered when the MoD was being built, and rather than knock it down they incorporated it into the basements, although the builders apparently had to shift it sideways by nine feet and down by twenty. We were taken, like, two floors beneath street level, and then we were led into a big underground space. In the middle there was this old structure with projecting bits of brick and mortar and stuff, not looking terribly impressive. Inside, though, was a different story – arches and a carved roof and everything. Terrible wine though. But it was a cellar, so nobody was ever meant to see the outside – only the inside. And this reminds me of that.'

Bex smiled at Bradley's obvious enthusiasm. 'Well, I can't promise that the inside of this thing will live up to the promise of Henry VIII's wine cellar, but let's take a look, see what they've done.'

She led the way across the warehouse space towards the construction in the centre. Up close she could see exposed nails, screwheads, splashes of paint and bits of plaster. It was, just as Bradley had said, like looking at the outside of something that was only meant to be seen from the inside. Or, she suddenly realised, like looking at the back of a theatrical set – the bit that was never meant to be seen by the audience. She could also smell more than just the sharp odour of fertiliser that Kieron had identified – she could detect fresh paint, and sawdust as well. The familiar scents of decoration. For a moment it reminded her of home, and her father turning his garage into a play space for her.

The most ordinary thing there was a door. She opened it, and led the way inside.

Which was a revelation.

It was an office. It was absolutely, and in every way, an office, looking like it belonged in some financial building or university. And she recognised it. Even though she'd never been in that room in that warehouse before, she recognised it. The construction team had done a perfect job. This was exactly like the MI6 Operations Control Room in Edinburgh that she and Bradley had visited, down to the battered desks in the centre, the bits of Blu-Tack on the wall where some posters had once hung and the ceiling tile that was missing a corner and had a strange brown watermark on it. Even the fluorescent light tubes were exactly the same, although these were powered from the electrical cables outside, plugged into a three-phase power supply over on the far wall.

'Very good,' Bradley said, looking around and nodding. He pointed to the floor. 'They've even got the spilled coffee stains right.'

'We'll need to do something about the smell,' Bex pointed out. 'Fresh paint and sawdust are not right.'

'As I remember,' Bradley said, 'the real ops room didn't smell of anything much. The air-conditioning was very good. It had to be, given that it's actually in the middle of the fifth floor of the MI6 outstation in Edinburgh and doesn't have any windows to open. If anything, there was that faint electrical smell you get from computer fans if they've been on for a long time.'

'We can deodorise this place,' Bex said decisively. 'There's sprays you can get in supermarkets to do that.'

Sam had moved across to the far wall, and was examining it closely. 'Amazing the way they make the paintwork look *old*,' he said. 'From the outside you can tell it's just been built, but on the inside it's perfect.'

'Those guys earned their money.' Bradley moved across to the screen that took up most of one wall. All the desks and monitors had been arranged so that the operators were facing that screen. More like a school IT room than an office, Bex thought. Bradley rapped it with his knuckles. It gave off a wooden sound. 'I'm guessing the money didn't stretch to making this thing operational though.'

Bex shook her head. 'No. I told them we'd just overlay graphics on it using CGI.' She nodded towards Kieron. 'I got that off him,' she said. 'There was no point making it operational – we don't know what kind of images MI6 put on the real one when it's working. If you remember, they had it turned off at the party for security reasons. They didn't want us seeing their operations in action.'

'So what are you going to tell this technician you're kidna— sorry, I mean *borrowing*?' Sam asked.

Bex shrugged. 'If he asks, we'll tell him the system's been taken down for maintenance. Or we'll say there's a VIP visit going on, and it's been turned off so it doesn't give away anything top secret.'

She and Bradley spent the next half-hour or so checking the room from top to bottom and side to side, looking for anything that might give the game away. There were little things that, if you looked closely enough, showed it was a fake, but for their purposes it would do. They weren't going to give Scott Bailson much of an opportunity to look around. After they finished they closed the warehouse up and booked into a nearby hotel. They weren't going to spend that long in Edinburgh – hopefully – but it made sense to have a local base where they could rendezvous if something went wrong and they got split up. Bex knew that no operation ever went completely to plan, and it was crucial to have a fall-back option.

They had dinner at a local pizza place. The conversation was strained – they were all tense, and they knew that they couldn't really talk about what was going to happen later, so they ended up chatting about their families, their lives, the things they loved and the things they hated. To Bex's surprise, Kieron talked about his dad. He was apparently from Mauritius, although Bex would never have guessed it. Kieron had inherited his mother's skin tone, and only the darkness of his hair and eyes gave away his heritage. From the way he spoke he had a mixture of bitterness and affection for the man who had walked out so early in his life. Maybe, Bex considered, it was the fact that his mum seemed to have a new man in her life that had provoked him into thinking about his real dad.

'Do you still see him?' Bradley asked quietly.

'Maybe at Christmas,' Kieron said, looking down at his plate. 'That's when he seems to remember that he's got a kid.'

'Where does he live? Locally?'

Kieron shook his head. 'Down south somewhere. Coventry, I think.'

'Your dad was a moron,' Sam said.

Bex and Bradley looked at him, shocked.

'Well, he was,' Sam went on. 'My mum and my dad both said so. They knew him.'

They went back to the hotel shortly after that. Bex made it clear that they were going to have to get up before dawn to catch Scott after his night shift, and they needed to get as much rest as possible.

She slept badly, dreaming for some reason about her family, and the time she'd broken her leg climbing a tree, or rather falling out of it, as a kid. Her leg had been in plaster for what felt like forever, and she remembered, in the dream, how she'd been convinced that when the plaster was taken off her leg would look different from the unbroken one – twisted, maybe, or wrinkled, or a different colour. It hadn't, of course.

Her alarm went off at five o'clock in the morning. She quickly washed, dressed, and woke the others. Fifteen minutes later she and Kieron were sitting in the car, waiting, while Bradley and Sam lurked somewhere in the shadows outside the MI6 HQ. She had opened the windows a fraction, so that the glass didn't get steamed up. Kieron had wanted the radio on, but Bex had ruled that out. She didn't want anything to draw attention to them.

'I've got to say,' Kieron said quietly to Bex, 'this makes me nervous.' He held up his hands. 'I'm sweating, there's this strange metallic taste in my mouth, and it feels like something's trapped in my chest and struggling to get out. I mean, isn't this illegal?'

'Well,' Bex said cautiously, 'that depends what you mean

by "illegal". Technically, taking someone off the street, rendering them unconscious and taking them somewhere they weren't expecting to go is, I suppose, in contravention of the law of the land. But look at it this way: is it any worse that a bunch of friends kidnapping a mate and taking him off to Bratislava for a stag weekend?'

'Yes,' Kieron said, 'it is. Scott Bailson doesn't want to go with us, and we're not his friends.' He sighed. 'That feeling in my chest isn't getting any better. If anything, it's getting worse.

Bex sighed. 'OK,' she said patiently, 'but consider this: if Scott knew everything that we do about what's happening with the PEREGRINE satellite network, don't you think he'd be eager to help us?'

'No. No, I don't. I think he'd want to report it to his bosses officially, not engage in some kind of off-the-books attempt to put things right without anyone realising.'

Bex gazed at him. 'You're a hard nut to crack, aren't you? All right – consider *this*: there's a higher cause here which we are serving, and by committing a small crime in the scheme of things we are making a positive contribution to something much bigger.'

'It's still illegal,' Kieron said mutinously.

'If I said I'll slip five hundred pounds into Scott's pocket while he's unconscious, along with an anonymous apology for any psychological trouble we've caused him, would that make you feel better?'

'I suppose. A bit.'

'Then that's what I'll do.'

116

Bex glanced outside, sensing movement. For a moment she couldn't work out what had triggered her to look, but then she saw a fox slink from underneath a bush and walk calmly but watchfully across the grass lawn outside the MI6 building, an old Victorian manor house made out of grey-and-red stone. A sign on the wall outside said, 'Square Triangle Consulting'. The fox stopped halfway across the lawn, sniffing the air cautiously.

'Do they actually do any consulting?' Kieron asked. 'I mean, I don't know what "consulting" actually means, not really, but do they do any? Is that how a cover story works – you actually have to do the thing you're pretending to be before you can do the real secret-agent stuff?'

Bex shook her head. 'Not usually. They probably have a couple of junior agents maintaining a fake website and some social-media accounts, but they won't actually take any work on. If anyone asks, they'll quote a price which is too high, and the customer will go somewhere else.'

'What about security? I mean, we're parked in front of their building. Won't they have cameras, and guards, and stuff?' He suddenly looked panicked. 'Won't the guards be armed? Aren't we in danger here?'

Bex shook her head. 'They're pretending to be a legitimate company. They can't have security that looks too out of place. Yes, there'll be cameras, but they'll be focused on the doors and the windows.'

'OK,' Kieron said cautiously. He didn't sound convinced. He checked his watch – something he'd been doing every few minutes since he'd got into the car. 'We've got twenty minutes before the next gap in satellite coverage. What happens if this bloke is late leaving? We need the ARCC system to knock him out, but if it's not working then we've got no way of doing that!'

Bex could hear rising panic in Kieron's voice. He was obviously deeply uncomfortable with the idea of kidnapping an MI6 agent – and, despite what she'd said earlier, it *was* kidnapping, even if it was only temporary and the victim might never realise he'd been taken. 'If the system goes down, then Bradley will hit him over the head,' she said firmly.

'*What?*'

'I'm winding you up, Kieron. If Scott is late and the SIS-TERR capability is down then we'll catch him later, or wait until tomorrow. This is going to work.'

The main door to the Victorian block suddenly opened, and a man came out. Startled, the fox ran for cover. It was difficult to tell at that distance, but Bex thought that this was the same man she'd met briefly at the outstation office party, and seen more recently in Bradley's selfies: Scott Bailson. He crossed to a bike rack by the side of the building and unchained a bike.

'That's awkward,' she muttered. 'We'd assumed he would walk home – it's only twenty minutes. Bradley and Sam are going to have to reach him before he gets on the bike.' Her brain suddenly flashed up an image of Bradley and Sam chasing a bike-riding Scott Bailson down the road, and she giggled.

'This isn't meant to be funny,' Kieron pointed out, obviously dismayed. 'It's *serious*.'

'I know – I'm sorry. Sometimes when I'm tense I find myself laughing at the smallest thing.'

Kieron unexpectedly laughed too. 'Yeah, I remember that Sam and I once went into uncontrollable hysterics in a maths lesson. I can't even remember what we were laughing about, but the teacher had to send us out. It took ten minutes before we could stop, and breathe again. We got detention for that.'

As they watched, Scott wheeled his bike along the path that led from the door of the office block to the gate in the wall.

'They're leaving it a bit late,' Bex murmured. 'Get ready. Phase One.'

Kieron slipped the ARCC glasses on and reactivated them from their sleep mode. Bex knew that glowing menus would be suddenly appearing in his field of vision.

'Do you see what we see?' Kieron asked. He paused as Sam replied, then glanced at Bex through the ARCC lenses. 'Sam's ready. So's Bradley.'

Scott was perhaps ten feet from the gate when Sam appeared from behind a bush. They'd all agreed that it had to be Sam: he would present less of a threat to Scott than Bradley would have done. Nobody would seriously believe that someone as young as Sam could be an enemy agent.

'Excuse me,' he called. 'Mister?'

Scott kept moving, but turned his head slightly. 'Can't stop,' he called. 'Sorry.'

'I just need some help,' Sam said, holding his arm as if he'd been hurt. 'I fell over and sprained my wrist. I was hoping you could call an ambulance for me.'

'What happened to *your* phone?' Scott asked. He was

almost at the gate by now, and still not looking back.

'Broke it when I fell.' Sam shrugged. 'And besides – sprained wrist. Can't hold it properly. And I'm out of credit.'

'What are you doing out at this time? Shouldn't you be at home?' Now he did turn around to look at Sam. 'You're just a kid.'

'I was in the city centre with some mates. I want to go home now, but I'm hurt.' Sam sounded genuinely frightened.

Bex saw Scott sigh: a little rise and fall of his shoulders. He was a good Samaritan at heart. 'OK,' he called reluctantly. 'Stay where you are. I'll call an ambulance.'

He was at the gate by now, and he leaned his bike against it. Sam stayed well back, as if trying not to look threatening.

Scott pulled his phone from his pocket.

'Moving to Phase Two,' Bex said. 'Ready?'

'Always,' Kieron responded, but he didn't look ready. He looked terrified. Quickly he activated the macro command Bex had seen him program in earlier.

As Scott raised the phone towards his face, the ARCC software connected with his mobile phone provider's computer systems, momentarily taking them over. It sent a special command to Scott's mobile; one that took control of the operating system and then wormed its way into the software that controlled the screen.

Bex stared hard at Scott, holding her breath. If they mistimed this, he would have the mobile up at his ear and the plan would fail.

Scott looked at the screen as he typed something into the keypad: presumably '999'.

The special ARCC software took control of his mobile. Suddenly his face was illuminated by a flickering light as the screen cycled from black to white and back to black again several hundred times a second. Bex wasn't sure, but she thought Scott's eyes widened slowly as he continued to stare at the screen. And stare. And stare.

'He's paralysed!' Kieron said, amazed.

'Phase Three: time for you to do your thing,' Bex said, pushing Kieron towards the door. He opened it and stepped out. He turned to look back through the window at Bex, face white and strained, but instead of saying anything he took a deep breath and ran towards the lawn, where Scott Bailson was still frozen, face flashing light and dark, light and dark, with the screen held in front of his face. The problem now was that the battery on his mobile would drain rapidly, and also that it would be almost impossible to bundle him into the car and drive him to the warehouse with the phone still held up to his face. His hand would move, or the phone would fall from his hand, and suddenly he wouldn't be transfixed by the flickering screen any more.

Bradley and Sam moved to stand on either side of Scott. Bradley was looking around, making sure that nobody else was passing by. The MI6 local HQ was located in a quiet part of town – and not by accident. That made their job a lot easier.

Kieron got to where the three of them were standing and waved his hands in the air, obviously accessing the virtual menus on the ARCC glasses he wore. He tore the glasses off his face and handed them to Sam. Bex could see that his eyes were screwed shut, just in case. Sam immediately put them on Scott's face, earpieces over the MI6 operative's ears, just as the screens projecting onto the lenses began to flash at the same rate as Scott's mobile – another ARCC app that Kieron had created. Bradley took the mobile from Scott's hand and turned it off before its flickering could affect himself, Sam or Kieron. With Scott now safely kept unconscious by the ARCC app, Bradley, Sam and Kieron were able to move his hands down to his sides, lean him backwards and then carry him to the car. And all without anyone seeing them – apart, presumably, from the fox that had passed by.

One of the back passenger doors opened, and Bradley and the boys manoeuvred Scott inside. Bex could see a faint flicker coming from behind the lenses, reflected off Scott's face, but Bradley draped a pillowcase over the MI6 agent's head so the flashing couldn't leak out and affect them. Obviously, having Bex slip into unconsciousness while she was driving would be a bad thing. Immediately Sam and Kieron climbed into the car on either side of the unconscious Scott, keeping him upright and blocking anyone outside from seeing him through the windows, while Bradley got into the passenger seat next to Bex.

The drive to the warehouse only took ten minutes, and Scott didn't move at all during that time. Once they arrived, Bradley and the boys carried Scott gently out of the car, across the warehouse and into the fake office while Bex locked the car and then raced ahead of them to check that everything inside the artificial set was as perfect as they could make it.

Scott was placed in an office chair, and the boys left the room. Bex and Bradley sat down too.

'Ready?' Bradley asked.

'Go for it,' she replied. It was either going to work or it wasn't. Time to see which one.

Bradley pulled the ARCC glasses off Scott's face and slid them into his own jacket pocket, turning them off while he did so. Scott's eyes were open, pupils dilated, as he stared straight ahead.

'What do we do if he doesn't, you know, wake up?' Bradley murmured.

'That's not going to happen,' Bex muttered back. 'OK, let's get into character. Phase Four.'

'Phase Five,' Bradley said. 'Phase Four was the drive here. Actually, Phase Four was probably us putting him into the car while Phase Five was the drive here.'

'Whatever.' She leaned back casually in her chair and said in a louder voice, 'And then he had the nerve to ask me for identification! *Me!* I mean, we'd only known each other for twenty years!' This was the script that she and Bradley had agreed the night before.

'It's the rules,' Bradley said loudly, shaking his head. 'I remember when I grew this beard, the security guards wouldn't let me in because the photo on my ID was me clean-shaven. They didn't believe I was the same person.'

'As if someone with a beard would try and get in using fake identification showing someone *without* a beard,' Bex responded. From the corner of her eye she could see Scott blinking. That was a good sign. 'What did you do?'

'I got out a felt-tip pen and drew a beard on my ID.' Bradley laughed. 'They let me in once they saw I looked like the picture, but then they reported me for defacing an ID card. Some days you just can't win.'

Scott suddenly sat upright in his chair, looking around in confusion. 'Ah – what happened?' he said loudly. 'I was – I was –'

'You were outside,' Bex said. 'Don't you remember? You were leaving just as we were coming in, and you fell over. We caught you and brought you back in, so we could make sure you were OK.'

Scott frowned. 'I remember going outside, and then – there was a boy? Wasn't there? He'd injured himself.'

'We didn't see any boy,' Bradley said, shaking his head. 'We just saw you fall over.'

'And we caught you,' Bex said, repeating herself deliberately in an attempt to create a picture in Scott's head, one that in his vulnerable state he would accept as a memory. 'Then we brought you in here to make sure you were OK.'

Scott looked at them both in confusion. 'Do I know you?' He frowned. 'Yes, I remember – you were here for Derek's leaving drinks. And I've seen you around a couple of other times as well.'

'That's right,' Bex said. 'We're part of the PEREGRINE programme.'

'Independent contractors,' Bradley added. 'I'm Bailey, and this is Rachel.' They'd chosen the names to sound something *like* their real names, just in case Scott had some vague memory of 'Bradley and Rebecca', but different enough that even if he remembered them after all this was over, nobody would be able to trace them.

'Yeah, right,' Scott said. He raised a hand to his forehead, exploring the skin. 'Did I hit my head? Is there any blood?'

'I don't think so.' Bex leaned forward and looked into his eyes. 'Your pupils seem fine – I don't think you've got any concussion. We managed to catch you before you hit the ground –'

'– And carried you back in here to make sure you were OK,' Bradley continued, reinforcing the story again.

'Do you want a coffee, or some water?' Bex asked. Before Scott could answer, she reached out and put her hand on his forehead just as he took his own away. 'I think you might be running a temperature. Maybe you've got a virus.'

Scott nodded slowly. 'I've been pulling twelve-hour shifts recently. I wouldn't be surprised if my immune system was compromised. I've been telling the bosses that for a while now – if they insist on us working overtime, then it's going to make us ill.'

Bex glanced at Bradley and raised an eyebrow. Bradley had been right: Scott *was* a bit of a hypochondriac, obsessed with his health.

'Actually,' Scott went on, 'I think a glass of water would be good. I've got a bit of a headache.' He frowned. 'And my eyes hurt.'

'It's a virus,' Bex and Bradley said together.

'I'll get you that water,' Bradley said, standing up and moving towards the door that led out to the warehouse. They had some bottles of water stored out there, just in case.

'There's definitely something going around,' Bex said, distracting Scott from Bradley and the door. She didn't want Scott seeing anything that he shouldn't through the doorway when Bradley went outside – like Kieron or Sam or the empty warehouse space. 'I've got friends who've had this same thing. You should take a couple of sick days to get over it.'

'I think I will,' Scott said, checking his forehead again, but this time to see if he was feeling warm. 'Yeah, my skin's definitely too hot. I need a few days in bed.'

'Good idea,' Bex said. 'Oh –' she added, as if a thought had just occurred to her – 'is there anyone who can –'

'Why is the screen off?' Scott asked, staring at the blank floor-to-ceiling LCD screen. 'It was OK earlier.'

'Preparing for some VIP visit,' Bex said smoothly. This was the moment of truth. This was the point where they would either get the information they wanted, or not.

'I wasn't informed,' Scott said, irritated.

'That's why we're here,' Bradley said, coming back in with a bottle of water. He handed it to Scott as he went on, 'We're giving a presentation to whoever's visiting – I think it's an MP or something. We've been told to brief them on PEREGRINE.'

'But that's a top-secret system!' Scott protested.

'Maybe it was one of their constituents.'

'Unlikely – it's an automated system. We program it remotely from here.' Scott looked around, still obviously confused. 'Where is everyone? This room is supposed to be continuously manned.'

'They're preparing for the visit,' Bex said smoothly. 'Yeah,

apparently this MP is interested in PEREGRINE because –'
she glanced briefly at Bradley – 'the PEREGRINE system
control station has something to do with their constituency.'
This was it: would Scott take the bait or not?

'I can't see how,' Scott said, still looking around, 'unless
they're the MP for the Falkland Islands. Do the Falkland
Islands even have an MP? I don't think so.'

Bex kept her expression neutral, but inside she felt partly
triumphant and partly crestfallen. Triumphant, because
Scott had told them where the PEREGRINE control station
was located. Crestfallen, because it was apparently in the
Falklands, thousands of miles away, out in the Atlantic
Ocean, off the coast of South America. Probably unreachable.

She looked over at Bradley. He was wincing.

'Phase Six?' she asked.

He nodded.

Scott's mobile began to ring. He reached for it
automatically. 'I must be feeling ill,' he said, shocked.
'I should have handed this in before I came back in the
building!' He frowned at Bex. 'Or you should!'

'Answer it anyway,' Bex advised. 'It might be important.'
As Scott – apparently still suggestible, after the previous
hypnosis event – complied, she glanced towards the door.
Outside, Kieron should be waiting to trigger the flickering
screen again, so they could take Scott home and leave him
there to wake up, confused and unsure what had happened.

The Falkland Islands. That was going to be a problem.
A really *big* problem.

CHAPTER SEVEN

'Are you absolutely sure about this?' Kieron asked, looking around what had been described as the 'departure lounge' but which to him looked more like a large school staff room, with its faded old carpet and vinyl-covered seats.

'We've been over this,' Bex said quietly, head turned away from the other people in the room – some of whom were in RAF or Army uniform while others were dressed casually, in jeans and Barbour jackets. They all looked like they were expecting cold weather though, which didn't fill Kieron with any great joy. He really wasn't looking forward to this. 'There's only one civilian flight to the Falkland Islands each week. It goes via Chile, and the next one is six days from now. We haven't got time to wait. The Ministry of Defence provide *two* military flights each week, and civilians can buy tickets. That means we can get there and do what we have to do more quickly.'

'Infiltrate a satellite communications facility without anyone knowing,' Kieron said, feeling his spirits fall with every syllable that came out of his mouth.

'Hey,' Bex said, 'if this was easy, someone else could do it.

Team AARC specialises in doing the impossible, the almost impossible and the improbable.'

'Team ARCC?'

Bex shrugged and smiled. 'I'm going to have to work on that, aren't I?'

'Thanks for the pep talk,' Kieron said.

'Did it work?'

'Not so you'd notice.' He sighed. 'I'm not complaining, but wouldn't it have been much easier if you and Bradley had gone on this trip rather than you and me?'

'Yeah. The problem is that Bradley had to stay behind and do what he could to optimise the ARCC kit. There are some little tricks he can play with the software that might increase the time the equipment is usable for. He was talking about reducing the level of the signal-to-noise ratio filters so that the glasses can be used with a lower quality of signal, but that's only going to help a bit. And he had to do it somewhere with good Internet connectivity, and I don't think the Falkland Islands counts for that. Also, I wanted him to keep an eye on Scott Bailson, just in case he causes any trouble.'

'It's just that I think my mum's getting suspicious of the number of times I go missing from the house for a few days. We've pulled the "winning a trip to America in a competition" trick and the "school trip to Venice" card, and pretty soon we're going to run out of ideas. We can't tell her that I'm staying with Sam, because it's too risky – my mum knows his mum, and if they meet up in the supermarket or at the doctor's surgery she'll ask how I'm doing and Sam's mum won't know anything about it.' He frowned, thinking. 'What did you do this time? All I got was a message on my mobile telling me that she was going to be away for a few days and she'd left fifty pounds beneath the toaster in case I needed to buy any food. But not takeaways. She was very particular about that. You didn't arrange for her to go away on another work-related trip, did you? That excuse is going to wear out.'

'You're not going to like this.'

'Just tell me.'

Bex hesitated, then said, 'I sent this new man in her life an email, and I faked it to look like it came from an Internet travel site. It said he'd won some vouchers that he could exchange for a luxury weekend in a spa hotel, with all kinds of massages and beauty treatments thrown in, but the vouchers had to be used on a certain weekend. I had a pretty good idea that he'd invite your mum to go away with him. Sorry.'

Kieron closed his eyes and sighed. 'You've paid for my mum to have a dirty weekend away with her new boyfriend. That's great. That's just *great*.'

'Look on the bright side,' Bex said brightly, smiling. 'Another year or two and you can tell her you're staying at your girlfriend's place. Talking of which, how's it going with –'

'We're not talking about that,' Kieron said flatly. 'I do get to have a personal life, you know.'

'Sorry.'

Kieron looked around again, for what felt like the five-hundredth time. 'I'm guessing that if we'd gone on the civilian flight we could have left from Heathrow or Gatwick or somewhere civilised. Not from some RAF base.'

'All military flights go from RAF Brize Norton,' Bex pointed out.

'Even the ones with civilians on board?'

'Even the ones with civilians on board.'

'Please tell me there'll be in-flight entertainment!'

'I wouldn't bank on it,' Bex said carefully.

'Food, at least? It's a twenty-hour flight!'

'With a three-hour stop on Ascension Island to refuel. I'm sure there'll be food. It might be sandwiches though.'

Kieron breathed a sigh of relief. 'At least that's something. What is there to see on Ascension Island?'

He saw Bex wince slightly. 'Actually, they keep us in the airport terminal for the whole time. It's largely a military base these days. We won't be allowed out.'

'Great.' Kieron sighed. He glanced at Bex, and noticed a slight smile on her face. 'You're enjoying all this, aren't you?'

She nodded, looking slightly ashamed of herself, but only slightly. 'My dad was in the Royal Air Force. I've flown out of Brize Norton on my way to his postings more times than I can count. It's just – nostalgic, I guess.'

Kieron glanced again around the depressing, old-fashioned lounge, filled with people in uniform and, presumably, Falkland Islanders, and at the large lounge windows, through which he could see several passenger aircraft that looked like they'd seen better days. In fact, it looked like those better days might have been before Kieron had been born. Everything in here felt like he thought the 1970s must have been: drab and brown and boring. 'I can't see the attraction myself.'

Bex looked around as well, and it was as if she was suddenly seeing the place for the first time. 'To be fair,' she said, 'it's probably an acquired taste.' She shook her head suddenly, as if banishing thoughts of the past. 'OK, we've got two hours before the flight. Let's go over our cover stories again. Who are we?'

'I'm Ryan Drewe and you are Chloe Drewe.'

'And why are we going to the Falkland Islands?'

'Because you're a location scout for a TV series that's supposed to be based there, and I'm your birdwatching-addicted brother.'

'Well done.' She suddenly pulled a small illustrated book from her pocket and turned to a random page with a photograph of a bird on it. 'What's this?'

'It's a bird,' he sighed.

'What kind of bird?'

He looked closer. 'A seabird, I think. Maybe a seagull.'

'You're going to have to do better than that if you want to pass muster as a birdwatcher.' She glanced at the photo. 'It's a white-tufted grebe, apparently. Still, you've got twenty-three hours and no in-flight movie, so you'll have time to do your research. Give me a potted history of the Falklands.'

Kieron stared at her. 'Nobody said there would be a test.'

'We're undercover. Every moment is a test. Go!'

Kieron closed his eyes, trying to remember the stuff he'd read online. 'Seven hundred and seventy-eight small islands off the coast of Argentina, only two of which are of any real size. Variously claimed by Spain, France, Argentina and the UK, although they've been a UK Overseas Territory for over a hundred years. Subject of a limited war in the eighties when Argentina tried to take them back. Population small, British and proud of it.'

'And why are they important?'

'Oil, fish and access to Antarctica. Apparently everyone wants to have land close to Antarctica because it gives them a better claim on the territory.'

'Well done. If there was a GCSE in the Falkland Islands, you'd have passed.'

'Oh joy.' He glanced over at the tiny cafe area, which looked like something you'd find in a shed in a park. 'What do you reckon my chances are of a brie-and-bacon panini?'

'Honestly? Fairly small.'

The next twenty-four hours were among the most boring Kieron had ever experienced. The flight attendants on the creaking aircraft were uniformed RAF personnel, the food was terrible, there was no in-flight entertainment so he had to make do with his mobile – all the games and movies on which he'd already played or seen – and Bex spent her time reading. Worse than that, all the seats faced *backwards*.

'What's the thing with the seats?' he asked Bex as they sat down. He felt dangerously close to mutiny.

'It's apparently safer that way,' she said, already pulling her eBook reader from her bag. 'If we crash, we'll be thrown backwards, into our seats, rather than forward into the hard backs of the seats in front of us. All military passenger planes have the same arrangement.' She rapped the seat in front of her with her knuckles as if to prove a point.

'That's very reassuring. How much of this flight is over water?'

'All of it.'

And it was. Whenever Kieron looked out of the tiny window by his seat all he could see was either the tops of clouds or glittering water, far, far below. The occasional ship was just a dark point on the waves. Kieron slept, a lot.

When the aircraft started its descent to Ascension Island, and the announcement came over the intercom that all passengers should sit down, put their seat belt on and raise their seat into the upright position, Kieron woke up. Looking out of the window, all he could see was water. No land. Just water.

The aircraft got lower and lower, and still there was no land. No sign of the island.

Kieron looked around, worried. Nobody else appeared to be taking any notice.

He looked out of the window again, nose pressed against the glass. The aircraft was now so low that he could see its shadow on the water, getting larger and larger.

He looked up, and along the length of the aircraft. The RAF personnel were strapping themselves into their own seats now. They didn't seem worried.

Outside the window the aircraft was racing its own shadow. Still, just the water.

And then land suddenly flashed beneath them, rock and then a grey expanse of tarmac. Moments later the wheels touched ground. A shudder ran through the aircraft as its engines shifted into reverse, slowing it down rapidly. Kieron started breathing again.

The arrival/departure lounge at Ascension Island was the spitting image of the one at RAF Brize Norton. The only difference was, it was about fifteen degrees hotter. And humid with it.

Getting back onto the aircraft and taking off again was almost a relief, but it just meant swapping one monotonous hell for another. Kieron tried sleeping, tried replaying games he'd finished weeks ago, and ended up sitting there with his eyes closed, imagining a story that he thought he might be able to turn into a graphic novel some time – once he'd taught himself to draw. Of the limited number of career paths open to him, creating his own graphic novels and then having them turned into movies seemed like the best bet. Being a secret agent was turning out to be a lot more boring than he'd expected.

That took up two hours. After that, in desperation, he pulled out the book of birds that Bex had given him and started memorising them. The striated caracara, the Magellanic penguin, the Falkland steamer duck – he filed them all away in his brain as if they were cards in some collectible card game – their appearance, their diet, whether or not they lived exclusively on the Falklands or were distributed more widely, everything and anything. Normally – if anything in his life could properly be described as 'normal' at the moment – he would have used the ARCC glasses to give him this information if he needed it, but he couldn't rely on them now. He had to do this old-school.

Seeing one illustration of a particular bird, he giggled. Bex glanced up from the book she was reading. 'What's so funny?'

'There's a bird called the Imperial shag!' he said, and giggled again.

Bex raised an eyebrow. 'Nice to see you're learning stuff.'

Landing at Mount Pleasant Airport was a repeat of landing on Ascension Island: water, water, more water and then the sudden appearance of land. The only difference was that the overalled RAF mechanics standing outside the hangars on the airfield were holding up large scorecards with numbers on them, presumably rating the pilot on the quality of his landing. That was how boring life here on the Falklands must be for the military, he realised.

'They have to make their own entertainment here,' Bex said, looking past Kieron at the mechanics. 'An eight, a seven and a nine – that's a good score.'

'I guess the time to worry,' Kieron said, 'is when you're landing, and you look out of the window and see that the scores are down around one or two.'

They deplaned down a mobile stairway, and were led across the runway into the immigration area. Kieron looked around at the landscape. Bumpy, grassy and windswept, with either small mountains or large hills in the distance. The sky was an absolutely pure blue, but apart from that it didn't look any different to him than the countryside outside Newcastle. The weather was cold, with a sharp, biting wind. He was glad he'd dressed warmly.

'What are you doing on the Falkland Islands?' the immigration official asked him in a bored tone.

'My sister's researching locations for a TV series,' he said, reeling off the cover story they'd agreed, 'and I'm taking the opportunity to do some birdwatching. There's some really neat birds on this island you can't see anywhere else.'

'Any ones in particular you want to see?' the man asked.

Kieron turned to where Bex stood behind him in the queue, listening without appearing to listen. She stared at him. 'I want to see penguins,' he said.

'That shouldn't be a problem here. So where are you staying?'

'We've got hotel rooms reserved at Port Stanley,' he replied. It was what Bex had told him earlier.

'And how are you getting to Port Stanley?

'We've rented a car. It should be waiting here for us.'

The man stamped his passport. 'Welcome to the Falkland Islands.'

After everyone from the aircraft had been processed through Immigration, they were all taken into a large room with lots of chairs facing a map of the islands that had been pinned to the wall. The airfield at Mount Pleasant and the main population centre at Port Stanley were clearly marked.

'I'm going to be briefing you on mines, and how to avoid them,' the man said without any preamble or introduction. He sounded as if he'd given this same presentation a thousand times before. 'Following the ten weeks of the Falklands War an estimated twenty thousand anti-personnel mines and five thousand anti-tank mines were left behind, scattered across 113 known minefields. Many of them are still where they were left. What I am going to do over the next twenty minutes is tell you what to look for so you can avoid stumbling into a minefield or stepping on a mine. Nobody has been injured or killed by a mine here on the islands in the past thirty-four years, and our aim is to keep it that way . . .'

Kieron shook his head slightly, amazed at how boring a presentation on live minefields could turn out to be.

After the presentation was over, they reclaimed their luggage, along with a large plastic crate that Bex had handed over to the RAF at Brize Norton. He'd asked her at the time what it was, and she'd just smiled and said, 'You'll find out.'

A woman with a clipboard was waiting for them when they left the luggage area. 'Ms Drewe?' she said, looking at Bex. 'I've got your car.'

'Porsche?' Kieron asked hopefully. 'Lamborghini?'

'Land Rover,' the woman said without breaking a smile. 'And not a new one. Let's walk over to it, and I'll give you some tips about driving here, and how to avoid the penguins. There's a map in the car. You'll be needing that. All the known minefields are marked.'

The drive from Mount Pleasant to Port Stanley took just over an hour, and they saw only three other cars in that time. The sky was a vast blue dome above them, without any hint of cloud. Kieron didn't think he'd ever been in a place before where he could look around and see nothing, literally *nothing*, apart from the horizon all around him.

About twenty minutes in, Bex pulled off the road onto an area of scrubby grass. A side road – more of a muddy track than anything easily drivable – led off into the distance. She got out of the car and, when Kieron had joined her, pointed off to one side. In the far distance Kieron noticed that something *was* actually breaking the monotony of the hills and mountains in the distance: a collection of white satellite dishes pointing upwards. A small number of futuristic buildings, looking more like huge white Lego bricks than anything else, clustered at their bases.

'That's the PEREGRINE control station,' she said. 'We've got to get in there.'

'Now?' Kieron asked nervously.

'No. I want to wait until nightfall, when we can get closer without being seen.'

'So what do we do until then?' Kieron looked around. 'I could do with a bath after that long flight, and some food as well, and there's nothing out here. I mean, literally *nothing*.'

'We'll drive on to Port Stanley,' she said, 'and check into our hotel. If we don't, people will get suspicious. They know we arrived on the island, and if we go missing someone will come looking for us.'

'So we'll drive back after dark.'

'Not drive,' she said. 'There aren't that many cars on the island, and besides, noise travels. We need to be stealthier than that.' She stared at the distant buildings. 'I can see a fence,' she said, 'and I can see cameras on poles. Probably infra-red cameras so they're covered at night as well as during the day. I've brought some stuff with me that'll help get us in.'

'Do they really need that level of security on the *Falkland* Islands?' Kieron asked.

Bex moved back towards the car and started to get in. 'Given that the PEREGRINE satellite network has been compromised, apparently they need a *better* level of security.' She started the car up again. 'Let's head for Port Stanley before they think we've driven into a minefield.'

Port Stanley turned out to be a collection of largely white buildings with coloured roofs – green, red, blue, yellow and purple. It looked vaguely like the villages he'd seen in Norway, Kieron thought, when he and Sam had rescued Bex and Bradley from the Asrael organisation. Their hotel rooms were small, but comfortable, and he luxuriated in a large, claw-footed bath tub for so long that he twice had to run some of the bathwater out and top it up with hotter water. When he finally got out he dressed in dark blue and dark grey clothes – Bex had told him to dress dark but to avoid black. Black clothes, she said, tend to make you look like a black hole against the night. Dark grey and dark blue provide just the right level of contrast.

He went for a walk along the quay before dinner. People in parka jackets and woollen hats nodded at him in a friendly way as they passed. He stopped beside a fishing boat that was unloading its catch of silvery fish on the quayside. They were being stacked in crates of ice, and when eventually he turned around to return to the hotel he realised that a woman was wheeling three of the crates in the same direction, heading from the quayside to the hotel. She got there just ahead of him, and disappeared around the back while he went in the front. That, he suspected, was going to be dinner tonight – fish that had been alive only a few hours before, taken straight from the ocean, cooked and put on his plate.

Life here didn't seem to be too bad. He'd wondered if the sheer distance between the Falkland Islands and anywhere that he would consider to be 'civilised' would mean that life there was hard and primitive, but he'd been wrong. The air was fresh, and so was the food.

Dinner was a choice between fish or lamb. He chose the fish, and it was the tastiest fish he'd ever had. Life here was better than 'not too bad'; it was good. He even managed to find a free wifi hotspot for his mobile.

After dinner, Bex took him back to her room. She'd somehow managed to get the black plastic crate up the stairs, and it was open on her bed. Inside were what looked suspiciously like two pairs of walking boots that had been surrounded with struts, braces, wires and tightly stretched rubber ties.

'I don't like the look of this,' he said cautiously.

'We have to get to the satellite control station,' Bex replied, pulling one of the boots out of the crate, 'and this is how we're going to do it. These are exo-boots. Bradley managed to get hold of two sets from a contact he has.' She indicated a leather collar-like strip that was connected to the boot but would be positioned up above it, just below knee level, Kieron guessed. 'You strap yourself into it, and these rubber things act like elastic bands. They multiply the power you're putting into walking by a factor of ten. And you see these bits here? They're pistons, driven by these fuel cells down here in the heels. They add even more power, so you can move faster and further than any Olympic runner. It's like having motors in your legs.'

'It's like a cheap version of Iron Man,' Kieron said. 'And just think how many more bones you'll break if you trip over,' he added, imagining in his head all the possible ways these things could go wrong.

'Don't worry. They come with gloves, knee pads, elbow pads and a padded helmet. Using these things we can go cross-country and approach the satellite control station from the fields rather than from the one road that leads there. If there's anything wrong at the control station, if someone has taken it over for instance, then they'll be watching the road. We can surprise them.'

'Shock them, more like,' Kieron said. 'If they see us in these things they'll die laughing.' He picked up one of the other boots from the crate and examined it critically. 'If there's a fuel cell and a piston then they must make quite a noise when they're operating. If there are any bad guys in the control station, won't they hear us coming?'

Bex shook her head. 'You know you can get noise-cancelling headphones, that get rid of external noise when you're listening to music, or you just want a bit of quiet in your life?'

'Yeah,' he said. 'They pick up the sound of the noise and then replay it half a cycle out of phase, so it actually cancels out the original sounds.'

'Well, these boots have a similar system built in.

Whatever noise the mechanical bits make is cancelled out. They're completely silent.'

'Wonderful. Can I just mention one word? Minefields.'

'None between here and the satellite control station.'

'You've checked the maps?'

'Twice.'

'What if there are minefields out there that aren't marked on the maps?'

Bex shook her head, a patient smile on her lips. 'There aren't.'

He sighed. 'I'm not going to be able to get out of this, am I?'

'Nope. Now get some rest. I'll wake you up once this place has gone quiet and we'll head off.'

Four hours later, a muffled knock on Kieron's door woke him from a deep, dreamless sleep. It was Bex, holding both pairs of exo-boots along with the padded protection. She passed one set to Kieron and gestured to him to follow her.

Once downstairs, they slipped out of the front door and, keeping to the shadows, moved quietly through town. Port Stanley seemed to shut up shop completely once the sun went down. Apart from one solitary man walking his dog, they didn't see anyone, and fortunately the dog was too interested in finding out what messages other dogs had left on the lamp posts to worry about Bex and Kieron.

Fifteen minutes later the houses were behind them, and the huge black expanse of the night-time countryside lay ahead. Looking up, Kieron saw more stars than he had ever seen in his life. He could even see the belt of the Milky Way – the galaxy in which Earth and its sun were located – stretching diagonally across the sky. He'd never realised just how many stars there were.

Bex helped Kieron put the boots on and strap his legs into the harnesses to which the mechanical bits were connected. While she was putting her own boots on, Kieron bounced up and down experimentally. It was like being on a trampoline, he decided, except that he was wearing the trampoline. This might actually be fun. He did feel a bit top heavy though – as if he was standing on a box made of rubber.

Bex handed over a small remote control. It was surrounded by rubberised padding and had a lanyard attached to it. 'This clips to your belt,' she said. Her voice was loud amid the absolute silence of the night. 'The big red button turns the boots on, and the two arrowed buttons increase or decrease the power. I suggest you start off on the lowest power setting until you get used to it. Now, you head off and I'll follow once I know you're OK with it all. There's a light at the front of your helmet, so you can see where you're going. We can use the ARCC kit to communicate and navigate – we're in an active window at the moment.'

Tentatively, Kieron started to walk. For the first few steps he felt strange, as if he was trying to move in some strange combination of walking boots and high heels, but pretty soon his body got used to it, and he started to run. The exo-boots magnified his movements, making him feel like a superhero. Cold air whistled past his head, filling his ears with a rushing sound. The landscape seemed to blur as he moved through it. This was fun!

His right foot caught on a clump of grass and he almost fell, but managed to get his leg out in front of him just in time to stop himself. Chastened, he decided to slow down before he tripped again. Despite all the padding and the helmet, he really might break his neck if he hit the ground at that speed.

He glanced over his shoulder. Bex was a few yards behind him, her legs pumping and arms swinging in an exaggerated way as she bounced across the landscape. Kieron could see a huge grin on her face. She was enjoying this as well.

Past Bex, Kieron could just about see the lights of Port Stanley on the horizon. They'd already moved a lot further than he'd thought.

He slowed to a walk and checked the map display on the ARCC glasses, superimposed faintly over the landscape. They were perhaps a quarter of the way to the satellite control station now. He estimated that they'd arrive in about twenty minutes.

Bex overtook him while he was checking the display. She obviously trusted that he was safe with the exo-boots now. Either that or she couldn't stop.

Kieron started running again, doing his best to catch up with Bex but stay behind her. A bird suddenly took flight from a patch of gorse, startled by the two intruders. It flew off in the same direction they were headed in, and for a few seconds, before it veered away, Kieron found himself running at the same speed it was flying. He glanced sideways at it, seeing the way its wings flexed and its feathers ruffled as it moved without apparently moving. It was an experience he'd never had before, and he had to catch his breath at the sudden wonder of the moment.

He realised that he could feel a dull ache in his calves and his thighs, as his muscles were forced to work in ways they hadn't done before. His cheeks and his ears felt numb with the passing cold air, and the tips of his fingers tingled fiercely, as if they were on fire. Within a few minutes the ache in his legs had turned into a regular stabbing sensation, and he could feel a similar pain starting up in his shoulders because of the exaggerated way he had to swing his arms to keep his balance as he ran. Suddenly this adventure didn't seem as much fun as it had.

Ahead of him, Bex started to slow. She raised her right arm and waved to him to slow down as well. The two of them gradually came to a halt over perhaps a hundred metres of countryside.

Ahead, on the horizon, Kieron could make out the dark shapes of the satellite control station's dish-like antennas blocking out the light of the stars.

'We're nearly at the fence,' Bex's voice crackled in his ear. 'Let's go slower now. We don't want to rouse a fox or something. In fact, let's take the exo-boots off. We can't really hide behind bushes or take advantage of dips in the ground while we're wearing them.'

'At last!' Kieron exclaimed. 'I thought we were going to have to jump over the fence using the exo-boots.'

'Oh, that's an idea!' Bex replied, frowning. 'I hadn't thought of that!' She saw the horrified expression on Kieron's face and burst out laughing – quietly. 'Don't worry. I wouldn't ask you to do that. Far too risky. You'd land badly and break every bone in your body. And, to be fair, so would I.'

Having left the exo-boots beneath a large rock, and marked the location on the map on the ARCC glasses, they proceeded slow and low, side by side, towards the fence, and the buildings beyond.

When they got to within ten metres of the fence, Bex stopped, and Kieron stopped with her. He stared ahead, through the darkness. The meagre light from his headband lamp illuminated a grid-like wire fence strung tightly between ten-foot high poles. At the point where the wires passed the poles Kieron could see that they were fed through ceramic insulators.

'Electrified,' he whispered.

'To be expected,' Bex confirmed quietly. 'Probably more to stop wildlife than people, but if we interfere with the signal we'll trigger an alarm.'

'So what do we do?'

'We don't interfere with the signal.'

Just as Kieron was about to ask what she meant, Bex started creeping forward. When she reached the fence she got up on her knees and took something out of her jacket. Kieron couldn't see what she was doing because her body masked that part of the fence.

He looked around. Darkness everywhere. The light from his headband couldn't penetrate more than a little distance before it petered out, defeated by the infinite blackness.

The back of his neck tickled. He shivered. He had the sudden but overwhelming impression that he was being stared at. He looked back at Bex, but she was still working on the fence. Panicking, he stared around again. Nothing. And yet he knew that someone, some*thing*, was watching him.

He closed his eyes for a moment, trying to control his breathing but also trying to work out which direction he was being stared at *from*. It was up high, in front and off to the right, he thought.

He opened his eyes and looked in that direction.

A bird sat on top of one of the fence poles. It seemed to be a hawk: curved beak and black eyes, glinting in the weak light from his lamp. It stared right at him without blinking, without moving. Maybe it was trying to work out whether or not it could swoop down and plunge its claws into the back of his neck.

Bex waved to him to come and join her. He glanced in her direction, then back at the hawk. It had vanished. He gazed wildly around and upwards, hoping desperately that it wasn't silently riding the air currents, heading directly for him under the impression that his neck tasted like a particularly fine mouse. He couldn't see it. The bird had flown away. He *hoped* it had flown away.

Still feeling twitchy, Kieron crawled over to where Bex was kneeling. He saw that she had cut a hole in the fence, severing several of the horizontal and vertical strands, but then joined the ends of the strands together with longer sections of wire she had brought with her, which were now attached to the bare metal with spring clips. Presumably those longer wires still carried the current, so the alarms wouldn't go off, but there was enough of a gap that they could both crawl through.

'I'd like to see a fox do that,' she said, grinning.

'To be fair,' Kieron responded, 'they *are* very cunning.'

They crawled through, and onwards, towards the futuristic buildings. After five metres or so Bex put her hand up, stopping them in the shelter of a clump of low bushes. She pointed ahead, to where more poles had been placed in the ground. These ones didn't have a fence attached to them, however; they had cameras on top. For a moment Kieron wondered what use they were at night, but then he remembered what Bex had said earlier about infra-red cameras. They could see in the dark! How were the two of them going to get past?

Bex pulled something out of her jacket and handed it to Kieron. It was a flat packet. As she watched, he unfolded it into what looked like an oversized 'onesie' jumpsuit, but made out of some kind of soft grey plastic. It had a plastic zip running up its back, and it was warm to his touch.

'Put it on,' Bex mouthed silently.

'What is it?'

'It'll keep all your body heat inside, so the cameras won't see you. We just have to wear them until we get to the other side of the poles.'

Quickly he climbed inside the onesie. It was large enough that he could keep all his clothes on. A hood covered his whole head, with a transparent plastic screen across his face. Small holes allowed him to breathe, but not well, and he could already feel himself heating up.

'Now. Quickly,' Bex said. She'd struggled into her own onesie, and together the two of them crawled out from behind the bushes and towards the cameras. Kieron waited tensely for alarms to go off, but nothing happened. Within a few moments the cold night air had been replaced with his own body heat, reflected back to him. Beads of sweat prickled on his forehead and down his spine. Halfway to the poles he could feel whole drops of sweat trickling down his sides and across his scalp. Breathing was an effort, as was crawling. His hands were damp, and he could feel the sweat making the fingers of the onesie unpleasantly damp. His T-shirt stuck to his back as he moved. His knees actually *squelched* as they pressed against the fabric of the onesie. This was horrible.

And then they were past the poles and the cameras, and both he and Bex were climbing quickly out of the onesies. Bex's hair was plastered across her forehead, and her face was flushed. Kieron knew that he probably looked the same.

'Let's not do that again,' he said as they folded the onesies up roughly and placed them together in the shadow of another bush.

A sound up ahead made them both stop. Not a natural sound, but the clink of metal touching metal. Bex crouched down and Kieron followed.

White light suddenly flared in the darkness, shockingly bright. It blinded Kieron for a few seconds, and he had to blink several times before his eyes adjusted. He found himself looking at the face of a woman, about ten metres ahead of them, illuminated by the light of a mobile-phone screen. She was holding it up and checking something on it. Her face looked Asian to Kieron. Japanese, he thought, or perhaps Korean.

'*Oi, hikari keshite!*' a voice called. Definitely Japanese: he recognised the sound of the language, although not the words, from the many anime films he'd watched online.

'*Hai*,' the woman said. The light of the mobile screen moved as she transferred it to a pocket in her jacket. As it did so it illuminated the dappled green camouflage jacket she wore, and, Kieron noticed with a shiver, a black metal weapon hanging from a strap over her shoulder. It looked something like a chunky black pistol with a long cylindrical barrel, but it had a second handgrip located in front of the main one, just below the barrel, making it look more like a sub-machine gun.

'Interesting,' Bex said quietly. Her voice was almost too quiet to hear, but the ARCC equipment picked it up and transmitted it to Kieron's glasses so he could hear her clearly.

'There's no reason someone Japanese shouldn't be working here,' Kieron pointed out, 'and this is a sensitive establishment. We were expecting guards, weren't we?'

'Not holding a Minebea 9mm machine pistol,' Bex said. 'That's not standard issue in the British Army, MI6 or any other organisation that might be guarding this facility. I think the place has been taken over.'

CHAPTER EIGHT

Bex's mind raced as she tried to process this new information.

'Let's assume that the station's been taken over,' she said softly, half to herself and half to Kieron. 'Let's also assume that the attackers are Japanese, because at least two of them speak that language. We can worry about why later. Let's also assume that the technicians who normally operate the base are being held captive, rather than having been killed, because the attacking force will need at least some of them to operate the equipment, take the PEREGRINE satellites offline and send status reports back to MI6 and the Ministry of Defence in the UK so nobody suspects anything. That means we need to get in there and rescue the crew, so they can get the satellites operational again. We know there's at least one armed guard out here, so either she's meant to patrol the site on a regular route or there are other guards and this is her station. More likely there are several guards, set around the perimeter of the site. Not sure how many – that depends how large their team is. Probably at least four. One on each side of the site.' She shook her head. 'Sentry duty at night is tricky. If you're walking around then you can get too focused on the sound of your feet and your breathing. If you stand in one spot you become very familiar with that location – the way it looks in the dark and the way it sounds – and you can easily spot any changes, but it does get boring and you have to keep your alertness levels up. We're lucky she's not wearing image-intensifying goggles – if she was, she'd have spotted us before we spotted her.' Bex hesitated for a moment, thinking through the next set of actions. 'OK. I'm going in alone. I'll sneak past this guard; she's obviously bored, and easily distracted.'

'Are you going to . . . to knock her out?' Kieron asked. Bex suspected that he'd been going to say 'kill her' but had stopped himself at the last moment.

'No,' she said. 'She's probably got orders to check back with whoever is giving the orders on a regular basis. If she doesn't make that report, then they'll raise the alarm. No, I'll just get past her. You stay out here and provide me with whatever support you can via the ARCC glasses. Stay low and keep as quiet as possible.'

'I want to come in with you,' Kieron said mutinously.

'That's not going to happen,' she explained patiently but firmly. 'These people have guns, and I suspect they're willing to use them. I'm responsible for your safety. Besides which, I'm trained in things like hand-to-hand combat and you're not.' She reached across the space between them and gripped his shoulder. 'And if none of that changes your mind, just remember that I *need* your help out here. You can give me details of the floor plans of the buildings and alert me to any threats that I can't see. OK?'

'OK,' he said, but he had a tone in his voice that Bex didn't particularly like.

'Don't talk to me while I'm moving towards the buildings, unless you need to alert me to a threat. If I'm close to the guard she might hear your voice coming out of the glasses.'

She squeezed his shoulder hard, then headed diagonally across the ground, staying low and quiet, hoping to get past the guard without being spotted or heard. It was fortunate that the guard had got bored and checked her mobile – fortunate because it meant that Kieron and Bex had spotted her in time, but also because the bright light of the screen would have completely disrupted her night vision, and it would take twenty minutes or so before she would be able to see properly in the dark again. She was obviously not a professional.

Bex kept her weight on her back foot as she moved, extending her leading foot to check for low obstacles. Each time she set her front foot down she slowly shifted her weight forward, absorbing the movement in her knees and ankles. She only let the ball of her foot make contact with the ground, acting as a cushion. She moved in a crouch, with her hands out to the sides at waist level to detect any bushes or saplings that might make a noise if she accidentally brushed against them. She kept her breathing shallow and slow, and made sure to take air in through her mouth rather than her nose because the nostrils can add strange sniffs or squeaks if you're trying to be quiet. It took an agonisingly long time, and Bex was very aware of the regular thudding of her heart as she moved. She was also very aware of the sounds of the night: the distant hooting of an owl, and the soft *swish*es made by what she assumed were bats swooping above her head and picking insects out of the air.

The guard cleared her throat. The sound placed her behind Bex. Again, that marked her out as something of an amateur – professionals had a range of techniques to stop themselves coughing, sneezing or making other noises like that. Throat lozenges were a good start, along with anti-allergy medication and nasal sprays.

The buildings were closer now: patches of deep black against the starry night sky. The dishes loomed high above her. As she got closer she could hear more noises: muffled voices, the low throbbing of a generator, a radio playing classical music.

Bright white light suddenly flared behind Bex, casting her shadow across the grass. She froze; fighting the urge to duck down or throw herself to the ground to avoid being seen. The light would be blinding the guard again, but someone else – another guard, or someone looking out of a window in the buildings – might catch sight of Bex, illuminated by the screen's brightness. The problem was that movement would be spotted. She was better off being a dark stationary object that might be mistaken for a bush. What she did do, however, was to bring her gloved hands up to cover the whiteness of her face. She counted her heartbeats, waiting for the woman to turn the phone off again. Ten . . . fifty . . . one hundred . . . She was on 118 when the light vanished again. Emails read, or social media checked. This guard was easily distracted.

Eventually Bex could reach out her hand and touch the corner of one of the buildings. It was cool and smooth – enamelled metal, she thought. Probably some kind of prefabricated pod, shipped out here and then fitted with power and water. If there were any windows in those exterior walls then they were curtained so well that no light escaped.

'Kieron?' she said quietly.

'Yes,' he replied through the tiny loudspeaker in the ARCC glasses she wore. He sounded tense. 'Are you OK?'

'I'm at the buildings. Now I need your help. Have you managed to locate any site plans?'

'I had to hack into the Ministry of Defence main computer server, which was fun, but I've found what you need.'

'Right, talk me through the layout.'

'There's six buildings in total, all pretty much the same size. Four of them are set like the sides of a square, but there are gaps at the corners where you can get into the middle. You're at one of those gaps now. The other two buildings are in the centre of the square, side by side, with space between them. They're arranged so that when you go through the gap you're standing in front of one of the central buildings. It runs off to your right, and the second one is on the other side of it. There are also three satellite control dishes of different sizes, but they're in a separate area way off to your right.'

'OK, got that.' She considered for a second. 'Which building is the main control room?'

'I don't know. The buildings aren't labelled. Sorry.'

'Are the locations of the power and data cables marked?'

'Ye-es,' he said, obviously checking.

'Which building has the most cables going into it?'

'Oh, good thought.' A moment's pause, and then he went on, 'It's the furthest one of the central ones.'

'Great. Thanks.'

She started to move through the gap, sensing rather than seeing the black bulks of the two buildings on either side of her as she passed them and a third one straight ahead. The buildings were single-storey, smooth and cold to the touch, with vertical ribs – probably some kind of structural bracing – sticking out every ten feet or so. Windows were set between each rib. The blinds on these windows weren't so good: light spilled around the edge of the frames, illuminating the space between the buildings. In its brightness she could see scrubby grass clinging to the walls on either side, with muddy paths in the middle made by years of booted feet walking from one building to another. Part of her wanted to avoid looking at the windows, because she didn't want her own night-vision ruined, but she was going to have to go inside at some stage, so it was best if she got acclimatised to the light now.

Moving to the end of the nearest building, past a closed door, she put her eye to the edge of the window frame. A slight gap between the blind inside and the frame allowed her to see in. It was a bunk room, with perhaps twelve beds in it. She couldn't see anyone inside, either awake or asleep. She wasn't sure, from the angle she was looking from, whether the door she'd just passed gave onto the room, to another room or to a corridor between rooms.

What to do? If she could be sure the door would get her straight into the empty bunk room then she could take the risk of entering, but she might end up in a crowded canteen or rest room.

While she was debating, the door suddenly opened.

Two things saved Bex: the fact that the door opened outwards, not inwards, and the fact that it opened in such a way as to hide her, not expose her. She turned, ready to hit or kick out if anyone emerged and turned towards her, but whoever stood in the doorway didn't step outside. All they did was to throw the contents of a cup onto the ground, then close the door again.

Bex started breathing again.

She decided not to risk going into that building. Instead she moved quietly on, past the window, to the space between this building and the next. She glanced down the gap; nobody there. After hurrying across to the next building, she flattened herself against the wall and waited. Nothing.

'Are you OK?' Kieron asked in her ear.

'So far.'

With her back against the white-enamelled metal wall, Bex slid along the side of the building, edging out whenever she got to one of the projecting ribs and ducking down whenever she passed a window. When she got to the corner she glanced around it briefly, and when she saw there was nobody on that side – the shorter side – she quickly slid along to the next corner. Across the gap was the second of the central buildings: the control room. Maybe there she would find out at least *something* useful.

She moved quickly across the gap. 'Kieron, I'm at the control building – the one with all the power and data lines going into it. Are there any rooms inside, or is it just one big space?'

'Just one big space, as far as the plans tell me,' he said.

'Right – stand by. I'm going to need you in a minute.'

She reached into one of her many jacket pockets and pulled out a small case. From it she removed a compact battery-powered drill. She quickly selected a diamond-tipped drill bit from the selection inside and clamped it into the chuck. The drill had been specially designed to deliver high torque at slow rotation, meaning it could bore through a wall making minimal noise. The diamond tip also helped minimise vibration, and that kept the noise down as well, while the high-density battery would ensure that she didn't lose power. She should be able to get through the metal wall without anyone inside hearing her.

She placed the drill bit against the side of the building and began to drill. The bit spun slowly, but with her weight against it the diamond tip immediately started to bite into the surface. Spirals of white-coated metal emerged like bizarre mechanical worms as she worked. When she felt the drill move forward a little faster than it had been, she pulled back. She'd got through, and hopefully without alerting anyone.

Bex pulled the bit out and carefully packed the drill away again. Neatness was an agent's friend. Next she pulled another item from her jacket – a pencil microphone, thin enough to slide through the hole she had made. She pushed it in, holding her breath and hoping that the drill bit hadn't come out behind a framed picture that she was now pushing further and further away from the wall. Someone might spot that.

A thin cable led away from her end of the microphone, and she clipped the end of it to the ARCC glasses she wore.

'Kieron, I've placed a microphone in the control room. I'm guessing the people in there – if there *is* anyone – will be speaking Japanese. Can you run a simultaneous translation for me?'

'Will do,' Kieron said tersely.

Bex activated the microphone by clicking the switch on the end that emerged from the building.

A voice suddenly spoke in her ear. Not Kieron's, but an older man, speaking Japanese.

'*Shisutemu no stehtasu wa?*' he said, but suddenly his voice got a lot quieter and another voice, calm and male and obviously computer-synthesised, started to speak over the top of him, saying, 'What is the current status of the system?'

A female voice inside the building began to speak, and within a second the ARCC kit was translating for Bex, this time with a synthesised female voice. Bex forced her mind not to listen to the Japanese words but to concentrate only on the English translation.

'All of the PEREGRINE satellites have now been shut down.'

'Good,' the man said. 'Our work is done.' The computer-created voice didn't sound pleased, but that was just a function of the software. 'It's time to get out of here. Akitsugu, prime the bomb. I want it to go off thirty minutes from now. We will be halfway to the ship by then.'

Bomb. Bex's mind immediately fixed on that word. She hadn't been expecting a bomb.

'I understand that we have to destroy the satellite control equipment,' another male voice said. The Japanese version, which Bex had been trying hard not to hear, sounded a lot younger. The ARCC translation was done in the same voice as before, however, which made it sound like the first man was having an argument with himself. 'Otherwise someone might be able to reverse the work we have done, even though we've password-protected everything. I also understand why we have to take the system encoder with us – so we can access the satellites from our Shinjuku base. Is it really necessary to kill the technicians, however? They're not bad people. One of them even speaks some Japanese. Not good, but he's trying.'

'Don't get soft on me,' the first man interrupted. 'They have seen our faces. Besides that, we need to erase all fingerprints and DNA evidence, and a bomb is the best way to do that if the explosion is big enough. Who knows, it might even be blamed on an electrical fault, and nobody will know we've been here!'

'Yes, of course. I obey.'

'Nashiko, get the others on the radio and tell them to come back here to the car park. Tell them to start up the cars. We're heading back to Shinjuku.'

The microphone picked up the noise of people moving

161

around, and then several *beeps*. That, Bex thought darkly, was probably the sound of the bomb being primed. Thirty minutes.

'Bex?' Kieron sounded scared. She didn't blame him.

'Yes.'

'A bomb?'

'I know.' Her mind seemed to suddenly be operating at several times normal speed. A bomb, with a timer and activated remotely. That meant it wasn't in the control room. The younger man had asked whether it was necessary to kill the technicians. That suggested the technicians were all being held together in the same place as the bomb. Five buildings to check, not including the control room. This wasn't good. Not good at all.

Bex heard a door open around the corner of the building and several people come out. She listened to see if she could tell which way they were going. She was at the short end of the building, and the door was in the long side that faced out, towards the outer 'rectangle' of buildings. With luck the Japanese terrorists – that was how she had started thinking of them – would head away from her, towards one of the open corners that would lead them out.

The multiple footsteps moved away from her. She breathed a sigh of relief. She was safe.

A door in the building in front of her – the first one she'd checked out when she'd got inside the 'rectangle' – opened.

Bex glanced around desperately. Climb up to the roof using the window ledges? Too slow, and she'd be caught with her back to whoever was coming out. Run? Same problem. Her only advantage was that their eyes would still be light-adjusted rather than dark-adjusted.

Bex threw herself to the ground and pressed herself as far into the corner between the cold metal wall and the cold earth as she could. She was wearing dark clothes. With luck, whoever came out would assume she was a shadow, not a person.

A stalk of grass tickled her nose. She tried not to sneeze.

More footsteps. A slammed door. The footsteps moving away. No shouts, no sounds of surprise.

'*Karo-san wa gijutsu-sha o korosu tsumori desuka?*' a female voice said. The voice must have been picked up by the microphone in Bex's ARCC glasses, because moments later a flat, synthesised translation in her ear said, 'Karo is going ahead with killing the technicians?'

'*Kare wa sono mokuteki o shinjiteru,*' a second, male voice said. 'He believes in the cause,' said the translation.

'*Watashitachi wa min'na mokuteki o shinjite imasu. Demi shinjinai hito o koros anakereba naranai wakede wa arimasen.*' 'We all believe in the cause. That doesn't mean we have to murder everyone who doesn't.'

'*Karo ni wa anata ni iwa semasu.*' 'I'll let you tell Karo.'

The footsteps receded around the corner.

Bex counted to ten, then pushed herself up to a standing position.

Somewhere in the distance a car engine started up, followed by another. The roar was loud in the quiet of the night.

'Bex, you've got twenty-nine minutes to get those

technicians out,' Kieron said nervously, 'and get clear of the buildings.'

'I know, but there's a problem. If that bomb goes off, then we won't be able to regain control of the satellite network. Whoever these people are, they'll be able to control it from wherever they come from.' She sighed heavily. 'First things first: let's get the technicians out and to safety.'

'But we don't know where they are!'

'True.' She thought for a second. 'Searching all the buildings is going to take too long. We need to do something clever.' Her mind was spinning; facts and suppositions and possibilities all circling one another without settling. She took a breath and exerted all her willpower, forcing her mind to slow down to the point where she could see any links, any pattern. And it worked. 'Right, Kieron, here's what we're going to do. You're going to get a staff list of all the technicians working at this site, you're going to find their mobile phone numbers, and you're going to use the ARCC equipment to phone as many of them at the same time as you can.'

'OK,' he said uncertainly. 'Doing that now, but if they could make and take phone calls, surely they would have phoned someone for help by now.'

'Not the point,' Bex said. She closed her eyes, concentrating on what she could *hear*. The night had seemed quiet, but now she was deliberately listening she could make out several distinct sounds. Loudest was the noise made by the Japanese terrorists as their vehicles drove away, but that noise was getting fainter and fainter with each passing second. Then there was the distant noise of a radio or an MP3 player, then the wind and the swooping of bats, and beneath all that was the sound of her own breathing and the pumping of her heart.

'Got them,' Kieron suddenly said, shockingly loud. 'Phoning now.'

'OK.' Bex concentrated.

And she heard a mobile phone ringing. And then another one. And another.

The sounds were coming from over on her right. She followed them, past the two central buildings and towards another that formed one of the sides of the outer square. There must have been a dozen mobiles all ringing now, all with different ringtones, but one by one they fell silent.

'Going to voicemail,' Kieron said. 'All of them.'

'Doesn't matter – I've located them.'

Confident that all of the Japanese terrorists had left, she approached the building without slowing down or trying to hide herself, and pulled the main door open.

It was a restaurant/cafe area. Tables and chairs in two-thirds of the room, with a counter separating them from the kitchen and food preparation area where there were several ovens, several freezers and a large refrigerator. A dozen people, a mixture of men and women, all of them looking scared, had been herded together in the kitchen area, handcuffed to the heavy ovens. They glanced up as Bex entered, obviously tense and scared. Somewhere in the room, music was playing. Something inappropriate – a Strauss waltz, she thought.

'I'm a friend,' she said quickly, holding her hands up. 'Who's in charge?'

A middle-aged man with a grizzled beard held up his hand, as far as he could with his wrist imprisoned in a metal cuff. 'John Petersen. Who are you? Are you with –'

'I'm your last, best hope of getting out of here alive,' Bex said. She wasn't going to give them her name, just in case it ever got back to MI6 or Avalon Richardson in England.

'All our phones went off just now. Was that you?'

'Yeah. I had to locate you.'

'What's going *on*?' a dark-haired female technician asked. 'We were all rounded up at gunpoint three days ago and locked in here. They were guarding us right up until a few minutes ago, then they left.'

'Cutting a long story short,' Bex said, 'they're terrorists, they've cleared out, I'm here to rescue you, and there's a bomb in the control centre.'

'How long until –' another female technician asked. Her voice was tense, but she wasn't panicking. That was good, Bex thought. She had to concentrate on freeing these hostages and then finding and defusing the bomb, not on calming hysterical reactions.

'Just over twenty minutes. She glanced around. 'I doubt the terrorists did anything as helpful as leaving the keys for the handcuffs behind. Are there any tools around here?'

'Bolt-cutters, over by the freezer,' Petersen said, gesturing in that direction with his head.

Bex moved quickly to get them. They had been left upright, resting against the side of the freezer: long handles and

166

thick, chisel-like blades. 'I'm not complaining,' she said as she picked them up and moved towards Petersen, 'but why keep bolt-cutters in a kitchen?'

'We needed to cut up a frozen lamb carcass so it would defrost faster, and the only tool that would do the job was the bolt-cutters. We never bothered taking them back to the garage.' He nodded towards one of the technicians. 'Get them free first. Leave me till last.'

It took just a few minutes to cut the handcuffs off everyone, but Bex was acutely aware that, somewhere close by, a bomb was ticking down towards detonation. As she freed Petersen she said, 'Get everyone away from here. I've got to find the bomb.'

'Leave the bomb,' he said urgently. 'This is a satellite control station. That's not worth risking your life for.'

'I have to try,' she said.

Petersen turned to one of the technicians. 'Get everyone to the road,' he said, then turned back to Bex. 'In that case, I'm coming with you.'

Bex stared at him. She could tell from his expression that there was no point arguing.

Outside the building, all the technicians headed one way while Bex and Petersen ran towards the satellite control building.

'Are you sure that's where they've put the bomb?' he asked breathlessly.

'It's where I would have put it. Right next to the thing they want to blow up.'

The control room was dominated by a big screen showing

an electronic map of the world, with curved lines like sine waves showing the paths of the satellites. Around the walls, white-shelled computer servers hummed quietly, pumping out heat that made the room uncomfortably warm. Several desks had high-end computers sitting on them.

One desk had been cleared, and placed right in the centre of the room. On it was a bomb. *The* bomb.

It was a simple package wrapped in sticky parcel tape. A circuit board and an antenna had been attached to the package with rubber bands. Several black wires ran from the circuit board to the package. It all looked very clumsy and home-made, but Bex didn't let that fool her. This was a functional bomb, and if that was plastic explosive then there was enough there to destroy all the buildings, and probably the dish antennas as well.

'Is that it?' Kieron said in her ear.

'I think it just might be,' she replied, staring at it and trying to work out the best means of rendering it safe.

'Talking to yourself?' Petersen asked.

'It's a bad habit.' She sniffed. She thought she could detect a slight smell, something like motor oil. C-4 explosive? It was likely to be either that or Semtex, and the only way of telling would be to make a slight cut in the sticky tape, pull a bit of it back and take a look. C-4 was a putty-white colour, while Semtex was orange. Not that it really mattered at this stage. Explosive was explosive.

'I can't help but notice,' Petersen said nervously 'that the wires are all the same colour.'

'It's only in movies that the wires are different colours,

and you have to choose whether to cut the red one or the blue one,' she murmured. 'In reality, a bomb maker just cuts lengths of wire off a spool. It's all the same.'

'That's ruined movies for me.' After a pause, he went on, 'And there's no big timer counting down. Is that normal?'

'Again,' she said, leaning closer and tracing the paths of the black wires with a finger, 'that's the movies. No bomb builder *ever* puts a nice glowing red timer on their bomb. I mean, what's the point?' She saw that the wires all entered the package of plastic explosive through small cuts that had been made in the sticky tape. At the end of each wire she knew there would be a detonator – basically just a small explosive charge that could be triggered by a current. When the circuit board decided that half an hour had passed, a small electrical charge would be sent down the wires to the detonators. They would go off – small explosions, barely more than a slight 'pop', but that would set the otherwise stable plastic explosive off, and that would be *much* more serious. 'Who's going to be looking at it?' she went on. 'The builder's long gone. In fact, if you ever *do* see a timer on a real bomb, you have to wonder if the builder put it there for a joke and it's giving you completely the wrong information. That's what I'd do. Set the timer so it says you've got half an hour to deal with the bomb, when it's actually going to go off in ten minutes.'

'OK –' Petersen sounded really nervous now. 'So you can't tell which wire to cut and you don't know how long until it explodes. What are you going to do?'

'This.'

169

Bex reached out, grasped the black wires leading to the plastic-wrapped packs of plastic explosive, and pulled them. They slid out – the wires and the tubular detonators, which were about the same size and shape as five cigarettes.

Bex heard a simultaneous intake of breath from Petersen and from Kieron.

'Is that – actually safe?' Petersen asked.

'Perfectly,' she replied. 'You defuse a bomb by separating the components. Most importantly, you separate the explosive from the thing that makes it explode. Simple. I've done the course.'

'But –' he sounded almost disappointed – 'seriously, what about all that stuff they do in the movies? All the checking, and the snipping of wires, and so on?'

'All just to ratchet up the tension.' She breathed out, aware that despite her calm demeanour she'd been holding her breath. 'To be fair, if the bomb builder thinks their bomb might be found, then they'll build in tricks and traps – trembler switches that can detect if the bomb gets moved, for instance, or wires that are set so if they're pulled out that actually activates the explosive. But these guys here, they didn't expect *me* to turn up, and they were pretty sure that the technicians wouldn't be able to get free. They didn't expect that anyone would discover the bomb. So, no booby traps, and so I could be reasonably sure that I could just pull the wires out safely.'

'Reasonably?' Kieron asked in her ear.

'Fairly.' She quickly removed the rubber bands and shifted the circuit board, antenna, wires and detonators away from the plastic explosive, placing them outside the cardboard box, on a different table.

'Fairly?'

'Kind of.' She turned towards Petersen. 'I've got to go,' she said. 'I suggest you phone someone for help. I'm guessing there'll be a twenty-four-hour manned guard at the Mount Pleasant base. And don't worry if, in about quarter of an hour, there are five small "pops" from this thing. The bomb won't go off. I've made sure of that.'

He gazed at her with a mixture of admiration and confusion on his face. 'Thank you,' he said. 'Whoever you are.'

'Don't mention it.' Bex turned away, then turned back. 'I mean, seriously, don't mention it. To anyone. Just tell them the terrorists didn't bother finishing the bomb and you managed to reach your phones.'

Before he could say anything else, she left.

She ran through the cold night air towards where she'd left Kieron. She wasn't worried about being seen: the terrorists had gone now, and even if the infra-red cameras were recording, it didn't matter. She and Kieron had their backs to them. Nobody would be able to see their faces.

She grabbed Kieron from where he'd been sheltering behind a bush and together they sprinted towards the hole in the fence. The fresh, cold air on her face made her cheeks tingle. It seemed to flush the tension and worry of the past half-hour from her mind, scouring it clear.

'What now?' Kieron asked.

'Now,' she said grimly, 'I try to catch up with those terrorists. I want to find out where they're going!'

Once past the fence they located the exo-boots and quickly strapped them on.

'Are you up for a sprint?' she asked breathlessly. 'It could be risky.'

'You've just defused a bomb,' Kieron said, grinning. 'I can risk falling over. It's the least I can do!'

With the exo-boots amplifying her every step, making her feel like the world's greatest Olympic sprinter, Bex led the way. With Kieron behind her, and the scrubby grass and bushes of the Falklands landscape flashing past underneath, she navigated them both around the boundary of the satellite control station and towards where the single road that led out of the site would be, where she'd heard the vehicles leave.

'Do you think I'll get to see a penguin?' Kieron said breathlessly in her ear.

'What?'

'A penguin? Do you think I'll get to see one?'

She laughed. The question was so perfectly inappropriate at that particular moment. 'Kieron, I have no idea!'

Once they got to the road, the going was much easier. It was barely more than a gravelled dirt track, flattened by years of tyres, but it was much easier to run along than the countryside had been.

Ten minutes went past in what seemed like just a few seconds, and Bex was feeling the burn in the muscles of her legs. It wasn't that the exo-boots took much effort to use, it was more that they were making her use her muscles in different ways and her legs had decided to protest. She could hear Kieron's breath rasping in her ears; he was getting tired. Maybe they ought to stop. The Japanese terrorists might be too far ahead to reach by now. Or they might have taken a different route, a track she hadn't noticed.

They were heading down a slight slope now, towards what looked like the top edge of a ridge with some kind of drop on the other side. Bex couldn't see what was beyond the ridge, but Kieron must have been checking, using the ARCC glasses map function, because he suddenly said, 'We're heading for a beach!'

The edge of the ridge suddenly turned orange. Sunrise? Surely that was still hours away! Flames, then.

'What's that?' Kieron asked nervously.

'The terrorists have set fire to their cars,' Bex said grimly as the two of them cleared the ridge and half ran, half fell down the bank on the other side and onto the sandy beach. And they had: two people-carriers sat there on the beach, flames bursting from their windows. The terrorists must have seen no point in taking the cars with them, but wanted to avoid leaving evidence behind. And, illuminated by the flames, she saw a ship a little way out. Bigger than a fishing vessel but smaller than a car ferry. Mostly just a black shape against the glittering tops of the waves, heading out into the Atlantic.

'We've lost them,' she said despairingly, slowing to a walk. The soles of the exo-boots caught in the sand, making her stumble.

'But we can –' Kieron said, then stopped. 'What about –' Again he couldn't finish the sentence.

'Did you hear what they said, back there, before they left the satellite control room?' she asked, feeling her heart sink. 'They'd transferred control of the PEREGRINE network from here to their base in Japan. We've failed! They still control the satellites, and they can break the whole thing whenever they want, or use it for their own purposes! We've lost the ARCC kit for good!'

'There must be something we can do,' Kieron said. 'I'm sure there is.'

'We've lost,' she said dully.

Kieron sighed, then suddenly drew a surprised breath. 'Bex . . .' he said.

She turned to look at him. He was staring along the beach. She followed the direction of his gaze.

There, a few hundred yards away, several hundred penguins were watching them, and the burning cars.

'At least I've seen a penguin,' Kieron said. 'We can go home now.'

CHAPTER NINE

Kieron travelled back from the Falkland Islands on his own. By himself. Alone.

It was a scary experience. Every time he'd flown before it had been with Bex or Bradley or Sam. Yes, he'd felt grown-up and important, going through the security scanners at the airport, asking the cabin crew for another orange juice and handing his passport to an immigration officer for checking, but he'd always had his friends there as backup. Now it was just him. And he was scared that he would get it wrong somehow, and end up either in a different country by accident or trapped in a foreign airport, unable to leave because he hadn't filled in a form correctly and didn't speak the local language so couldn't explain the trouble he'd got himself into.

But he managed. After Bex dropped him off at Mount Pleasant Airport he got through the security checks with no problems. When he was asked why he was leaving after just one day he gave the answer that Bex had made him memorise: 'My mum is ill and I need to get back to England to see her,' and when he was asked if anyone was meeting him at the other end he simply said 'Yes.' He mostly slept all the way to

Ascension Island, and from there back to England he played games and watched movies on his mobile. Time seemed to freeze; whenever he looked at his watch, or the time display on the tablet, it took a while before the numbers made sense.

When he slept, which happened in short, broken stretches, he dreamed about flying fast and close to the ground across the rough landscape of the Falklands, but his dreams always seemed to end with him circling around the satellite control station and watching helplessly as it exploded and burned. But that wasn't what had actually happened. He and Bex had saved the technicians and she had defused the bomb. Dreams where it all went wrong were probably just a combination of stress and exhaustion.

When he and Bex had got back to the hotel after their adventures he had been desperate to get to his room and sleep, but she pulled him to one side. 'We're going to have to split up,' she'd said quietly. 'We know their base is in Shinjuku, which is an area of Tokyo, so I'm going there to try and track down where these terrorists – or whatever they are – are based and stop them taking full control of the PEREGRINE network, and you're going back to Newcastle.'

'But –' he'd started to say.

She had put her finger against his lips. 'No arguments. Your mum will be coming back from her free spa weekend, and you need to be there. If you're not, she'll wonder what's happened to you, and everything will start to unravel. So, you're going back.'

'You promise you're not just doing this to keep me out of danger?' he had asked.

Bex had shaken her head. 'That's not it,' she had said. 'You've proved yourself time and time again. I know I can trust you, and I know I can rely on you, but now we have to go in different directions. Obeying orders is hard, if you don't agree with them, but this is the way it has to be.'

As the aircraft descended towards RAF Brize Norton, Kieron stared morosely out of the window. The blue-grey of the ocean gave way to the fields and forests of southern England, illuminated by a rising sun that cast long shadows over the green countryside, and he felt a sudden rush of homesickness. Usually, coming home after an adventure, he felt a combination of elation at succeeding against the odds and regret at leaving wherever he had been, but now he just wanted to get back to normality. Maybe he was growing up. Maybe it was time to leave this part of his life behind and do something sensible, like get a job, or go to college. Or set up that computer repair business with Sam.

RAF Brize Norton was exactly as he'd left it: a combination of highly expensive, high-tech military aircraft alongside buildings that seemed to be trapped in the 1960s. No mobile people-conveyors that joined up to the aircraft doors and allowed the passengers to walk in the warm and dry all the way to where their luggage would be waiting for them here; as in the Falklands, an old wheeled set of stairs allowed the passengers the privilege of walking across a stretch of racked concrete to the arrivals building.

He checked his watch. It was nine o'clock in the morning. Another day had begun, although as far as his body was concerned, time seemed to have stopped.

He slipped the ARCC glasses on and activated them as he waited for his luggage to arrive in the retrieval area. All he could see was an expanse of blue, just like the sea he'd been looking at from the window of the aircraft, with the exception of the block of white words sitting in the centre:

CONNECTION LOST. UNABLE TO ESTABLISH LINK TO SECONDARY ARCC EQUIPMENT. PLEASE CHECK LINK.

Bradley was waiting for Kieron when he got out of the baggage reclaim area. He ruffled Kieron's hair, grabbed his rucksack and led the way to the car park.

'I've heard a little bit about what happened from Bex,' Bradley said as they drove out of the base gates, 'but you know what she's like. She never gives me any of the exciting details. So I want you to tell me exactly what happened. Don't leave anything out.'

Kieron spent the next half-hour briefing Bradley as they drove. Bradley nodded several times, but didn't interrupt. When Kieron finished he took a moment to consider, and then said, 'OK, so the bottom line is that these bad guys, whoever they are, have disabled the PEREGRINE network from the Falklands, and they've transferred the codes back to their facility in Shinjuku so they can maintain control and stop anyone from using it. They've disabled access to the network from all the other sub-control stations, like the one in Edinburgh, and they think they've blown up the control station in the Falklands, so they're the only ones who can control the satellites, but Bex saved the Falklands station from destruction, and the staff there are currently fighting to regain control of the satellites. While they're doing that, Bex is heading to Tokyo to try and find their control station, and presumably destroy it the way they were trying to destroy the Falklands station. Is that about right?'

'Bex and me,' Kieron said. 'I was there too.'

'Bex and you; I'm sorry. But is that it?'

'That's exactly it. How's the ARCC system looking?' Kieron asked. 'I didn't get a chance to check when I landed.'

'It's back up to about fifty per cent operational,' Bradley said. Kieron couldn't help noticing that his gaze kept flicking to the rear-view mirrors every few seconds. That attack against him and Bex on the motorway had spooked him. He was obviously nervous that it might happen again. 'From what I can see, it's a fight between them and the bad guys in Tokyo. They bring a satellite back online, and then half an hour later the bad guys take it down again. Stalemate.'

They stopped at a service station on the M1 for food, and Kieron took the opportunity to call his mum.

'Hi, kid!' she said brightly.

'Hi, Mum. Where are you?'

'I'm at home. We checked out of the spa hotel this morning and drove back.'

'Did you enjoy yourself?'

'I had a great time,' she said. 'But what about you? Have you been eating properly?'

'Yes,' he said patiently, 'I've been eating properly.'

'I mean vegetables. And tomato sauce and jalapeño peppers on a pizza don't count as vegetables in my book.'

'I've been eating properly,' he repeated. He remembered the meal at the hotel restaurant in Port Stanley. 'I had fish the night before last. Fresh fish, not frozen.' No need to mention the terrible pasta he'd been given on the RAF flight.

'Fish? That's good. I'll have to start getting some salmon from the supermarket.' She hesitated slightly. 'We had some really good meals at this spa hotel. You know Tyler's a chef – well, even he was impressed, and his cooking is incredible.'

'Is everything . . . OK?' Kieron asked carefully.

'Everything is perfect,' she said, and hearing her tone of voice Kieron believed her.

'I'm glad.'

'Where are you? You're not here.'

'Obviously,' he said. 'I'm talking to you on the phone.'

'What I mean is, I guess you're over at Sam's place?'

Kieron sensed a slight rise at the end of the sentence: an implied question. He knew what his mum wanted to know but didn't want to ask. 'Don't worry,' he said, 'I didn't spend any time over at Beth's house, and she didn't come to our place.'

'It's none of my business,' his mum said. 'Just as long as you're happy, you're safe and you're being careful.'

A sudden vision of a burning satellite control centre flashed through his head. 'Yes, I'm being careful,' he said. 'Look, I'm going to see Beth for a while, and then I'll come home and we can get a takeaway. Or you can cook salmon, if you want. You can even cook vegetables and I'll eat them. But not asparagus – that's just rank.'

'That sounds great,' she replied. 'See you later.'

'Love you.'

'Love you too.'

He held his mobile in his hand for a while after the call was over.

'Everything OK?' Bradley asked eventually.

'I guess,' he replied. 'It's just – things in my life seem to be changing, and I'm not sure what they're changing into.'

'That,' Bradley said, 'is life. Life is change. If nothing's changing then you're not living.' He frowned. 'I think I read that inside a Christmas cracker once. Or maybe it was a fortune cookie in a Chinese restaurant. Either way, it's good advice.'

It was early evening when they returned to Newcastle. 'Do you want me to drop you off at your place?' Bradley asked. 'I need to get to the apartment soon though. Bex's flight is doing a stopover in Australia, and we arranged to talk.'

'Let's go to the apartment together,' Kieron decided. 'I'd like to hear Bex's voice and know she's OK.'

When they arrived, Sam was already there. Bradley had called ahead, and Sam had cups of coffee and ham-and-cheese toasted sandwiches ready for them, and while they waited for Bex to call, Kieron repeated the story of his adventures to Sam. His friend just sat there, nodding every so often. When Kieron got to the end, Sam looked over at Bradley and said, 'Those exo-boots – is there any chance I could have a pair for Christmas?'

'Absolutely not,' Bradley replied.

Bradley's mobile rang five minutes later. He put it in the centre of the coffee table and set it on speakerphone.

'Hi, Bex,' he said. 'I thought it was best to do this via mobile so the boys can listen. Plus the ARCC kit is only useable about half the time at the moment.'

'Good idea. At least it's still working *some* of the time. So who's there?' Bex asked. Kieron thought she sounded tired, but that wasn't surprising. *He* was tired.

'Me, Kieron and Sam,' Bradley said. 'Where are you?'

'Sydney Airport. I've got half an hour until my flight to Tokyo boards.'

'I've booked a hotel for you, and I've arranged for a car to pick you up at the airport. I assumed you'd be too tired for public transport.'

'You were right. I'm guessing they'll be looking for Chloe Drewe?'

'That's the name I gave them. Any idea what you're going to do when you actually *get* to Tokyo?'

Kieron heard Bex sigh. 'No. I've been thinking about it and I've not come up with anything approaching a plan.'

'From what I can see at this end,' Bradley said, 'the guys you saved in the Falklands keep trying to get the satellites up and running, while the bad guys keep trying to take them down again. It's a bit of a stand-off. Or a chess game.'

'Except,' Bex pointed out, 'that as far as I can see, the bad guys have got the advantage. They have the technology to change the access codes for the Falkland Islands. The only reason they *didn't* do that is because they thought

182

the bomb was going to do their work for them. We still have to stop them from doing that when they get to their control centre.'

Bradley opened his mouth to say something, but Bex continued, 'They're calling my flight now. I need to catch it. I have a terrible feeling that I'm in a race with the bad guys from here on out. I'll call again when I land in Tokyo.'

'OK,' he said. Turning the mobile off, he glanced at Kieron and Sam and took a deep breath. 'Right,' he said, 'I've still got to get the false control room up in Edinburgh taken apart, and I need to keep an eye on Scott Bailson to make sure he isn't remembering anything about the experience we put him through. I can do most of that from here, but it's going to take up a lot of my time and attention. What about you two? What are you going to do?' He glanced at Kieron. 'You ought to get some sleep. You're probably jet-lagged.'

Kieron shrugged. 'I feel tired,' he said, 'but I'm not sure I can sleep. My body doesn't really know what time it is. I think I'll stay awake for a while and see how well or how badly the ARCC system is doing – whether things are swinging our way or the bad guys' way.' He hesitated. 'I need to go and see my mum as well.'

'I should probably go to bed,' Sam said, nodding. 'I've been up for quite a while.'

'Waiting to make sure Bex and I got to wherever we were going OK?' Kieron asked, touched at Sam's concern.

'No,' Bradley said. 'He's been playing computer games.'

Sam looked shocked. 'Yeah, but I've been worrying on the *inside*,' he protested. 'I was only playing to distract myself.'

Kieron and Sam left together. The journey to their respective homes in Newcastle took them along the same route for half the distance, then they just waved at each other without saying anything and went off in different directions.

Kieron's mum was just preparing an early dinner when he got back. And yes, it was salmon. They sat and talked, and he realised that, while he had been away, things had somehow changed. The landscape of their lives had shifted in some subtle way. It wasn't like a mother talking with her son any more; it was two adults chatting about what had happened to them, what they liked, what memories of the past they shared. They talked about his dad, her husband, and how things had gone wrong in the family a long time before either of them realised. He told her about Beth, and she told him about Tyler. They both laughed, and they both cried a bit. Kieron even had a glass of wine, while his mum *only* had a glass of wine. It was, he thought as he took the plates and cutlery into the kitchen so he could put them in the dishwasher, a perfect evening. Somehow, somewhere in the past few days, they appeared to have renegotiated the relationship between them without them noticing it was happening. But it was good.

When he got back to the living room, his mother stood up and hugged him for a long time without saying anything.

'You're a great kid,' she said eventually. 'More than that – you've grown into a great person. And I know I haven't been around as much as I should have been –'

'You've been around just as much as you needed to be

for me to feel safe and loved,' he interrupted. 'You haven't done anything wrong. I, on the other hand, have been moody and adolescent.'

'True, but that's something that couldn't have been avoided.' She released him and held him at arm's length, staring intently into his face. 'The teenage years are like a long, dark tunnel,' she went on. 'You enter one end at about the age of fourteen, and you exit the other at about eighteen or so, and in that tunnel there are all kinds of things that might happen – some of them good, some bad, some dangerous and some safe. All I can do, as your mother, is stand at the far end of the tunnel yelling things like, 'Go left!' or 'Slow down and watch where you put your feet!' I can't stop you going into the tunnel – I *shouldn't* stop you going into the tunnel – and I can't go in there with you, mostly because I went through it myself years ago. I just have to pray you'll come out the other end safely.'

'Mum, I –'

'Shut up. I'm talking.' She took a deep breath, and said, 'I'm proud of you. I don't think you're out of the tunnel yet, but you've managed to get through most of it without falling over or getting into trouble.'

'Well, I knew I had you standing at the far end, waiting for me.' He looked down at the carpet, embarrassed and unable to meet her gaze. Trying desperately to change the subject, he asked, 'Does Tyler have any kids?'

'Yes. He's divorced, and he has a daughter.'

Kieron looked up, horrified. 'It's not Beth, is it?'

His mum laughed. 'No, she's nine years old.

'That's a relief!' He stared at her, and it was as if he could see right into her mind. 'You miss him already, don't you?'

She nodded. Now it was her turn to be embarrassed. 'I know I only said goodbye to him at lunchtime, but yes, I do miss him. Kieron, I think he's the one.'

'Give him a call. See if he minds you going over to his place for a glass or two of wine. I'm sure he wants you to call. He's probably too embarrassed to do it himself.'

Her eyes went wide. 'Do you think that would be OK?'

'That would be fine.'

'He won't think it's too clingy?'

'I think he'd love it. Take a Blu-ray. Settle down on the sofa and watch something together.'

He heard her calling Tyler while he was in the bathroom, cleaning his teeth. By the time he came out, she had her coat on.

'You were right – he was thinking of phoning *me*. I just got in first. Are you *sure* this is OK?'

'It's fine. *I'll* be fine. I'll see you tomorrow.'

He had the ARCC glasses with him and he slipped them on as the door of the flat closed, wanting to check the status of the PEREGRINE network before he settled down to sleep. Or, more likely, several hours of lying in bed *wishing* he could sleep.

The ARCC system seemed to be in one of its 'on' phases. Bex was probably still in the air, or maybe she'd got to her hotel in Tokyo and just collapsed. Whatever the reason, she hadn't switched on her end. Kieron just spent half an hour or so going through virtual screens of test programs and diagnostic routines, making sure that the glasses were still functioning the way they ought to.

He realised that the virtual screens were blurring in front of him, and he was having difficulty focusing on them. Perhaps it *was* time for bed after all.

'Hi.'

It was Bex's voice. He turned his head, not believing that she could be there, in his living room.

But she was.

He couldn't believe it. He'd tried hard to keep the various parts of his life – school, home, Bex and Bradley – apart, but here they were, colliding. Crashing together.

'Bex! You're supposed to be in Tokyo.'

'I know,' she said. Her face was serious, almost emotionless. She stared at him with an intensity that he found frightening. 'I need your help.'

'Sure, but –'

'Don't worry about why or how I'm here. Look, there's been an accident. Something bad has happened.' She raised a hand to her head. 'My taxi got hit by another car as we were leaving the airport. I think it was deliberate. I think someone chose to crash into us.'

He stood up abruptly, and suddenly felt dizzy as his vision shifted unexpectedly. Bex's figure seemed to shift slightly as his eyes unfocused and then refocused. 'Are you OK?'

'I managed to get away from the crash, but I hurt my head.' She held her hands out beseechingly. 'I can't remember anything! I need you to tell me who I am and what I'm doing here!'

Kieron felt like his world was sliding sideways, taking him with it. 'But you need to get to hospital! Get yourself checked out!'

She shook her head. 'No, I have a mission to accomplish – I just can't remember who I'm accomplishing it *for*.'

Kieron abruptly felt like a little kid, confronted with something that only adults could deal with. 'I need to tell Bradley about this! He'll know what to do.'

'Bradley who?'

'Bradley Marshall. Don't you remember him?'

'I don't remember *anything*.'

'OK.' He took a deep breath. He could do this. 'There's Bradley Marshall, and there's Sam Rosenfeld, and there's –'

He stopped. Something was wrong.

'Bex, what are you wearing?'

She frowned, confused. 'Why is that important?'

'Because those look like the clothes you were wearing when we were on the Falklands. When we managed to get inside the satellite control station.'

'Yes. What's the matter with that?'

'Those were your operational clothes: black and loose and anonymous. That's not the kind of stuff you wear when you're travelling.' He thought back to the last time he'd seen her, as she'd dropped him off at Mount Pleasant Airport and headed off to take the hire car back. 'And that's not what you were wearing when we said goodbye. You had jeans and a kind-of turquoise blouse, with a grey jacket. Why did you change back?'

'That's not important.' She waved an impatient hand, dismissing his concerns. 'What were you saying – Bradley Marshall, Sam Rosenfeld and you. But who are you? What's your name? And what's *my* name? You said I was called "Bex" – is that right? Bex what?'

'This doesn't make any sense.' Even though it was a cliché, he pinched the skin on his arm to check that he wasn't dreaming. The pain convinced him that this was real.

A possible explanation occurred to him, but it was too bizarre, too horrible in its consequences to contemplate. But he had to.

He moved his head slightly, letting his eyes drift sideways, to the doorframe beside Bex.

Her body seemed to drift momentarily towards the frame as if she was floating above the carpet, before she snapped back to where she had been standing.

'What's the matter?' she asked. Her expression was still as serious, as emotionless, as it had been when he'd first seen her there, but he realised now that it was more . . . blank. She wasn't controlling her emotions; she didn't *have* any emotions.

He reached up and took the ARCC glasses off with a sweep of his hand.

Bex vanished. There was nothing in the doorway.

He put the glasses back on again.

Bex reappeared in the doorway.

'You're just an illusion, projected by the ARCC kit,' he murmured. 'You're Avalon Richardson, or someone who works for her.'

Again her expression didn't change, but she said, 'I would say you're very clever, except that you've just made three fundamental mistakes.'

'What?' he demanded.

'Firstly, you mentioned Mr Marshall, which confirms that I'm talking to someone who knows Mr Marshall and Miss Wilson. Secondly, you mentioned Avalon Richardson, which confirms that Miss Wilson and Mr Marshall have worked out who their enemy is. And thirdly, you mentioned Sam Rosenfeld. I didn't know that name before. That information is useful to me. Thank you.' Now, finally, Bex's expression changed. She smiled, and it wasn't a humorous smile. Not the smile of someone who had heard something funny. It was the smile of someone who had won.

Abruptly, the figure flickered and vanished. The doorway was empty.

Kieron swept the glasses off again and chucked them away from him. They had been poisoned. He couldn't trust them. Anything they showed or told him could be a lie.

His brain raced. What exactly *had* he told Avalon? *Was* it useful?

If this was Avalon Richardson, and not the people in Japan using the ARCC system and sneaking a simulated image of Bex into his field of vision, then she already knew Bex Wilson and Bradley Marshall's full names, so he hadn't given anything away there. Bradley would have rented the apartment in Newcastle under a false name because that's the kind of thing he would do, so her people wouldn't be able to trace where their base was.

But they now knew Sam Rosenfeld's name. They could trace him.

With a sickening sensation that the ground had suddenly dropped out from beneath his feet, Kieron realised that he had inadvertently put his friend's life at risk! The bad guys would be able to check on where a Samuel Rosenfeld lived in England. They would be able to get his address, and his family details. And they could take Sam captive and use him as leverage to get Bex to stop pursuing them!

Kieron had to get to Sam as quickly as he could.

He grabbed his mobile phone and pressed the memory button for Sam's number. It rang, and rang and rang. He hopped from one foot to another impatiently.

Voicemail.

Kieron started running. He had to get to Sam's home before the bad guys did, or his friend's life was in danger, and so were the lives of his family . . .

CHAPTER TEN

From Mount Pleasant Airport on the Falkland Islands, Bex flew to Chile's Punta Arenas, sleeping from the moment they took off to the moment they set down. She'd been expecting a small aircraft, maybe with a propeller – something that would skim low over mountains and close to the sea, frightening the passengers, but actually the flight was on an Airbus A321 jet, and very comfortable.

Punta Arenas was a surprisingly modern airport, and she managed to get some South American street food from a stall in the transit lounge. She ate it while sitting beside a massive sculpture of an ice crystal that looked like a prop from one of those science-fiction series that Bradley loved to binge-watch. Through the large glass windows she could see ice-capped mountains. It looked cold out there – not surprising, considering the airport was at the furthest tip of South America and this was the closest she'd ever been to the South Pole. She let the landscape and the familiar-yet-strange airport lounge soothe her as she tried not to wonder what exactly she thought she was was doing.

With a change of aircraft, but not aircraft type, she flew

north to Santiago Airport. The journey took her right up the thin ribbon of land running between the Pacific Ocean on one side and the Andes mountains on the other. That was Chile: 4,300 miles long but only 360 miles wide at most. Again, she slept most of the way. Her adventures rescuing the satellite technicians from the Japanese terrorists had exhausted her – especially all that running in the exo-boots across the uneven Falklands terrain.

And all for nothing. That's what her brain kept telling her, whenever she was awake. The PEREGRINE satellite network was still compromised, although she hoped that the technicians could recover it. The problem was that she'd heard the Japanese terrorists talk about having password-protected what they'd done. All control of the satellites had passed to their facility in Japan, and all the travelling, stress and pain she and Kieron underwent had been for nothing.

Well, maybe not for nothing. If it hadn't been for her and Kieron, then the technicians would be dead, killed by the bomb, and nobody would know who had control of the satellites. At least Bex knew that her next target was in Japan.

But she needed to sleep first, to get back her strength.

She managed to wake up enough at Santiago to transfer onto a Boeing 747 heading for Sydney, Australia. She ate dinner on the aircraft and slept again. At least, she thought it was dinner, although it might have been lunch; her body clock appeared to have stopped completely. Hell, she decided – and not for the first time – was to be perpetually travelling but never arriving.

At Sydney she had a spare two hours. She ate, even though she wasn't hungry, and managed to snatch a few minutes talking to Bradley, Kieron and Sam on her mobile, which reassured her. At least Kieron had got home, and the technicians at the Falkland Islands control station appeared to be fighting back against the bad guys. But if the bad guys made it to Tokyo with the encoder and connected it into their system, then all bets were off.

After cutting the connection with Bradley, she looked up and across the sea of people in the terminal. Her brain went blank. Where was she? Obviously it was an airport, but she had suddenly lost track of exactly where in the world she was. She tried to get a clue from the faces, the accents and the languages around her, but there were ten different skin colours or shades within fifty metres of her, and probably ten times that many languages being spoken. The departures boards were in English; that was a clue. She tried to remember where she had come from, where she had started her journey, but everything was blank. A rising panic made her chest feel like straps had been secured around it. The tannoy language! The announcements were being made in English as well, and the voice had an accent. An *Australian* accent!

Australia! Sydney! It all came back to her in a rush. She'd flown from the Falklands to Chile, then an internal flight within Chile, then to Sydney, and she was flying *on* to Tokyo! The momentary lapse of memory left her shaken; even though she had slept on the various flights it hadn't been *proper* sleep, more of a light doze interrupted by announcements over the aircraft's PA system and cabin crew offering her juice or sandwiches. She needed eight hours in a proper bed. Her reflexes and her mental resilience were shot to hell at the moment.

The flight to Tokyo was boarding. Bex quickly stopped at one of the airport pharmacies and bought some earplugs, an eye-mask and a blister-pack of herbal sleeping tablets – herbal because she didn't particularly like putting pharmaceutical drugs in her system, and an ordinary sleeping tablet would probably leave her feeling groggy.

With the earplugs and eye-mask blocking out the sensory input from the aircraft, and the valerian and hops in the herbal tablets relaxing her, she managed to get a fair amount of decent sleep while the aircraft was in the air. She had set her watch to Tokyo time before take-off, so that every time she glanced at it she would orient herself further. With all of those factors working in her favour, when the aircraft touched down in Tokyo she felt surprisingly good.

As Bradley had promised, a driver was waiting for her in arrivals, once she had got past immigration control and luggage retrieval. He wore a black suit, and held a sign saying *Chloe Drewe*. She discreetly looked around while she walked towards him to make sure there wasn't anyone else looking for a Chloe Drewe. It wasn't like she thought that the bad guys somehow knew she was coming *and* knew her cover name, but it was a sensible thing to check, just like never taking the first taxi you saw. She nodded to him and smiled. He bowed, and she bowed back. She was definitely in Japan.

Bradley had secured her a room in a hotel in the Shinjuku district of Tokyo. That was where the leader of the bad guys had said they were heading to, when he had been giving orders to his team back in the Falkland Islands control station. But although Shinjuku was small, it was densely packed; her research had informed her that although it was only eighteen square kilometres, it had a population of over one-third of a million people. Given that Shinjuku Station was apparently the largest and busiest station in the world, she was glad that she wasn't using public transport to get there.

Bex gazed out at the passing scenery, trying to get some feeling for where she was. The city itself reminded her of New York or Central London – towering office blocks and skyscrapers built in various impractical shapes – but behind them she could see white-capped mountains towering higher than the buildings. They were strangely similar to the ones she'd seen at the airport in Chile. Only the signs were different; every road sign, advertisement and shop front here was written in characters she couldn't understand.

A few years back Bex had thought about learning Japanese, to complement the other languages she had mastered over the years, but she had quickly found that there were three separate writing systems in Japan: *kanji*, in which a single character stood for an entire word; *hiragana*, in which a single character stood for a syllable and words would be built up from several characters; and *katakana*, which was a syllabic system like *hiragana* but used only for English words like 'computer' or 'soda'. As she sat there in the car, while it wended its way haltingly through the thick Tokyo traffic, she remembered trying to master *kanji* and discovering with horror that there were over fifty thousand of them to memorise. That had put her completely off learning the language. Now, as she looked out at the sea of information that surrounded the car, she regretted that she hadn't persevered. Advertisements in particular dominated the landscape; running vertically up the buildings to which they were attached rather than horizontally, as they would have been in New York or London. It was early evening, and the light was beginning to fail as the sun set below the tops of the buildings. The steep, geometrical canyons formed by the office blocks shadowed quickly, but the adverts had already lit up, forming a shining backdrop in every colour Bex could imagine. She had spent quite a lot of time half watching science-fiction films with Bradley, and it was only now that she understood how many of the futuristic cityscapes of those films had been based on Tokyo, and the Shinjuku region in particular.

The car dropped her off in front of a hotel located in a skyscraper, with just the lobby, a bar and a restaurant on the ground floor. It was part of an American chain, which meant that although the lobby and the bar had touches of Japanese art and style, the staff all spoke perfect English. With the ARCC kit malfunctioning, and unable to translate for her, that was suddenly very important.

She checked in quickly, and went to her room. It was on the twenty-second floor, and had an incredible view over ninety per cent of the other buildings in the Shinjuku area, out to the waters of Tokyo bay, glittering red now in the low radiance of the setting sun, and to the lights of the city of Chiba on the other side. Having said that, it was small, but real estate was at a premium in Tokyo.

She checked the ARCC glasses, but although the system was in one of its 'up' phases she couldn't get hold of Kieron. His end of the system was dead. That was odd, and rather unsettling; he knew what time she was getting to Tokyo – or, at least, Bradley did – and normally he would have been there for her, providing support. Right now there was nothing.

She checked her messages on the 'Chloe Drewe' phone, and found something from Bradley, sent some five hours ago.

Hope your flight was good. In case the ARCC kit is down, here's some information for you. I've traced sales of satellite dishes, tracking equipment and high-end comms stuff in Japan. I'm assuming that the bad guys – whoever they are – will have had to set up their own control centre, and that's not something you can do by buying online from a normal retailer. The only people who've bought that kind of stuff recently are, strangely, a religious organisation called Ahmya. That's Japanese for Black Wind, by the way. Nothing much is known about them, but I have their address. It's 11 Nakatomi, Shinjuku, Tokyo 160-0014. They were set up twenty years ago by a Japanese inventor who had made his fortune in robotics. His name is Ito Aritomo. I checked the Ahmya website and social-media accounts, and they

do actually have several members with the names
Akitsugu and Nashiko. I remember that you and
Kieron heard the guy in charge of the mission mention
them. Good luck, and be careful.

Bex lay back on her bed, feeling the stresses and strains of
the journey and the past few days melt away like ice turning
to water and trickling out of her body. A Japanese religious
organisation? That was not necessarily a good thing. Given
her training in intelligence and special operations, the first
thing Bex thought of when she heard those words was
the infamous Aum Shinrikyo cult from twenty-five years
ago. They had released nerve gas onto the Tokyo subway
system in some twisted plot to cause the end of the world –
something that only members of the cult would survive.
Thirteen people had died and over six thousand had been
made ill by the poison. Members of the cult, including its
leader, had been executed by the Japanese authorities and
the cult itself split into two smaller groups who were now
kept under observation by the Japanese police.

Cults. Interesting. Bex couldn't help thinking of the Blood
and Soil fascist group that had brought her and Kieron
together. There seemed to be a common theme here. Was
Avalon Richardson associating herself with cults and fascist
groups around the world, or was this Ahmya group up to
something else, by themselves? Something that required the
PEREGRINE network? Difficult to know for sure, unless
she did some investigation.

She sighed, and sat up. Much as she wanted to sleep for

the next eight hours, she didn't have time. She had to find out where the system encoder had been taken, and why? Time for a shower, then she'd get out on the streets.

Half an hour later she left the hotel and headed out into the chaos and madness of Tokyo, letting her mobile phone guide her with its mapping function. Still no ARCC kit to help: she was going old-school now.

The Tokyo pavements were narrow, and crammed with people despite the time of day. Most of them held mobile phones up; not to their ears but so they could see the screen. The light from the screens illuminated their faces in strange ways. Were they FaceTiming, looking at maps or watching movies? Bex couldn't tell. Many of them had medical masks over their face; white, handkerchief-like bits of cloth held over their mouth and nose by white ribbons tied behind their head. The sight made Bex think about Aum Shinrikyo again, and she shivered, but she guessed the masks were more to stop people breathing in pollutants from the hundreds of taxis and ordinary cars that were crawling down the wide road.

She walked along the pavement. There seemed to be a flow to the pedestrians that surrounded her; two separate ribbons of people going in opposite directions, meaning that if you wanted to cross the ribbon that lay between you and a shop, a hotel or a restaurant, then you had to take care to avoid crashing into anyone. As she walked Bex could smell hundreds of different sweet, spicy and savoury odours drifting out of the many restaurants, and she suddenly realised she was hungry. Very hungry. But no time for that now.

She passed several pod hotels as she walked, and gave a silent prayer of thanks that Bradley hadn't booked her into one of them, but somewhere more upmarket. Pod hotels were something that only the Japanese could have invented – instead of rooms they had 'capsules', which were roughly the width and length of a standard single bed, and just high enough for the occupant to be able to crawl inside and sit up. They were usually made of plastic, with walls that were a sterile white in colour. Sometimes they had a television screen and power sockets, but no toilet, bath, shower or basin. If you wanted a shower, you had to go to a shared area, like in a sports centre, and if you wanted a bath then you might end up in a communal one with ten other people. If you were staying in a pod hotel then you had to give up your clothes when you arrived and change into a traditional Japanese *yukata* robe that was provided by the management. The worst thing about them, as far as Bex was concerned, was that the capsules were stacked up in rows, and to get to the higher ones you had to climb a ladder. It must be a bit like living in a beehive, she thought, and shuddered. She guessed they were mainly used by businessmen, students and travellers trying to save money, but to her they sounded like a form of hell on Earth. People stacked up like produce in a warehouse. She wanted privacy and comfort from her hotel experience.

Eventually her phone told her that she was where she wanted to be. She looked up. Squeezed between a ramen noodle bar and a shop selling mobile phones and tablet computers, she spotted a doorway with a sign above it in English: Ahmya. Just that one word, and nothing else.

Nice of the bad guys to actually advertise their location, she thought. It made the whole process so much easier. This must be the traditional Japanese politeness and eagerness to please.

'Would you like a free personality test?' a voice said from beside her.

She turned. A small Japanese girl, maybe a few years younger than Bex, stood beside her. A small bubble of space seemed to have appeared around them; the two streams of human traffic passed by on either side, going in opposite directions, but they were isolated. The girl held a tablet computer in her hand. She had black hair, cut short, and her face seemed to shine with an inner radiance. Or it was very subtly and very competently made up to look that way. She wore a badge with 'Ahmya' written on it, along with a logo that featured a single black water droplet and the girl's name, 'Midori'. Quickly looking around, Bex could see four or five other young Japanese people with similar tablets. *Probably bought from next door in bulk*, Bex thought. They were intercepting passers-by.

'Oh,' Bex said, trying to sound surprised. 'That would be nice.' Actually, she had been expecting something like this to happen. Cults tended to be one of two kinds: those that kept to themselves, and mainly increased their number by members having lots of babies and bringing them up in the cult, and those that wanted to recruit new members off the street. That recruitment process often started out with a personality test or something similar, but it was always rigged to convince the person taking it that there was a hole in their life that only the cult could fill.

Midori smiled, even more than she was already smiling. 'Let me start,' she said. She touched her finger to the screen of the tablet, and said, 'Do you normally bite your fingernails, or perhaps chew the end of your pencil or pen?'

'Why, yes,' Bex said. Not true, but she wanted to see where this would lead.

Midori ticked a box on the tablet screen. 'Do you normally speak slowly, or fast?'

'Slowly,' Bex said. Actually she hadn't got a clue what speed she normally spoke at, but she had a feeling that the answers didn't really matter. Whatever she said, Midori was going to tell her that she had personality issues and should come inside to talk to someone about it. That was the way it worked. And somewhere down the line, once she was hooked, they would ask her for a financial contribution to keep the cult going. After *that*, when she was totally indoctrinated and separated from the real world, they would ask for her bank account details. Of course, she wasn't going to let things go that far.

'Do you think that your life is a constant struggle to achieve your goals?'

Bex considered the past six months of her life. 'Oh yes,' she said honestly.

And so it went on. Some of the questions were trivial, some were absurd and some were quite personal.

Eventually Midori looked up from her screen and said,

'That completes the test. May I show you the results?'

'Yes, please,' Bex said, trying to look eager and vulnerable at the same time.

Midori turned the screen round so that Bex could see it. It showed a graph with a straight red line running horizontally across it, and a jagged black line that sometimes rose above the red one but mostly stayed below it. 'The red line is a normal, healthy person with a good mental state,' Midori said, sounding like she was reading from a script, 'and the black line is you. As you can see, there are some issues with the way you interact with the world. You probably already know this: maybe you feel insecure, or uncertain, and often you feel unhappy without knowing why.'

Don't we all? Bex thought. It was a clever scheme, she had to admit: playing on people's basic weaknesses. They probably showed everyone the same graph. It was like horoscopes in newspapers; you could show the same horoscope to people who belonged to any of the twelve star signs and they would find a way of linking what was said to their own history and issues.

'If you like,' Midori said, 'you could come inside and talk to one of our counsellors. They can give you some advice on how to change your life for the better.'

And start the process of pulling me into the cult, making me more and more dependent, Bex thought angrily, knowing that some people – impressionable teenagers usually, but also middle-aged people going through some kind of life crisis – could get sucked into this really fast, just because someone was showing an interest in them.

'It's completely free,' Midori went on, taking Bex's hesitation as uncertainty. 'We in the Ahmya Order just want people to be happier in their lives. That is our goal, and our joy.'

'That sounds great,' Bex said, suppressing her anger. She had to look like a potential victim here. She tried to put on a hopeful expression.

'Here.' Midori reached out and pinned a laminated cardboard badge onto Bex's jacket. It was blue, with the Ahmya symbol above the words 'Ground Floor Only'. 'This will get you into the building. Someone will guide you to a counsellor. I am sure they will make you feel much better, and give you hope for the future.' She bowed.

'Thank you,' Bex said, bowing as well. She headed towards the doorway, but slowly, as if she was still unsure. Two people moved ahead of her on the pavement, trying to get past: one of them had a blue badge like hers, but the other had a red badge. Quickly trying to read the red badge as its owner went past, she made out the words 'All Floors' beneath the black raindrop.

That was what she needed; access to all floors of the cult's HQ.

Bex listened out behind her as she drifted towards the doorway. Midori might be watching her, and she didn't want to look like she was getting away. When she heard the girl's voice say, 'Would you like a free personality test?' to someone else on the street she slipped sideways, into the crowd, merging with the stream of humanity that was passing by the Ahmya doorway.

She let the crowd carry her, past shoe stores and clothes stores and restaurants and hotels, until she spotted a print shop – somewhere you could get photocopies done, or things printed from USB sticks. She struggled sideways, out of the crowd and into the shop.

'Can I help you?' the teenager behind the counter asked in good English.

Bex held up the laminated badge. 'I need fifty of these done, but in red and with a change of words,' she said. She shrugged apologetically. 'I've got a conference going on at a hotel nearby, and we've had far more people turn up than we were expecting. It's some kind of administrative foul-up. We can't let any of the attendees into the presentations and workshops they've signed up for unless they have a badge. Can you help me?'

The teenager took the laminated badge and looked at it. 'I can scan this,' he said, 'then change text and background colour. Maybe I won't get the shade *exactly* right, but I can get close.'

'The would be fine,' Bex said, relieved.

It took just twenty minutes for the badges to be printed off and laminated. The teenager didn't query why Bex wanted copies of badges – either her cover story had convinced him or he just didn't care. Bex only needed one badge – but just asking for that might have made the boy suspicious. She kept one badge and dumped the rest in a bin just down the street as she left.

As she approached the Ahmya doorway, Bex swapped the blue badge she had been given for a red one and put the blue one in her pocket. She glanced around to find Midori. The girl had cornered a Japanese boy, who looked mesmerised by her, and was going into her spiel. Knowing that Midori was distracted, Bex walked straight up to the door and pressed the entrance button.

The door opened. She walked in as if she had every right to do just that.

The entrance gave out into a large white lobby with a huge reception desk and a walk-through security scanner that looked more like it should have been located in an airport than in the headquarters of a religious organisation. A huge banner hung from the ceiling with a photograph of a kindly, smiling Japanese man with bushy white hair, beard and eyebrows. This, she presumed, was the inventor, robotics expert and founder of the Ahmya cult: Ito Aritomo. On the other side of the barrier Bex noticed a side lobby with three lifts.

Movement on the edges of her vision caught Bex's attention. She glanced left and right, and froze where she stood. Two *things* were approaching her from alcoves on either side of the security scanner. For a moment her mind went blank as it scrabbled to identify what she was seeing. Finally it came to her with a rush of amazement; they were robots! They looked a bit like mechanical centaurs, she supposed, with four legs and a stocky body about the size of a small pony, and an elevated front end topped by a 'head' sporting video cameras and lights. From their 'shoulders' extended two arms, that looked like they had more joints than a human limb. The arms ended in things that were halfway between hands and claws.

Each robot had a red 'All Floors' badge attached to the centre of its chest.

Bex glanced at their bodies. She couldn't *see* any weapons, but she wouldn't be surprised if they were there. Hidden.

Ito Aritomo *was* a robotics expert, or so Bradley had said in his message. He obviously trusted robot security guards more than he trusted people.

Bex put her fingers beneath the red badge and pulled it away from her body, displaying it to the two robots. They dipped their heads, taking in the image of the badge through the lenses of their cameras, then moved back to where they had been standing.

'You may enter,' a mechanical voice said. The robot was obviously clever enough to spot from her face that she was not Japanese.

Bex walked towards the security barrier. She moved through it as if she did the same thing every day. There was a *beep*, but nobody tried to stop her. She wasn't carrying any guns or explosives. Maybe the scanner was calibrated to look for recording devices as well; most religious cults had an issue with journalists trying to get inside, looking for stories. She was OK; she didn't have any of those either.

Once past the barrier, Bex walked towards the lifts. A sign beside the lift doors labelled in both Japanese and English indicated that the 'Ahmya Institute' occupied ten floors in the building. The ground floor was *Reception and Processing*; the next three floors were labelled *Presentations and Induction*; floor five was *Administration*; floors six to eight were labelled *Outreach and International* while the top two floors had been reserved for *Executive Operations and Directors*.

Where to go? Bex had to keep moving, otherwise people would start to suspect her. Everyone around her was well dressed, perfectly coiffured and smiling. They smiled at each other, and they smiled a thin air if nobody was around them. Obviously the Ahmya Institute was a happy place to be. Or maybe there were punishments if they didn't keep smiling.

Administration. That was probably the best place to start. She entered the leftmost lift of the three and pressed the button for the fifth floor.

She was the only person in the lift, and she took a moment to breathe calmly and compose her face into a happy smile before the door opened and she walked out again.

Another robot security guard stood just by the lift doors. It scanned her badge, and its 'head' nodded briefly before it turned away. She was safe, for the moment.

The administration level contained numerous desks with computers on, and rows of young people sat at them, working. They all wore headsets with microphones, and they all wore the same clothes – white shirt or blouse, and black trousers or skirt. Most of them were talking to someone via their headset. Bex heard Japanese being spoken, along with maybe ten other languages, including English, German and Chinese. This looked like a massive fundraising exercise. The workers at the desks were probably phoning people around the world, using numbers from a database that Ahmya had either built up themselves or bought, a database of targets who might be inclined to make donations to a religious organisation. People who had suffered a bereavement recently, or people who had just come into an inheritance or cashed in their pension, sad and lonely people who would welcome the chance to talk to someone sympathetic on the phone and would be liable to give out their bank details.

Bex hated it. She hated anyone who tried to take advantage of those who were grieving, or uncertain, or vulnerable in some other way.

No photographs, she noticed. No pictures of parents or siblings or pets. No potted plants or vinyl figures of characters from films, games or graphic novels. Nothing personal at all. Each desk was perfectly anonymous. This was probably a hot-desk setup, where the kids came in at the beginning of their shifts and took the first available space.

All of the desks were occupied. That was a problem. Bex didn't want to just stand there, waiting for a spot to become free.

She felt a giggle well up inside her, and ruthlessly suppressed it. Her mind had just thrown up a picture of the beginning of a shift, with all the kids turning up at the same time and then scrambling for desks like some kind of work-related version of musical chairs.

Yes, the darker part of her mind piped up, *but what happens to the kids who can't get a desk? Do they get punished?*

She had to move before the security robot got suspicious. She walked up to the end of a row, where a teenager with acne and long hair pulled back into a ponytail sat talking into his microphone. He was speaking in English, which was why she chose him. She tapped him on the shoulder. He turned his head.

'You are required in Induction,' she said firmly.

His face took on an expression of horror. 'Me? Now? What have I done wrong?'

'Only you know that. Go. They're waiting for you.'

He tore his headset off and scrambled out of his seat and towards the lifts. Bex felt guilty about what she had just done, but it was necessary, and the best way to get what you wanted in an authoritarian regime was to assume authority and give orders. People were likely to follow them without question.

Bex slipped into the vacated seat. She probably had five minutes to do what she needed before the poor kid got down to Induction and realised that nobody was waiting for him.

She reached into her pocket and took out a small USB device that Bradley had provided. It took her a few moments to work out where the USB sockets were on the computer – on the left-hand side of the screen, she realised. She reached out and plugged the device in. Instantly a green LED started flashing, indicating that the device was hoovering up as much data as it could from the system. It was possible that the kid only had access to superficial levels of the computer network, but as Bex didn't know exactly what she was looking for, she had to start somewhere.

Maybe remove the LED bulb, she thought. She would have a word with Bradley. She was uncomfortably aware of it flashing away, attracting attention. She looked around for something she could use to hide it, but there was nothing on the desk she could use. Literally nothing.

After what seemed an eternity, the light stopped flashing. The device had absorbed all the data it could find.

Bex pulled it out.

A metal hand clutched her shoulder.

'You do not belong here,' an artificial voice said.

She turned her head, making sure to keep smiling. 'Is there a problem?' she asked.

One of the robotic security guards stood beside her. Its expression was inflexible – metal, glass and wires – but it *looked* fierce. 'The Ahmya Order does not allow intruders, thieves or investigators on its premises. You will come with me.'

Its metal claw-hand tightened painfully on her shoulder, compressing muscle against bone. She grimaced, hoping the thing knew when to stop. Humans were so much more vulnerable than robots.

CHAPTER ELEVEN

Sam lived twenty minutes away from Kieron's house. Twenty minutes' walk. What was that in running time? Ten minutes? Maybe five? Kieron already felt a stitch in his side, and he'd barely made it to the end of the road.

He dimly remembered from his biology lessons at school that you got a side stitch because more blood was being forced through your liver and it wasn't coping very well. Lovely to know this in theory, but the reality meant that he felt as if somebody had stabbed him just below his ribs on the right-hand side of his chest. The pain seemed to radiate from one side to the other, and from front to back. It hurt so much that he was running virtually lopsided, bending over to try to stop the pain.

It was mid-evening now. The sun had gone down, and the cloudless sky glowed with a profusion of stars, like glittering diamond dust floating on black water. It really *did* look to Kieron like the stars were floating on something because his vision was blurring, and his head felt swimmy. Everything around him was coming in and out of focus, and moving around in strange ways. He had a horrible feeling he was about to pass out.

He slowed down, holding his side to contain the agony. Maybe if he'd worked a bit harder in PE this wouldn't be happening. If he was the kind of guy who could climb up a rope to the gym ceiling, or come in the top three in cross-country, or swim from one side of the pool to the other on one lungful of breath, then he wouldn't feel like this – in pain, and terrified. He'd always felt a secret contempt for the kids who were good at sports, but right now he would be happy to have even half the stamina they had.

He bent over; hands on his knees, breath rasping in his throat and whistling in his lungs. An asthma inhaler would be a great idea right now. Sam had one, but that wasn't much help. He had to *get* to Sam first.

Kieron looked around, hoping he would see something, *anything*, that might help. Nobody was around; the streetlights formed little pools of orange light around the base of each pillar. He could see televisions flickering in front rooms. Someone was practising the drums. Somewhere else he could hear the distant sound of Indian dance music. All so normal. So Newcastle.

It was no good. If he kept going at this rate he would be dead before he got to Sam's place. He had to ask for help.

Pulling his mobile phone from the pocket of his jeans he found *Tom Drewe* in the contacts list. That was the fake name Bradley's burner was entered under. A few seconds later he heard the beeps as the phone dialled the number.

'Yes?' Bradley's voice; cautious and non-committal.

'Tom?' Kieron said breathlessly. 'It's Ryan.' That was *his* fake name.

'Ryan, you sound like you've run a marathon. What's wrong?'

'It's about Craig.' That was Sam's undercover name. 'I think he's in danger.'

'OK.' No panic or confusion in Bradley's tone; he had snapped straight into professional mode. 'Where is he?'

'I don't know for sure, but at this time of night he's probably at home. He didn't tell me he was going out, and he always tells me. He virtually boasts about it.'

'And where are you? Don't be specific – just give me enough information to work it out.'

'At the end of my road. I'm trying to run, but I'm making a bad job of it.'

'And this danger?'

'The people you and . . .' He hesitated, trying to remember Bex's undercover name. '. . . Chloe don't like. It's them.'

'I'm sending a cab for you. Stay where you are, I'll do it online from here. I'll get one as well. We'll meet at Craig's place.'

'Thanks,' Kieron said, and meant it.

'Ryan . . .'

'Yes?'

'When you get there, be careful. Look to see if there's anyone else around before you go up to the door and ring the bell.'

'OK.'

'And one more thing: have you got the . . . the *thing* with you?'

Bradley meant the ARCC glasses. 'Yes.'

'Good. We can't let it fall into anyone else's hands, understand?'

'I understand.'

Bradley – or, rather, 'Tom' – cut the connection. While Kieron waited for the taxi, and as the pain in his side subsided, he pulled the ARCC glasses from his jacket pocket and put them on. He pressed the activation button on the side and waited as they booted up. A few seconds later he was looking at the translucent operating screens of the kit, projected onto the lenses over the dark background of the streets and the houses. They appeared to be still in the middle of one of the 'islands' of accessibility when the satellites were operational. Kieron quickly waved his hands in the air, accessing menus via the gesture control sensors built into the rims of the lenses. Within moments he had pulled up the menu that should be showing him what Bex was looking at, in Tokyo, but it was dark. Not switched on. Maybe she was asleep, or maybe she wasn't using the glasses just then. Difficult to tell. In a way he was grateful: if she'd been there, he would have had to tell her about what was happening in Newcastle, and she would start worrying about *that* rather than the mission she was meant to be on.

He felt a stab of concern, similar to the side stitch. Bex was out there, alone, with no support from Kieron or from the ARCC kit. He hoped she was OK.

'Are you OK, son?'

The voice from behind scared him. He turned, pulling the glasses off.

The man standing there wore an anorak and a cap. He held a lead, and on the other end of the lead was possibly the saddest dog Kieron had ever seen. It was some kind of crossbreed – a Labradoodle, maybe, with a Labrador and a poodle for parents. Or maybe a Cockapoo, with a cocker spaniel instead of a Labrador in its parentage. Its face looked sad, and it stared at Kieron with eyes that seemed to say, *Please, I want to go home. My paws are cold on these paving slabs.* Even its fur appeared to droop sadly.

'Yes, yeah, I'm fine. Really.' Kieron tried to look convincing, but he had a horrible feeling that his eyes were open far too wide. He tried to close them, but straight away he thought he probably looked like he was squinting suspiciously, so he stopped.

'OK.' The man looked like he was about to move on, but he paused. 'It's just that you were waving your arms around. I thought you were dancing, but I couldn't hear any music, and when I got closer I couldn't see any headphones.' He stared curiously at Kieron's right ear. 'Unless you've got one of those wireless doodads, and it's shoved in so far I can't see it. That could be dangerous, you know? What would you do if it got stuck in there?'

'No, I was actually –' Kieron's mind went suddenly blank. What could he say? What sounded likely? Not *I was operating a top-secret piece of undercover equipment*, obviously. 'Exercising. Yes, I was trying to keep myself warm. By moving my arms around. A lot.'

The man looked sceptical. 'If you're feeling cold, best

thing is to wrap up warm. You kids, you never wear enough clothes. Anyway, you're all right, son?'

'Yes, thanks. I'm fine.'

The man nodded, and walked off. The Labradoodle, or Cockapoo, or whatever, stared at Kieron in silent reproach before the lead pulled tight and it was dragged away.

A car swept up, almost silently, to the kerb near where Kieron stood. For a moment he tensed, ready to run, but it was a bright yellow Toyota hybrid. With the best will in the world, he couldn't see any bad guys driving a bright yellow hybrid.

'Tom?' the driver called. He was Asian; young, with short hair and a smile on his face.

Kieron was about to say 'No', and then he remembered. 'Yes, that's me.'

'Climb in.'

Kieron slammed the passenger door and put his seat belt on and the driver pulled away.

'Sorry it's so close,' he said.

The driver shook his head. 'No problem. Every journey starts with a step, and every fortune starts with a penny. That's what my mum taught me. Actually, I prefer a lot of short trips to one long one. I like the variety.'

Five minutes later they were approaching Sam's house. The car pulled over down the street from where Sam actually lived. Bradley was being cautious.

'Thanks,' he said, getting out. Up ahead, further along the road, beyond Sam's house, he saw the lights of another car approaching.

'No problem. Have a good evening.'

The car pulled off. Kieron wasn't sure whether to head straight for Sam's front door or wait for Bradley. Fortunately, he didn't have to make a decision. The car whose lights he'd seen up ahead pulled over a hundred metres away, and a man got out. Bradley.

'OK,' he said as he got closer, looking around cautiously, 'tell me everything.'

Quickly, Kieron brought him up to date about the phantom version of Bex that he'd seen in the ARCC glasses, and the things that it had said. By the time he finished, Bradley looked grim.

'Avalon Richardson,' he said, making the name sound like a curse. 'She'll use anything to get to us. Even you and Sam.' He shook his head angrily, then reached out and patted Kieron's shoulder. 'You did exactly the right thing. Right, let's go and see if Sam is OK.'

'Let me try his mobile again,' Kieron said. He pulled his phone out and selected Sam's contact details. The phone rang, and rang, and –

'Yeah, what?' Sam's voice asked. 'I'm halfway through a movie.'

'Are you all right?'

'Yeah, except that I'm missing the movie. What is it?'

'Why didn't you answer earlier?'

'Cos it was a good bit. What's the problem?'

'You might be in danger. Who else is in the house?'

'Nobody.' Sam sounded confused. 'Danger from who? Where?'

'Where are your mum and dad?'

219

'They've gone out to see some friends. They won't be home until after midnight. Kieron, you're scaring me.'

'What about your sister?'

'On a date. Haven't got a clue when she'll be back. Maybe never.'

Bradley tapped Kieron on the shoulder. 'Get him to come out to us.'

'Sam, you need to –'

Bradley's hand clamped hard on Kieron's shoulder, making him wince. 'No, stop.' He pointed down the road, in the direction from which he had come.

Kieron stared. He saw a car, illuminated by the light of the streetlamps, moving silently down the road. Its headlights were, strangely, off. Kieron wondered how the driver could see in the dark.

'Ops team,' Bradley whispered. He glanced in the other direction, the way Kieron had come. Kieron turned his head to look.

Another car was drifting silently towards them. Its headlights were off as well.

Bradley's hand was still clamped on Kieron's shoulder. 'Move slowly,' he whispered, pulling Kieron backwards off the road. 'If we're very, very lucky they will be concentrating on the house, and they won't see us.'

'Sam,' Kieron said quietly, even though the people in the cars couldn't possibly hear him, 'go to your back door. I'll meet you in your back garden in a couple of minutes.'

'OK.' His voice stopped as Kieron cut the connection.

'What's your plan?' Bradley asked, looking back and forth

as the two cars coasted towards each other. He pulled Kieron into the shade of a nearby bush before the headlights of the nearest car could light them up. 'I'm guessing you've got a plan. A plan would be good, because I'm out of options at the moment.'

'I,' Kieron said, trying to sound firm, 'am going to sneak around to the back of Sam's house and get him out through the garden. The reason I'm going to do that is, I know his back garden well and I can navigate my way there in the dark. *You* are not going to come with me, because if we get caught then the bad guys have *you*, but if they just catch me and Sam, then you can still get away.' He reached up and swept the ARCC glasses from his head. 'And you need to take these. We can't afford the bad guys getting hold of *them* either.'

Bradley's mouth twisted in a grimace, but he nodded reluctantly. 'Your logic is impeccable. I wish I could help, but –'

'Everybody has to play to their strengths,' Kieron said, feeling a heavy weight in his stomach. 'I know the ground, and I know Sam.' He hesitated. 'And I'm replaceable. You're not.'

Bradley's hand had moved off Kieron's shoulder, but he extended it again, for shaking this time. As Kieron took his hand, and felt Bradley squeeze his fingers, Bradley said, 'You're an impressive kid, Kieron. I'm proud to know you. And you're wrong: you're not replaceable. Just so you know.'

As he let go, the nearest car to them slid past, on its way to Sam's house. It was big and black – a Humvee, maybe.

Its lights were off and its windows darkened. It moved with a quiet purr – an electric engine, rather than petrol. Maybe it *was* a hybrid, Kieron thought randomly, but it wasn't yellow. He'd been right about that at least.

He turned his head to say something to Bradley, but his friend had gone; slipped away quietly into the night. Probably with regret, probably against his better wishes, but he had gone, like Kieron had asked.

Kieron felt a tidal wave of loneliness and responsibility sweep over him. He suppressed it all. He had a job to do.

Now that the first car had passed, and was slowing down as it approached the second one, Kieron ran quickly across to the other side of the road. Two houses along, in the direction of Sam's house, he paused. He knew that to his right a narrow walkway ran between two houses, but before he went down there he wanted to see what happened when the cars stopped.

They ended up bumper to bumper outside Sam's house. Their occupants seemed not to care about anyone else who might be driving down the road and find their way obstructed. Maybe that's what it was like when you worked for the intelligence services; you could do what you wanted.

Doors on both sides of both cars opened at the same time. Figures in black jumpsuits and black balaclavas climbed silently out. They held objects in their hands, and while Kieron was still trying to see what they were, each one suddenly emitted a thin beam of red laser light. For a few seconds the beams pointed in all directions – some up into the air, some down at the ground and some at nearby houses; a cat's cradle of intense crimson light. At a silent command the figures all swung around so that the objects they carried, which Kieron now realised were assault rifles, were all pointed at Sam's house. The battered wooden front door that Kieron had gone through so many times he'd lost count, painted red so long ago that it had faded to pink in the sun, suddenly became the focus of maybe ten laser target indicators. It was like a scene from a thriller, but it was real. It was Sam's house!

At least his family weren't home. Kieron just hoped that Sam had got out in time as well, and was waiting in his back garden.

Kieron pivoted and ran down the narrow gap between the two houses where he stood.

The ground was rutted and overgrown. Nettles slapped at his trousers as he ran. There were no streetlights down here; the only thing helping him was the light of the stars and his own memory of so many years playing with Sam around these back lanes. He leaped over the rusted carcass of a child's tricycle, not so much because he saw it but because he *remembered* it. He ran between the twin six-foot-high fences that bounded the back gardens; both twisted and rotted by years of rain and sun. At the end of the fences he nearly ran into another fence, right in front of him, but he swerved left into the lane that ran along the backs of the houses, separating the ones on Sam's road from the ones on the next road along. Nobody knew who owned it, and nobody used it except for kids playing and burglars presumably burgling. As Kieron ran, fragmented memories came back to him. This narrow stretch of land had been so many things to the two boys over the years: the equatorial canyon on the Death Star; a rocky defile down which World War Two soldiers quietly crept; a secret way into the Evil Lord's castle in a fantasy world, far far away . . . It was their childhood. It was every imaginary game they had ever played. How many times had one of them caught the other, raised his hand, made a gun shape and gone 'Bang!', or zapped him with an imaginary laser?

And now it was for real. Now, real people with real guns were chasing them.

Kieron stepped over a pile of bricks and dodged around an iron stake that had somehow become embedded in the earth. Maybe it had been a sword, back in the day. He counted the houses on his left as he went: number forty-six, where Mrs Merthan lived; number forty-eight, which had been separated out into flats and was occupied by four different Polish families; number fifty, which he and Sam had broken into one day when they were younger, to find bare boards, chalk circles and black candles that had burned out to leave wax puddles. And number fifty-two: Sam's house. Sam's *parents'* house.

There was no gate or doorway from the alleyway into Sam's back garden. Kieron went on to number fifty-four, where a music teacher from a local school lived. A door in the back fence could be opened if you slid a piece of wire up between the door and the jamb to lift the catch. That's what Kieron did, using a straightened paper clip that he and Sam kept hidden beneath a large stone for that very purpose. He crept quietly into the music teacher's back garden.

A cat yowled, and Kieron jumped, but it was somewhere in a different garden; nothing to do with him. He crept over to where he knew there was a gap in the fence between this house and Sam's house, caused by some storm years ago and which neither side had bothered to fix. The panel there had come loose at the bottom, and he squeezed through the gap into Sam's back garden.

The only light was still that from the stars, and Kieron nearly fell into the goldfish pond. He caught his balance, detoured around it and headed for the back door of the house.

'Sam?' he whispered.

'Kieron! What's going on?' The voice came from the darkness.

'Bad guys, out front. Got to get out.'

'How did they find me?' Sam hissed loudly.

Kieron decided that right then discretion was the better part of valour. 'Dunno,' he said. 'They just did. I've got to get you out.'

'What about my mum and dad?'

'The bad guys aren't after them, they're after us. Well, you right now. Come on.'

Sam emerged from the shadows of the conservatory. His expression – what Kieron could see of it – looked worried.

'It'll be OK,' Kieron said. 'Bradley's with me.' It wasn't quite the truth, but Sam needed reassurance, and there wasn't very much else Kieron could give.

They headed towards the loose fence panel that Kieron had come through, but he suddenly heard a nearby door open and a voice say, 'Go on then, if you have to.' He wasn't sure what to make of that until he heard the pattering of claws on concrete. The music teacher had let her dog out.

'OK,' Sam said, 'change of plan. Follow me.'

He ran towards the back of the garden. Kieron followed him, uncertain where they were going. There wasn't any door in the back fence, and no loose panels as far as he knew. What was Sam doing?

As the thought went through his mind, Sam suddenly jumped up, scrambling onto what Kieron now remembered was a low plastic storage unit in which Sam's dad stored his garden tools. Kieron followed, but by then Sam had scrabbled sideways onto the roof of a larger shed, where bigger things – old gazebos, lengths of wood that might come in useful one day, big rolls of wire netting intended for some gardening project that had never happened – were stored. From there he could get to the top of the fence panels that separated the garden from the back alley. He vaulted over them as Kieron watched. Seconds later, Kieron followed.

As he pushed off he heard someone say, 'Stop where you are or I'll shoot!'

Too late to stop. Kieron vaulted over the fence, following his friend. In the sparse starlight and still in mid-air he saw Sam trying to pick himself up, and a black-clad figure pointing a gun directly at Sam's head. A small red dot glowed on Sam's temple. The figure was moving forward along the alley, which meant –

Kieron kicked them in the head as he landed.

The black-clad figure flew sideways, hitting the back fence and bouncing off before they lay there, unconscious.

'OK, this *is* serious!' Sam said as Kieron hit the ground and rolled. 'Which way?'

Kieron straightened up, and looked both ways along the alley. 'Don't think it matters. Choose one.'

Sam pointed ahead, in the opposite direction to the way Kieron had come. 'That way. We can get a bus and go to Bradley's place.'

'OK.'

Sam ran, and Kieron followed, scooping up the bad guy's weapon as he did so. Numbers fifty-four, fifty-six and fifty-eight flew past. A pigeon suddenly flew up in a flurry of feathers, disturbed by their passage. Somewhere, a dog started to bark.

Up ahead, Kieron saw a black rectangle; the end of the alley. Beyond it was the road that ran perpendicular to Sam's road and the next one along.

He turned to look behind. He wasn't sure if anyone was chasing them or not; the alley was too dark.

Sam ran out of the alley, past the two houses that bracketed it and out onto the pavement. Kieron followed.

'Stop right where you are,' a voice said. Male, authoritative, used to being obeyed. 'If you do not stop, we will shoot.'

Sam put his hands up.

Kieron ran out onto the pavement. He looked left and right. Black-clad operatives, their faces covered by balaclavas and holding high-tech weapons, faced them from both sides.

He stared down at his chest. A cluster of five red dots circled over his heart like mosquitos looking for a place to land.

He looked up, into the eyes of the nearest agent. Well, not into their eyes – they were covered by what looked like low-light goggles. Into his lenses.

'Have you seen my cat, mister?' he asked plaintively. 'We've lost her.'

'Nice try,' the man said. 'You're coming with us.'

CHAPTER TWELVE

Bex stared into the 'face' of the security robot. There was no possibility of sympathy there, nothing she could play on; only a pre-programmed dedication to duty. Appealing to its better nature wasn't going to achieve anything.

She stood up suddenly. The robot was so close to her that she brushed against its uniform jacket, knocking the red 'All Floors' access badge off its chest.

'Oh, I'm so sorry!' she exclaimed. Before the robot could do anything she bent down and scooped the badge off the floor. Straightening up again, she reattached it –

– Except that the badge she attached wasn't the one that had fallen. It was the blue 'Ground Floor Only' badge she had been given earlier by Midori, outside. Fortunately the security robot didn't notice.

'Come this way,' it said, taking hold of her arm firmly with a metal hand about the size of her head.

As they got to the lobby area with the three sets of lift doors, she stepped firmly and abruptly away from the robot. Taken by surprise, and with its balance momentarily upset, it let go of her arm before it could be pulled right over.

The central lift doors opened. Three white-shirted young cult members stepped out, while behind them another security robot stood, patiently waiting for the doors to close again and the lift to take them up to the floor where it worked. Somewhere on the executive levels.

'Please!' she said, looking at the robot in the lift and trying to look concerned. Well, it wasn't much of a reach, to be honest. 'I don't think that this thing belongs here!' She pointed at the security robot. More particularly, she pointed at its badge.

The robot in the lift pushed the 'Door open' button. '*Kore wa shin'nyu-shadesu!*' it said loudly in the automated voice that all the robots shared.

Within moments, an alarm started to sound, and a recorded voice on the PA system shouted '*Shin'nyu-sha! Shin'nyu-sha!*' over and over. Bex guessed that was the Japanese for 'Intruder!'

The previously calm administrative floor suddenly became a scene of panic and chaos. The young people operating the phone lines all reached out and switched their computers off, then stood up as if to attention, holding their badges out so they could be seen. They must have been trained to do that, so that an intruder couldn't access information and would easily be identified and caught.

The 'head' of the security robot that had caught Bex looked around, then tilted so it could look at its own security badge. Bex thought she caught a slight flinch in its metal shoulders and a tensing of its legs. Bex didn't know what happened to intruders in the Ahmya building, but she didn't think it would be a firm telling-off before being escorted off the premises. It looked a lot more serious than that. She had no idea how much or how little of a real 'personality' these robots had – artificial intelligence was not her subject – but it seemed to know that something was wrong and it wanted to survive. It started to run – well, lumber, to be fair – towards a fire door off to one side. The emergency stairs, Bex guessed. She didn't know if it was going to try to head for the ground floor and hope nobody noticed or get to someone who could vouch for it and explain that a mistake had been made. She didn't actually care. She just wanted to get out herself.

The doors for the left-hand lift opened. Another security robot cantered out, holding what looked like a Taser. Bex slipped inside and pressed the button for the ground floor. The lift doors slid closed, and she took a deep breath.

The alarm was sounding on the ground floor as well. She straightened her back, smiled, and walked directly towards the exit onto the street. Everyone around seemed either paralysed or panicked by the repeating alarm.

Midori stood on the pavement outside, staring into the building. She glanced at Bex. 'Please, what is happening?'

'They're testing the fire alarm,' Bex said calmly. 'They've asked me to come back tomorrow, when they haven't got so much on.'

She walked off, feeling an itch in the middle of her back. *Nobody is looking*, she told herself. *Nobody is chasing after you.* But the itch kept itching until she had gone around the corner and was out of sight of the Ahmya building.

Halfway back to her hotel she stopped at a sushi and sashimi bar, partly to check that nobody was following her and partly to get some food. She was suddenly hungry, and some sushi seemed like a great idea right then. The place was small, with only ten seats, all of which were placed along a conveyor belt that came out of a hatch, travelled slowly along the length of one wall, then vanished into another hatch. Small plates covered with transparent plastic domes sat on the conveyor belt. The plates were various colours, and each one had a small portion of sushi or sashimi on it. Bex knew that the colours of the plates reflected the price, and a woman sitting at a till by the door was counting how many plates the leaving patrons had, and what colours they were. She sat and watched the food going past her, wondering which to take. They all looked so good.

The great thing about sushi was that it was quick; she ate, and was out of there within five minutes. Ten minutes after that she was back at her hotel.

She tried the ARCC link again, but this time it was actually down, inoperative, rather than nobody answering. It looked like she was going to have to do this herself, the old-fashioned way.

Her tablet computer had a USB port on the side, and the chip and memory had been upgraded by Bradley so that it was a lot more capable that it looked on the outside. Bex had also loaded it with high-grade security analysis programs that weren't generally available on the open market. She booted it up, and set the programs running on the data she had stolen while she had another shower. By the time she came back, refreshed, the programs had finished their work and were proudly displaying their results.

The software had been designed to take a raw set of data and pull out whatever patterns it could, displaying them as an overlapping series of windows. In this case, Bex could see organisational charts for the Ahmya order, lists of members and what level they had reached within the organisation, sites and properties owned by the order, people around the world who had contributed financially, and people who might contribute in the future . . . Basically, a full description of how the order was set up.

First, Bex checked the list of properties. The main office block that she had just left was listed, as well as several other properties scattered around Japan – mostly in rural locations. These were probably 'retreats', where recent converts were separated from their real life and family and pulled further into the cult. Five locations, however, were just listed as 'Operations Sites', with no further description. One of those was probably what she was looking for. Probably.

Next she checked for purchase records or financial transactions, to see if she could tie in the satellite tracking equipment whose sale Bradley had told her about with any of the locations, but if it was listed then it was under some generic name, like 'Electronic equipment' or 'Computer equipment' that she couldn't connect with anything. She sat back for a moment, considering.

Staff lists. The Ahmya team who had attacked the Falkland Islands satellite control station had included members with the first names Akitsugu and Nashiko. She quickly cross-referenced the personnel records of the entire organisation with the lists of where people had been posted.

Two of the mysterious 'Operations Site' locations had staff with the first names Akitsugu and Nashiko. But which was the one she wanted?

Ah. Geographical location. Nobody in their right mind would put a satellite control station in a valley, because its view of the sky would be blocked. Satellite control stations were generally in the middle of large open expanses of land, like the one in the Falklands, or on top of hills or mountains.

Bex checked the geographical locations of the two sites. One of them was right in the centre of the city of Kyoto. She could rule that one out straight away. The other sat at the highest point on a hill in Tochigi Prefecture, about 180 kilometres away. It looked like a rural, mountainous area. Remote.

If that wasn't her target, then she didn't know what she was going to do.

She phoned Bradley's mobile, hoping to be able to pass on the details of what she had found, but he didn't answer. Rather than leave a message she wrote a quick email, encrypted it, then sent it.

She tried the ARCC system again. In the time since she had last tried it, some of the satellites had obviously been turned back on. She could get a link to England, but neither Kieron nor Bradley was answering.

A feeling of dread swept over Bex, like a tsunami suddenly appearing on the horizon and sweeping in within moments to devastate a beach. Why couldn't she get hold of Bradley? Why wasn't anybody at the other end of the ARCC kit to give her support?

She phoned Kieron on his burner phone. No answer. She tried Sam. Again, no answer.

This was getting serious. Bex felt a sudden shiver run through her. What had happened back in England? Part of her wanted to throw everything into her suitcase, get a taxi to the airport and return home to see what was going on, but she stopped herself. She had a mission. She had to succeed at this end of things, and trust the others to succeed at theirs.

She stood at the window, gazing out at distant lights across the bay and trying to calm her racing heart.

She didn't often think about the other nine teams that were using the ARCC equipment. They were all freelancers, like her and Bradley, but it wasn't like they all got together once a year for a party. None of the nine teams knew who the others were. Bex and Bradley did their missions – using the kit they had designed, of course – and let the other teams get on with theirs. The problem was that with the PEREGRINE satellite network suffering from sabotage, and shutting down intermittently, those other teams were in the same position she was: an agent, undercover somewhere dangerous, suddenly unable to get access to the information and intelligence they needed.

Bex suddenly felt a real kinship with those other agents. She felt their anxiety and confusion.

She shook her head. The best thing she could do for everyone was to get to that mystery Ahmya site and stop them from trying to take control of the satellites – and maybe discover why the organisation wanted the PEREGRINE network at all.

Without the ARCC system. Without Bradley or Kieron. Without support.

What was that phrase Bradley liked to quote? 'When the going gets tough, the tough get going.'

Time to get going. Or just go; she wasn't sure how the grammar worked out there.

Bex took everything out of her rucksack apart from some basic tools and the thermal suit that she had worn in the Falkland Islands, then left her room. She wasn't sure if she would need the thermal suit, but it was better to have it and not use it than not have it and suddenly need it.

The concierge down in the hotel lobby arranged for a hire car to be booked for her. With typical Japanese efficiency, within twenty minutes the car pulled up outside the hotel – a black Toyota RAV4. The driver got out, gave her the keys, then flagged down a taxi to take him back to wherever he was based. Fortunately the Japanese drove on the left-hand side of the road, as they did in England, so Bex didn't have to mentally adjust her mindset. She got in and started the car.

The car-hire company had very kindly set the satnav system to English rather than Japanese, but Bex quickly discovered that it still wasn't much help. She tried typing in 'Tochigi', but the device's computer didn't recognise the name. Perhaps she had spelled it incorrectly. She tried 'Mount Nantai' and 'Mount Nyoho', which, according to the Internet were both peaks in the mountain range near where she wanted to go, but the system couldn't find them either. Obviously she was missing some subtlety in the Japanese language. She tried 'Nikko' and 'Kanuma' as well, which were nearby towns, but again they weren't recognised. How, she wondered despairingly, could she get 'Nikko' wrong? Eventually she decided that she just had to use the satnav on her phone, but she did make sure she downloaded the map of the area around Tokyo to her phone's memory first. The chances of getting an Internet signal out in the middle of nowhere seemed slim, and she didn't want to suddenly be told, two hours into her journey, that her phone had no idea where she was.

Setting out, Bex found herself driving north out of Tokyo. The first twenty minutes or so were stop-start, stop-start at the many sets of traffic lights, but soon enough she was heading through the suburbs and into the countryside. Once out of the city, traffic was strangely quiet, and also strangely slow. Even on the main motorway, Japanese drivers seemed to be very cautious, and also very polite. Most cars drove at speeds that were much lower than would have been the case on similar roads in England or America, and the cars that *were* going faster, overtaking the others, tended to be driven by Westerners. Or Japanese teenagers. Or a frustrated MI6 agent who was desperate to get to where she needed to go.

She also found, about forty-five minutes into her journey, that there were toll roads – and each of the sections of toll road appeared to operate in a different way. With some you paid in advance, at a toll booth, and were given a set of vouchers which you had to hand in at various stations along the road to be allowed to continue. With others you were given a single voucher and had to stick it into a machine every ten miles or so for validation, along with a payment, before you could go on. Bex had to improvise each time, feeling frustration and anger gnawing at her stomach. All the road signs were in Japanese, of course, and Bex had to rely on her phone to keep her going in the right direction. As she drove, she kept switching her attention from the phone's screen to the views outside the car, and then back again. She did manage to marvel at the Japanese countryside, however; the dark green forests; the snow-capped peaks of the distant mountains; the geometrically regular fields planted presumably with rice, soya and other crops. She passed what seemed to be several religious shrines and temples, presumably dedicated to one of the two main Japanese religions – Shinto or Buddhism. This was definitely Japan.

After about ninety minutes she found herself heading into a region of hills, backed by distant mountains. She was hungry, and every so often she passed a stall on the side of the road that was selling fruit or fish or meat, but she kept driving. She had a job to do, and every second might count.

The number of cars that were driving alongside or past her had progressively dropped, the further north she went, and the number of Western faces had also reduced, to the point where she appeared to be the only *gaijin* – Westerner – on the road or off it. Soon the road itself narrowed, and she was heading uphill along a series of switchbacks and sudden hairpin turns that, on her satnav, looked like someone had just scribbled on the screen rather than actually drawn a route. Now it was an event if another car passed her by. She had left the usual tourist highways and byways, and was truly in the heart of Japan – with only a satnav and an unreliable mobile-phone translation service to help her.

Eventually she had climbed so high that she emerged from the treeline to find herself almost at the top of what was either a very large hill or a small, wide mountain. She knew from long-ago geography lessons that the treeline was the highest point at which the trees could grow. Above that point the cold air and the lack of moisture meant that seeds would not germinate.

A mist had drawn in, or perhaps she was actually up in low clouds. Either way, it meant she couldn't see very far. What she *could* see, however, was a fence and, beyond it, a large, circular building, right on the highest point of the hill. Or the mountain. Whatever. This, according to her satnav, was her destination.

The building looked like a series of white plates of different sizes, placed upside down and arranged with the biggest at the bottom and the smallest at the top. On the flat surface on top of the highest and smallest 'plate' Bex saw what she assumed were the things that transmitted messages to and from the satellites. Rather than the large satellite dishes she had been expecting, however, like the control station in the Falkland Islands, the installation here was topped with five white domes made up of a series of smaller triangular elements. Maybe they had the satellite dishes inside, and were meant to be aesthetic, or a protection from the weather. They looked strangely like huge golf balls; which was ironic,

Bex thought, considering the apparent fascination that the Japanese had with golf. If it wasn't for the mist she reckoned she could have seen ten or fifteen golf courses on the flat landscape below.

She backed her car down into the treeline again, and parked it off the road, then spent a few minutes breaking branches off the nearest bushes to partially cover it from sight. No point in being obvious. Her breath clouded in front of her, and she could feel the cold air nipping at her fingertips, ears and cheekbones. She should have thought this through, she told herself ruefully. She should have brought some cold-weather clothing before she left Tokyo. Just a woollen hat and gloves would have helped. She half considered putting on the thermal suit that she had brought with her in her rucksack, but the problem with that was that it was *too* effective. She would suffer heat exhaustion if she kept it on for more than fifteen minutes.

Before leaving the car, she tried turning on the ARCC glasses again. Again, the system was in one of its blank times, where the satellites were unavailable. And somewhere in that building at the top of the hill was the force that kept turning them off. Frustrating.

She tried her mobile phone, but she couldn't get any signal. Hardly surprising.

She emerged from the treeline again on foot, keeping low, and crept towards the fence, rucksack on her back.

The road that she had been on went past the control station, with a spur leading off and up to a massive sliding gate set into the fence. The fence itself was topped with what looked like razor wire. Getting over that without slicing her hands and arms to shreds would be impossible. She could see no guards; no security booth; no way of getting in. She also couldn't see any cameras on poles, as there had been at the Falkland Islands control station. How did any authorised visitors enter?

As she got closer, she saw a box on a pole, just next to the gate. Presumably visitors would have a code, or the box contained a voice link to a security post inside the buildings. If the ARCC kit had been working, and if anybody had been answering her calls, she could have used it to hack into the box and open the gate, but that wasn't an option now.

She was just about to move out of cover and see if she could use the same trick on the security fence as she had in the Falkland Islands, when something moved off to her left. She ducked behind a bush.

A security robot, identical to the ones she had seen in the Ahmya building in Tokyo, trotted steadily along the perimeter of the fence. *Outside* the fence, where she was. And in its hands it held a very large and very powerful machine gun.

CHAPTER THIRTEEN

The black-clad troops acted with military precision as they bundled Kieron towards one of their black SUVs and Sam into the other one. One of them expertly searched Kieron and took away both his own mobile phone and the burner he'd been using to talk to Bex and Bradley. Neither of the phones would help the kidnappers. The problem was that they had Kieron and Sam as well, and each of them could provide a *lot* of information.

But what would the kidnappers do to get that information? Would they hurt the two boys? Torture them? Or maybe threaten their families? Kieron wasn't sure how much physical pain he could handle before he broke down and told Avalon Richardson everything about Bex and Bradley – he needed full sedation when he visited the dentist, rather than just a local anaesthetic – and if anyone threatened his mum he would probably snap straight away. He couldn't let anything happen to her.

As Kieron was pushed into the back of his SUV he glanced across to the other one. Sam was looking at him. Their gazes locked, and what Kieron saw in Sam's expression was probably what Sam saw in his: fear and panic, but also a resolve to cause the bad guys as much grief as possible before the end. Whatever the end might be.

He glanced up at the dark facades of the houses. No curtains were twitching; nobody was silhouetted against the light, looking out at them, wondering what was happening. If anybody in there suspected that something was amiss outside, they were keeping it to themselves.

The rest of the troops piled in, and the cars pulled away from each other; driving backwards at speed until they got to either end of Sam's road, then reversing around the corners before setting off – both in the same direction, but on parallel roads. They seemed to be heading out of Newcastle.

It occurred to Kieron that the bad guys hadn't blindfolded him, or blocked his ears so he couldn't hear them talk. That was a bad sign. It probably meant that they didn't care what he saw or heard, which probably meant they didn't intend releasing him. Or Sam.

That was the pessimistic interpretation. The optimistic one was that when the bad guys had finished with the two of them they would just tell them that if they said anything, if they gave anything away to anyone else, their families would suffer.

Kieron decided to look on the bright side. Maybe they would both get out of there alive.

But what about Bex and Bradley?

Kieron's car drove for about ten minutes, then pulled off the road and into a car park that had once belonged to a discount warehouse. The place had closed down a few years before, and the tarmac of the car park was cracked, with weeds poking up through the gaps. The burnt-out skeleton of a car sat over by the graffiti-covered metal shutters of the warehouse. On the other side, by the fence that separated the car park from the train track, a massive articulated lorry had been parked – the kind that supermarkets use to get their goods to the stores. As well as the cab it had two large sections, separated by a kind of hinged bar that would allow it to go around corners – although Kieron reckoned they would have to be pretty wide corners. Small roundabouts would be completely impossible.

Both cars stopped, and their captors bundled the boys out and pushed them across to the rear of the lorry. The doors had been opened, and a set of metal steps led up from the ground into the back.

One of the kidnappers shoved Kieron towards the steps. When Kieron turned around to protest, the man pointed his weapon at him, then at the steps. The implication was obvious.

Kieron climbed up the steps, into the lorry, and Sam followed.

Kieron wasn't sure what he was going to find inside: stacks of shrink-wrapped boxes, perhaps? Slabs of meat hanging from hooks? What he *wasn't* expecting was a cross between a conference room and a control room, with the front section taken up with two rows of computers, and the back half occupied by a narrow table with chairs set along both sides. A mug, a flask and a dish with paper packets of sugar sat at the far end of the table, near where a woman sat. She wasn't looking at Kieron or Sam. In fact, she was turned to one side, studying the last in the row of computers that lined that end of the lorry.

'Please,' she said, not looking at them, 'take a seat.'

Kieron walked down one side of the table and Sam down the other, until they were halfway along, and then they sat. There wasn't much room between the backs of their chairs and the sides of the lorry.

Two of the troops entered the lorry and stood at the back. The steps retracted automatically, folding themselves up, and the doors swung closed. Somewhere up ahead an engine started, and the lights flickered momentarily.

'You have seen me before, I think,' the woman said, still looking at the screen in front of her. 'It was about a year ago, in the Newcastle Arts Centre. We spoke then, briefly, and again earlier today.' Finally she did look up, glancing from Kieron to Sam and back again. 'Yes,' she said, staring at Kieron, 'you, I think. I'm not sure why, but you look like you might be in charge. Your friend looks like a follower.'

'Hey!' Sam protested, but Kieron shushed him.

'Yes,' the woman said, smiling slightly as she finally turned to face them, 'as I thought.'

Tell them your name, rank and serial number and nothing else! Wasn't that what they always said to do in war films if you were caught by the enemy. The trouble was, Kieron didn't even want to give her his name. Instead, he kept quiet.

He could feel himself shivering. He made a fist with his left hand and then put his right hand over it, trying not to let Avalon Richardson see how scared he was.

The container they were in vibrated slightly. Although they couldn't see out, Kieron had the distinct impression that the lorry was moving. But where were they going? And why?

'I know that you are both working with Rebecca Wilson and Bradley Marshall,' the woman went on. 'I'm not sure what exactly you are doing for them, except that I know they have allowed you to use the Augmented Reality Computer Capability equipment – which, by the way, is top secret and shouldn't be demonstrated to anyone who isn't cleared.' She paused, looking again from Kieron to Sam and back. 'I think you already know that Rebecca and Bradley have gone significantly beyond their job remit. They are supposed to find and deal with threats to the United Kingdom. Instead they seem to have employed amateurs and turned their attentions to *me*.'

'Because *you're* a threat,' Kieron said. He'd meant to keep quiet, but there was something about Avalon Richardson's calm tone of voice, and the fact that she was talking about his friends, that forced him to speak.

'Blood and Soil,' she said, nodding. 'That group of fascist thugs. Stupid, but useful. Yes, I'd already assumed that the four of you had connected me to them. The only thing I need to know is: do Rebecca and Bradley know who I am? Do they actually know my identity?' She paused again. 'Actually, that isn't everything. I need to know if they are aware of my plans for the PEREGRINE satellite network. While we are at it, you can give me their current locations, and the locations of their ARCC equipment.'

'We won't tell you anything,' Sam said bravely.

My plans for the PEREGRINE satellite control network. Her words struck a chord in Kieron's mind. Did she mean what had happened in the Falkland Islands, and what was happening in Japan? Was she connected with that as well? It made some kind of sense that Avalon Richardson was working with the people who had attacked the control centre in the Falklands. They had taken control of PEREGRINE for her, but what did they get in return?

'You will.' There was something about the calm certainty of Avalon Richardson's voice that sent a chill down Kieron's back. 'I have various methods of persuading you to talk. I can hurt one of you until you decide to tell me what I need to know. I can hurt one of you until the *other* one decides to tell me what I need to know. I can threaten your families so that you both tell me at the same time, rushing to see who can get the information out first.' She shrugged. 'If I had more time there are drugs I could use that would destroy your willpower and your resistance, and then you would love to tell me of your own accord. Believe me, there isn't any method of torture devised by humanity in the past three thousand years that I wouldn't be prepared to use to get what I want out of you.'

Kieron deliberated and rebelliously looked past her, keeping his mouth tightly closed. He focused his gaze on the screen of the computer Avalon Richardson had been looking at when the two of them entered. He kept wondering where Bradley was. He knew that Bex was in Japan and couldn't possibly help, but Bradley was there in Newcastle.

But what could he do against Avalon Richardson and

her troops? He was only one man. One man with partially working ARCC glasses.

'Your choices are very limited at the moment,' Avalon Richardson said. 'You can either give me Rebecca's and Bradley's locations now and tell me how much they know about me, and so save yourselves a great deal of pain and, I am afraid, lasting damage. Or you can foolishly try to brave it out, in which case you will feel agony such as you have never experienced before, and you will leave here with, what I think they call on the television news, "life-changing injuries".'

To distract himself from the mental picture that Avalon Richardson was deliberately trying to create, Kieron focused hard on the computer screen that she had been looking at when they came in. Something about it looked familiar. He squinted, trying to make it out. Suddenly he felt a flood of familiarity followed by a rush of excitement, and it took a moment for his brain to catch up and let him work out why. The screen was showing something very similar to the initial information Kieron usually saw when he switched the ARCC glasses on! He glanced down to the table where the keyboard sat. Yes, just next to the mouse was a headset and microphone, probably connected to the computer. This was the terminal from which Avalon Richardson had managed to infiltrate the ARCC glasses and talk to him when Kieron had been wearing them earlier. Or, more probably, one of her team had done it. Kieron didn't think Avalon Richardson had the computer skills to create an avatar of Bex that would be realistic enough to fool him into giving up information.

His thoughts raced as he tried to work out how this new information could help.

If he assumed that the computer was still connected into his ARCC glasses – which Bradley now had – then he might be able to get Bradley's attention. If the satellites happened to be up and running. But to do that . . .

He glanced across at Sam. His friend had a fierce expression on his face, but beneath that Kieron knew he was scared. They had known each other for as long as Kieron could remember. Sam was his best friend and he was Sam's. They knew each other so well that they could finish each other's sentences and make each other laugh just by saying a single word that reminded them both of something funny in the past. They sometimes phoned the other one at the same time. When they were playing against each other in multiplayer computer games each of them instinctively knew what tactics the other one was going to use. They were *linked*.

He had to trust that link now.

Kieron caught Sam's eye. Sam looked at him, glanced away, then looked back when it was clear that Kieron was still staring at him.

'GamR BlamR,' he said cryptically, hoping that Sam would remember the YouTuber whose gaming channel they'd been addicted to for a while, and who they'd actually met in Venice a few weeks before.

Sam nodded cautiously. Avalon Richardson stared at Kieron oddly, as if he had just started uttering random words. Which, as far as she was concerned, he had.

'Timeslice!' he went on. The word would mean nothing to Avalon Richardson, but Sam would recognise it as the last game they'd been playing online together; Kieron in his bedroom and Sam in his.

Sam nodded again, intrigued.

'Plan Omega,' Kieron said. That was one of the many tactics he and Sam had agreed on when they were playing online as a team, against other players scattered across the world. Sam would make his character step out of where he was hiding and sprint across the terrain, while Kieron would stay in hiding with a sniper rifle and pick off anyone who started firing at Sam.

Plan Omega. It meant 'create a diversion'.

Sam grinned, then suddenly half stood up and collapsed across the table, shaking.

The two guards by the exit raised their weapons, expecting some kind of attack, but Sam slid off the table and onto the floor, babbling incoherently in a loud voice.

Avalon automatically sprang out of her chair and moved towards Sam. 'What's the matter?' she demanded.

'He's having a hypo!' Kieron shouted.

'A *what*?'

'A hypoglycemic attack. His blood sugar is too low. This happens when he gets stressed. You need to help him!'

'You!' Avalon pointed at the guard on the left. 'Get him back in his chair. We need to make sure he doesn't choke on his tongue. I'm damned if I'm going to let him die before I want him to!'

She moved closer to Sam, obviously concerned. For a

second Kieron found himself wondering if she had kids. He just automatically assumed that all bad guys lived alone, in some kind of impressive futuristic apartment, but maybe Avalon was married, with two kids and a dog. He almost – *almost* – felt a twinge of empathy for her, but he pushed it down until it surrendered. She'd been happy to torture him. She didn't deserve sympathy.

He got out of his chair and moved towards the computer screen he'd been looking at. Avalon's attention was directed at Sam. So was that of the guards.

As Avalon headed round the corner of the table, towards Sam, Kieron sidled up to the computer. It *was* showing the ARCC screen. He let his gaze slide over it, looking for anything different. Actually the whole thing looked slightly different, because it was solid. Kieron was used to seeing *through* the translucent text boxes and images on the ARCC glasses to whatever was beyond. Here there was no 'beyond'.

There! A communications menu, listing all the times recently that this program had been active, and who it had been communicating with. Kieron scanned through the information, listening out for what was happening behind him. It sounded like Sam was thrashing around, knocking chairs over and shouting out random words.

The program had communicated through PEREGRINE to something called 'ARCC-1' about two hours ago, for ten minutes. That was pretty much the same time Kieron had seen the faked image of Bex on the ARCC glasses.

Kieron checked quickly over his shoulder. One of the

guards was pulling Sam up into a chair while Avalon Richardson was tearing open packets of sugar from the dish on the table and pouring them into her mug. Presumably she was going to treat Sam's fake diabetes attack with a massive amount of sugar.

Turning his attention back to the screen, he reactivated the link to ARCC-1 via PEREGRINE. He looked frantically for anything labelled 'Input'. The box he needed was half hidden behind another one, and he frantically clicked on it to bring it to the front. He selected 'Microphone' from the list of things he could link the equipment to. A box opened with the question: *Transmit local audio over PEREGRINE link to ARCC-1?* He clicked on *Yes*, then turned around quickly and stepped closer to the table in case Avalon looked his way.

He was only just in time.

The guard had the mug of sugary coffee up to Sam's lips and was forcing him to drink it. Avalon Richardson, looking stressed, turned back to Kieron.

'Maybe I should have just let him have his attack, and held back the treatment until you told me what I want to know,' she said tersely.

'Why didn't you?' Kieron asked, taking a step sideways while she looked over at Sam.

She turned back to him. He expected her to say something about having a similar problem herself, or having a child who did, but instead she said, 'Too difficult to control. When I torture someone, I want to know exactly how much pain I can inflict. I'm not familiar enough with his condition to know how long I could withhold treatment.' She shook her head. 'Enough delays, enough wasting time. I have things to do.' She snapped her fingers at the trooper who hadn't been helping with Sam. 'Take him,' she said, pointing at Kieron. 'Open the back door, half-extend the ladder and hold him over the road. I want that tarmac going past right under his nose.'

Kieron felt as if the world had dropped out from beneath his feet. She was really going to do this?

Apparently she was. The trooper moved towards Kieron, weapon pointed at Kieron's stomach. He – or she; it was difficult to tell with the bulky black jumpsuit and the facemask – nodded towards the back of the lorry, then backed away so Kieron could get past.

Once Kieron was facing the metal shutter, the trooper pressed a large red button on a box next to the shutter's edge.

The shutter began to roll up, hiding itself somewhere in the roof of the lorry. Suddenly the noise of the lorry's tyres against the road became much louder. Kieron could smell diesel fumes. The shutter moved steadily and remorselessly. It was up to his waist by now, and the wind whipping past the lorry and swirling behind it caught Kieron's trousers and made them flap against his legs. He could feel the cold air outside nipping at his skin. The low pressure caused by the vortices of air swirling in the lorry's wake dragged at him like some huge but invisible creature trying to pull him to his doom.

He turned to look over his shoulder at Sam.

'Don't tell her anything,' he said bravely, but he didn't feel brave inside. Not at all.

The trooper pressed another large button on the control box and the metal steps unfolded from the floor in front of Kieron's feet, extending downwards until they hung about thirty centimetres above the road. And as the shutter rolled up even higher Kieron could see the road itself; grey and blotchy, whipping past in a blur. Off to his right, white road markings flashed by; there, gone, there, gone . . .

The shutter retracted above his head, and he saw the surface of the road, extending away from the lorry. He'd hoped there might be a car following them that he could signal to, but the road was empty. Presumably Avalon Richardson had deliberately chosen a section that hardly saw any traffic. Maybe they were even on a deserted army base, off the beaten track and away from prying eyes. He tried to get sight of any buildings as they flashed past. They might have been old army huts, or farm outbuildings; he couldn't tell.

The wind plucked at his jacket and sucked the warmth from his hands. The edge of the lorry's floor and the first metal step were only half a metre away.

Something struck him between his shoulder blades and he fell forward. He tried to catch himself, to get his leg underneath him to prevent himself falling out of the lorry, but it was too late; his foot went right over the edge at the back, and by the time it hit that first step his weight would be too far forward and he would tumble out and hit the road. And probably die; scraped along the rough tarmac like a tomato on a kitchen grater.

A hand caught the back of his collar, stopping him from falling. He hung there, half in and half out of the lorry. He imagined his body was a perfect diagonal line, suspended by the hand of the trooper behind him. No going forward; no going back.

'How much do Rebecca Wilson and Bradley Marshall know about me?' Avalon Richardson's voice shouted above the roar of the wind. Kieron could hardly hear her. 'Either of you can answer.'

Kieron wasn't sure he *could* answer, even if he wanted to. It was hard enough to breathe, with the air being pulled from his lungs every time he opened his mouth. If he tried to speak his words would just be whipped away by the wind.

'I will ask again,' Avalon said, 'and then I will count backwards from ten. On zero the grip on the back of your friend's collar will be released, and he will tumble out to an unpleasant and very messy death. So, tell me: how much do Rebecca Wilson and Bradley Marshall know about me?'

Half of Kieron's brain was begging Sam not to answer, while the other half was begging him *to* answer so that Kieron didn't have to.

'Ten . . .' Avalon said calmly. 'Nine . . .'

This couldn't be it, Kieron thought despairingly. This couldn't be how it all ended.

'Eight . . . seven . . .'

There was so much he wanted to do with his life. Well, he didn't know quite what it all was, but he knew there were loads of things he would be missing out on if he died now.

'Six . . . five . . .'

And Beth. He'd only just *got* a girlfriend; he couldn't lose her now!

The grip on the back of his collar suddenly vanished. He fell forward, gasping so much that he couldn't even cry out. The road in front of him blurred.

The grip came back, almost choking him. He was nearly horizontal now, looking down at the steps and the grey tarmac. The trooper holding him was incredibly strong. Kieron guessed he must be holding onto a strap or a bar or something.

'That was just for fun,' Avalon said. 'Now answer the question. Four . . . three . . .'

Kieron opened his mouth to shout the answer as loudly as he could – and then shut it again. He couldn't betray Bex or Bradley. Not even if it cost him his life. He knew – knew for certain – that they would risk their lives for him. He had to do the same.

'Two . . . one . . .'

Still nothing from Sam. Kieron felt a warmth flow through him, and a strength. If his last memory, his last thought, was one of friendship, then so be it. What a way to go.

The roar in his ears suddenly became louder. He glanced up, shocked, as something moved in the corner of his vision. A car – no, a flatbed utility truck! – had suddenly slewed in from a side road and joined the road the lorry was pounding along. It settled in right behind the lorry, barely a metre away. Kieron stared at the windscreen. It took him a moment to realise that Bradley was driving. His expression was as fierce and determined as Kieron had ever seen it.

There was no way the three of them could coordinate their actions. What happened next was a combination of coincidence and hope; three people acting independently towards a single end result.

Bradley sent the ute into a handbrake turn. Amid squealing rubber, purple smoke and the smell of burning he managed to skid the vehicle through 180 degrees *and* slam it into reverse, so that he was still behind the lorry but travelling *backwards*. How long he could keep that up for, Kieron had no idea. Kieron found himself looking into the ute's rear end: a flat wooden bed surrounded by slats. And the gate at the back was down!

Sam, meanwhile, must have suddenly run full pelt at the trooper holding Kieron, because the man's grip loosened, and his whole weight hit Kieron in the back. He and the trooper tumbled out of the back of the speeding lorry –

– And fell into the flatbed of the truck.

Despite the bruises and scrapes Kieron had received, he knew exactly what had happened – and exactly what *would* happen if he didn't act quickly. Bradley was still driving backwards, but that wasn't a viable long-term strategy. He would have to turn around, and that could send Kieron sliding and falling onto the road. He had to act.

Kieron was lying on his front, feeling wooden splinters from the flatbed digging into his hands. He wormed his way onto his back, and stared ahead of him in shock.

Directly in front of him, the trooper was trying to climb to his feet. Just off to his right, Sam clung to the wooden slats on the side of the van. He must have fallen out behind the trooper and Kieron. And a few metres away, from inside the open back of the lorry, Avalon Richardson stared with grim disbelief.

Kieron did what he had to. He kicked the trooper in the middle of his facemask. The man fell backwards, screaming and clawing at the air, but Bradley was slowing down now and the trooper's momentum carried him onto the metal steps at the rear of the lorry. He bounced off and vanished sideways.

Sam slithered down the wooden slats to the end of the truck, reached down with one hand and hauled the tailgate up. It clicked into place automatically.

Kieron grabbed hold of the side as Bradley skidded backwards to a halt, then threw the gears into 'forward' and started to speed away. Kieron could hear his *whoop* of triumph even above the squealing of the tyres.

'Please tell me you were filming that!' Sam shouted, grinning.

'No,' Kieron shouted back, 'but I'll remember it for as long as I live.' He stared at his friend for a moment. 'Thanks, mate.'

'No probs.' Sam gave a little salute with a free hand. 'Just goes to show that I really do have your back!'

CHAPTER FOURTEEN

Bex crouched under cover of a bush and watched as the robot sentry lumbered past.

It looked like something from one of Bradley's sci-fi films, something that intended taking over the world and wiping out all humans. Despite telling herself that it was just a collection of metal and plastic parts all connected together and moving around according to the dictates of a computer program running in its memory, Bex couldn't help thinking of it as something *alive*, even *alien*. Maybe it was the way that it had to steady itself every now and then, when it put its mechanical foot on a slippery patch of wet vegetation or a stone that moved beneath it. Or maybe it was the way its head moved to track aircraft flying high above them or suddenly twitched as it detected the movement of a flurry of leaves disturbed by the wind and made a decision about whether or not it was safe to proceed.

Bex had two problems; she had to get past the robot – and its friends – and she had to get inside the Ahmya complex. She smiled as she remembered the many times her dad had said to her, 'Sometimes, kid, a problem is just a solution looked at from the wrong angle.' As a child she had never quite grasped what he meant, but as an adult she realised the truth of his words. So maybe the robot was actually the key to getting inside the complex, rather than an obstacle to be overcome.

She had an idea, but she needed to test it.

As the robot reached its closest point to her on its sentry round, Bex prepared to act. At a moment when the robot's head was facing directly away from her she stood up and threw her rucksack at it, then ducked back into cover. The straps on the rucksack caught on one of a series of sharp metal spikes that seemed to be designed to stop people jumping on the robot's back, and hung there, swinging back and forth. The weight of the rucksack shifted the robot's centre of gravity slightly, and it had to trot sideways a couple of steps to recover its balance. The key thing from Bex's point of view was that it didn't bother twisting its neck or turning its head to see what had landed on it. It probably didn't even *know* that something had landed on it; there were no sensors on the outside that would pick up impacts. Why would there be?

She glanced around. There were no other robot sentries around to spot her.

She picked up a stone the size of a cricket ball and threw it over the robot's head. It landed about ten metres beyond the robot, making an audible *chink* as it hit another stone. Even better, it scared a bird that had been perched in a nearby bush. The bird took off in a flurry of feathers, making a whirring noise as it flew. The robot stopped walking and turned its head to track the bird.

While it was doing that, Bex snuck up, rolled underneath it and reached around its sides. Her fingers managed to locate places on the robot's flanks where two of the curved plastic panels that formed its 'skin' came together. She held on tight, pulling herself up so that her face was pressed against the 'chest' of the robot, then swung her legs up and wrapped them around its 'belly'. Her entire body was now hanging beneath the thing.

It started to walk off again.

The robot's four-legged gait meant that Bex's body swung back and forth as it moved. Her fingers managed to keep their grip on the edge of the plastic panels on its sides, but her arm muscles were burning. Fortunately the plastic side panels didn't glide together as the robot walked; that would have crushed Bex's fingers entirely. She had checked that out from a distance, but her weight might have changed things. Sometimes you just had to take a chance.

She couldn't stay hanging there for long – her strength wouldn't hold out. The robot would patrol the boundary fence unless Bex changed its behaviour – and she thought she knew how.

Just beside her head she could see the bulky mechanical joint of the robot's right front leg through the plastic panels covering its flanks. As well as the joint there were wires, and plastic tubes of hydraulic fluid. Tentatively, she let go of the side panel with her left hand. Her entire weight was now on her legs and her right hand, so she had to make this quick. She reached into the gap between the flank panels, to where the joint was hidden, and quickly pulled

261

one of the wires away from its connection.

There were no sparks, but the robot's entire body seemed to twitch. Bex had ridden horses when she was a child, and this was the way they reacted when bitten by a horsefly. She had caused the robot irritation.

It paused in its patrol, almost as if it was thinking. Bex hoped that, somewhere in its programming, a line of code had been activated that said something like: *When damage is detected, return to workshop for repairs.*

It occurred to her that the line of code might actually say: *When damage is detected, send alarm signal and wait for mechanic to arrive.* That would be a problem.

She returned the fingers of her left hand to their previous position; curled around the edge of a plastic panel on the robot's flank. Her right arm, which had been insistently trying to tell her that it was hurting, now told her it wasn't hurting *quite* so much.

The robot paused . . . and then, as if it had made a sudden decision, it turned around and trotted at speed back in the direction it had come, towards the main gate that led into the complex.

The jolting of this new mode of travel sent spears of pain through Bex's legs and arms. She couldn't even *feel* her fingers now; they were clamped so hard to the edges of the side panels that the circulation had been cut off.

Something moved at the edge of her vision. She turned her head. Another robot had come up alongside the one she hung beneath. For a moment she thought it had seen her, but then she heard the grating of the gate opening and she realised that the new robot had come to make sure that nobody snuck through the gate after the damaged one. Little did it know . . .

The grass inside the compound was shorter than outside; obviously regularly trimmed. Probably by robot lawnmowers. The ground was more even as well, which meant that Bex wasn't being jolted quite so much as the robot moved.

She craned her head, trying to work out what was happening. The robot seemed to be heading for a white section of wall on the circular compound building. As it got closer she saw the outlines of a door; one that slid open to let the robot pass through.

And she still hadn't seen a single human being.

They entered a wide white corridor, and the door slid closed behind them. The robot's clawed feet clicked on gleaming tiles, and the clicks echoed off the smooth white walls, sounding like a swarm of invisible crickets. She swung her head around, trying to see if anyone else was there, or any other robots, but the wide corridor seemed to be completely empty apart from her and her steed. If you could call it a steed, considering she was hanging underneath it.

She had no reason to stay on the robot. It was almost certainly heading for a workshop, which she had no reason to want to visit. She released her grip, and fell the metre or so to the hard floor. Quickly she pulled herself into a ball, hoping that the robot wouldn't step on her with its back legs. It didn't, and as it continued blithely onwards she stood up and tried to shake some life and feeling back into her hands. Her thighs ached with the effort of holding onto the robot's side.

She looked around. No people, no robots, and no signs either. Just white walls, white ceiling and white floor which joined together not at right angles but with a curve, which meant there were no perspective lines that she could follow. Concealed lighting as well, which made everything seem to glow too brightly. There was nowhere to hide. She felt like a cockroach in a neon tube.

To her left was the door leading outside. To her right was the corridor down which the robot was trotting. She didn't really have much choice, so she followed it.

After a hundred metres or so they came to a junction. The robot turned left and headed off that way. Bex stared ahead, then off to the right. Still no signs. Nothing to show her the way. This wasn't going well. A map would have been nice. Or some notices hanging from the ceiling, with helpful arrows. Or maybe coloured lines on the floor leading to the various destinations.

This place was pretty obviously part of Ito Aritomo's commercial robotics empire, rather than his religious cult activities.

Shrugging, she walked straight ahead. She didn't really have a choice. She could check every room until she found the satellite control centre, or she could head up to the top of the complex and destroy the communications dishes in the geodesic domes. That would be a crude solution, but it would be effective. The PEREGRINE network would be safe from interference.

A door, previously hidden by the white glow of the concealed lights, suddenly slid open as she passed. She froze. Another robot emerged into the corridor, but this was a different type. The top of its back was flat, and it didn't carry a weapon like the robot sentries had. On top of it were several boxes, secured by clamps. A delivery robot? That seemed likely. It trotted past without seeming to notice her. Maybe if you got past the sentry robots, then any other robots assumed you had a perfect right to be there.

Before the door silently slid closed again, Bex had a brief glimpse of what looked like an automated production point in the room beyond. Robotic arms hanging from the ceiling were constructing something; reaching out and grabbing components from racks on the walls and fitting them together. It looked as if they were making a robot. Robots making robots . . . Was this, she thought with a shiver, the future? Was there *anybody* human here?

Ten metres further on, she got an answer to her question. Another hidden white door slid noiselessly open, but this time the two sentry robots that emerged into the corridor were both staring directly at her through glass lenses. They moved out into the corridor, aiming their weapons at her head.

'You can't fire,' she said, trying to sound brave even though her stomach had turned to ice. 'Any blood would spoil the minimalist aesthetic you have going on here.'

'Blood would be contamination,' a voice said behind her, 'and I do not like contamination of any kind.'

Bex turned around – slowly.

A door in the opposite wall had opened, and *something*

had come through. For a few seconds Bex wasn't sure whether it was a robot or a person in some kind of vehicle, and then she realised that it was both.

The man she faced was hugely obese, to the point where he probably couldn't walk unaided. He didn't have to, though, because he sat cross-legged in a transparent bubble that was being carried around by a type of robot Bex hadn't seen before. This one had eight legs, like a spider, and no head. It was basically just a platform on legs. Its passenger had black hair, pulled back behind his pumpkin-sized head, and a black beard and moustache that drooped down onto his chest. He wore a white robe that had a single image of a black drop of water over where his heart would be. He held something like a complex game controller, which Bex assumed connected him with a mainframe computer somewhere, and with the robots.

'Ito Aritomo, I presume,' Bex said. She glanced around. 'I like what you've done with the place.'

'Rebecca Wilson,' Aritomo said. His voice was thin and high, almost like a penny whistle. 'I was warned you might be coming here.'

'You are trying to take over the PEREGRINE satellite network,' she said. As she spoke, she slipped her hands casually into her pockets. Maybe she had something in there she could use. 'My ARCC network depends on the PEREGRINE satellites to operate. I can't let you take the system down.'

'I'm not trying to take the system down,' Ito said, staring at her curiously. 'I am trying to use it.'

The only thing Bex could find in her pockets was the ARCC glasses. She hadn't been wearing them because either the network had been down or Kieron and Bradley hadn't been active at the other end, but maybe, just maybe, if the stars were all aligned and she had walked past enough four-leaf clovers on her journey, they might be there for her now. So she slipped the glasses on, trying to make the movement look perfectly ordinary.

'Forgive me,' Aritomo said, raising a hand, 'but there is something I need to do. This may cause you a little discomfort.'

An articulated arm with several joints unfolded from behind Aritomo's transparent bubble, arcing over his head like a scorpion's tail. Bex just had enough time to see that it ended in a nozzle rather than a claw before it emitted a spray of liquid at her. The droplets were tiny, almost a mist, and they felt cold on her skin. She closed her eyes automatically, and raised her hands to try to ward off the liquid, but it seemed to sink into her clothes and her skin. It gave off a sharp odour, like something you might smell in a hospital.

'Please turn around,' Aritomo said. 'If you do not, I will tell one of my robots to turn you around, and it will not be gentle.'

Bex did as she was instructed.

Facing Aritomo again, she dropped her hands to her sides. 'I'm guessing disinfectant,' she said, detecting as she did so the sharp, hospital taste on her lips. 'You seem like the sort of man who is terrified of germs and bugs and stuff like that.'

'I am,' he said. 'I also do not like people very much. They have their uses, and they make money for me – both through my robotics company and through my religion – but I do not like them. People are messy and unpredictable.'

'Todd Zanderbergen!' Bex said suddenly. She reached up and tapped her forehead theatrically, but her real aim was to turn the ARCC glasses on. Just in case. 'He was a bit like you. He developed a way to selectively kill people who had particular genes in their DNA.'

'I am aware of Mr Zanderbergen. His ideas were interesting, but DNA is a clumsy tool to use for such delicate work. Too much can go wrong. My idea is far better.'

Bex felt a sinking feeling in the pit of her stomach. '*Your* idea? I'm guessing that's what you need the PEREGRINE satellite network for?'

'Building and launching my own satellites would have taken too long, and cost too much,' he said, smiling. 'Using a network that someone else has built is far more efficient, and I like efficiency. Efficient and clean. That is the way I live my life.'

'This guy is seriously insane,' Kieron's voice said in her ear. 'He's working with Avalon Richardson, by the way. Or for her. I'm not sure exactly.'

Bex tried not to jump in surprise, but she couldn't help smiling, just a little bit. The ARCC system was alive – for the moment – and her friends were alive as well. The world seemed a lot rosier than it had just a moment before.

Aritomo's face creased into a frown. He had seen her smile, and misinterpreted it. 'You laugh at me, but I am the future – me, and people like me. We can sweep away all those people who do not agree with us, or who will not do what we say.'

'Look, we've obviously got a lot of catching up to do,' Kieron said in her ear from thousands of miles away, 'but the important thing is that Bradley, Sam and I are safe, and we've probably got half an hour of ARCC time before the network goes down again. The guys in the Falklands control centre are doing a great job keeping it up, but your madman there is doing an equally thorough job of taking it down again. So, if you can – who is he and where are you?'

'But it's just you, isn't it, Ito Aritomo?' Bex asked, goading the man but also making sure Kieron had the information he needed. 'Just you, here in your Tochigi facility. What can you do by yourself? You and your robots – you can't fight the entire world.'

'The liquid you were sprayed with *is* a disinfectant, you were right,' Aritomo said, still scowling, 'but it had something else added to it. Did you know that some chemicals are asymmetrical? They have a left-handed or a right-handed molecular form. Sometimes those two forms have the same chemical qualities, but sometimes they are different.'

'It's called "chirality",' Kieron said. 'I remember it from chemistry lessons.'

'The substance you have been sprayed with,' Aritomo continued, 'is innocuous in its left-hand state, but poisonous in its right-hand state. You have been sprayed with the innocuous version, and it has been absorbed through your skin into your flesh.'

'So you *haven't* poisoned me,' Bex said, confused.

'Not yet.' He smiled suddenly, and his wide, round face seemed to light up, like a child's. 'But this molecule can be "switched" from one form to the other with a simple radio signal. That energy, at a particular frequency, flips the molecule over. Imagine what would happen if water reservoirs in a particular country were contaminated with this chemical, or water bottles sold in supermarkets in a chosen city or two contained traces of it!'

'A poison you could switch on or off whenever you wanted to?' Bex said. The rosy glow that had flooded her body when she heard Kieron's voice had vanished now, replaced by a sick dread. 'That's madness.'

'That is control,' Aritomo said proudly. 'I now control you, and with the PEREGRINE satellite network I can control everyone in the world.'

'And how are you, in your little transparent bubble there, going to get that poison out to all those communities?' Bex asked, though she had already worked that out. The answer was obvious.

'I have a religious cult with ten thousand members,' Aritomo said proudly. 'They will take my poison everywhere, across the world, for me, and they will not question why.'

'I'm questioning why.' Bex shook her head. 'Is it money you want? Blackmailing towns and cities for cash, otherwise you kill them? Or will you sell your services to people like Avalon Richardson so they can get rid of people they think are somehow weaker, less "human" than they are?'

Aritomo's expression flickered at the mention of Avalon Richardson's name. 'You have made some clever connections,' he said. 'Clever, and for you very dangerous.'

'So help me understand this,' Bex said. 'You control the PEREGRINE network from here, and because it's a global network of seventy-six satellites, there will always be several directly above wherever it is that you want to poison, and you can transmit your switching signal.'

'Exactly.'

'But PEREGRINE currently runs the ARCC system.'

Aritomo shrugged, a slow rippling of his bulky body. 'I have no interest in your ARCC.'

'No,' Bex said, 'but I was thinking, if ARCC transmits through PEREGRINE, and PEREGRINE is connected to your satellite control station here, then ARCC can get into your main computer.'

Aritomo frowned at her in puzzlement, but then his eyes widened in shock. He quickly started typing something into the controller he held. The eight-legged robotic body that carried him around took several steps backwards.

'Funny,' Kieron said in her ear, via the tiny loudspeaker in the ARCC glasses, 'but exactly the same thought had occurred to me.'

Something went *bang!* behind Bex. She whirled around, to see that one of the two robot sentries that had been guarding her had shot the other in the leg.

'Just getting the hang of this,' Kieron muttered. 'Bear with me.'

The second sentry, teetering on three legs, brought its own

weapon up and fired a sustained burst of ammunition at its attacker. The head of the first robot exploded in flames and shards of glass and metal.

'What are you *doing*?' Aritomo screamed.

Bex grinned. 'I'm not doing anything. You may not like people, but I love them. One boy in England in particular. He's very quick on the uptake.'

'Your user interface makes it easy to control anything,' Kieron's voice said. Bex could hear the glee in his voice. 'And you ain't seen *nothin'* yet!'

'Stop! Please stop!' Aritomo was punching instructions into his controller, but they weren't having any effect. Instead, the three-legged robot had turned its weapon towards Aritomo's own robot transporter. As he desperately tried to get himself out of the way, the robot calmly and precisely shot out the transporter's legs, one by one. It crashed to the floor, with Aritomo screaming inside. Massive cracks spread across the bubble canopy that protected him from the world.

'And for an encore –' Kieron said.

Bex heard clicking coming from both directions of the corridor. Lots of clicking. If one robot's claws hitting the white ceramic of the floor had sounded like a swarm, this was a megaswarm. A swarm of swarms.

Robots appeared around corners Bex hadn't even seen in the sterile white glow of the complex's lighting system. Some were sentries, some were transporter robots, and some were types she hadn't seen before – cleaners, maybe, sterilisers, lifters and hefters. Rather than turn and run down the corridor towards Bex and Aritomo, however, they headed for each other in a wave of metal and plastic, colliding in a massive act of mindless robotic violence. Some of them just smashed into pieces, with arms and legs and heads flying off in all directions, but others must have ruptured whatever batteries or fuel sources they contained. Those ones exploded into flames.

Smoke billowed down the corridor towards Bex, but suddenly sprinklers appeared from hidden holes in the ceiling and sprayed water across the burning mechanisms, while huge fans buried in the walls started up and sucked the smoke away.

An explosion from above Bex's head made the ground shake. She looked upwards.

'That, if I am not mistaken,' she said casually to Aritomo, 'is your satellite control room, or possibly your computer mainframe.'

'Both,' Kieron confirmed. 'There's lots of robots up there as well. OK, not so many now, and the number is going down rapidly.' He giggled. 'This is great. It's like a computer game but real!'

Bex walked forward to where Ito Aritomo lay on his back amid the wreckage of his transporter robot. The broken bubble canopy around him looked like the remains of some giant egg.

Aritomo stared at her in horror. 'What . . . what are you going to do?' he moaned.

'Don't worry, I'm not going to touch you. I know you don't like that.' Bex reached down and picked up the scorpion-like tail of his robot, which trailed pathetically from underneath the metallic carcass – the device that had sprayed her with disinfectant and a harmless substance that, with just a simple command and a radio signal, could have been transformed into a poison. The liquid was still pumping weakly from the nozzle at the end, draining the tanks inside the robot.

Bex picked up the nozzle and held it over Aritomo's head. Disinfectant – and harmless poison – splattered on his hair and face.

'Now you are just as vulnerable as you wanted us to be,' Bex said calmly to him. 'How does it feel?'

CHAPTER FIFTEEN

'So what exactly is this thing?' Bex asked, staring dubiously at the glass Kieron had handed to her.

Kieron smiled. 'It's a milkshake,' he said, 'but it's made with one of those chocolate cream egg things you can get, all mashed up in a food blender with ice cream and milk.'

'It's a heart attack in a waxed cardboard cup, that's what it is,' she said, but she sipped at it experimentally.

They were at Manchester Airport, having met Bex's flight back from Tokyo. There hadn't been much chance to talk before she had taken off; although the Ahmya satellite control station had been largely destroyed, thanks to Kieron's attempt to turn the complex into a robotic mosh-pit, it was still taking the Falklands control station some time to regain control of all the satellites, and the ARCC kit was still a little flaky.

Bradley and Sam stood beside Kieron. They all had large smiles on their faces, smiles that had been there pretty much since Bradley had rescued them from Avalon Richardson's troopers. He had told them that he'd seen the two boys being taken prisoner, hot-wired the nearest vehicle – a flatbed utility truck – and followed them at a distance. When he saw Kieron being dangled out of the rear of Avalon Richardson's lorry he had decided to take his chance, and driven up behind them. The rest had been luck, and the kind of shared thinking that good friends could sometimes achieve.

'I'm going to have to introduce you to the idea of a carrot-and-ginger smoothie,' Bex said, smiling, 'but right at the moment I need the blood sugar. First, though: Sam, hold this for me.' She passed the cup to Sam, then stepped forward and hugged Kieron. He felt his face turning red, but he didn't try to squirm out of her embrace. Not too hard, anyway.

'Thank you,' she said, holding him at arm's length and staring into his eyes. 'For saving me.' She took the cup from Sam and gave it to Bradley, then hugged Sam. 'And thank you for saving him.'

'People are staring!' Sam complained.

'It's an airport. Everybody hugs.' Bex released him, then took the smoothie cup from Bradley and gave it to Kieron. 'Hold this for me.'

'Do we have to?' Bradley asked, but she grabbed him and hugged him too. 'Thank you for saving both of them.'

'We save each other,' he said, his voice muffled by her hair. 'That's what we do.'

Bex released him, and took the cup back from Kieron. She looked at each of them in turn, and Kieron saw that she had her 'serious' face on.

'This isn't the end though,' she said. 'We still have Avalon

Richardson to worry about – and she's shown a distinct desire to kill lots of people from races or religions that she doesn't like.'

'Actually,' Bradley said, 'maybe we don't have to worry quite that much.'

Bex frowned. 'What have you done?'

'Well,' Bradley started, 'Kieron turned on the ARCC program that Avalon had running on her computer, and started it transmitting everything that she said –'

'And Bradley, while he was driving to rescue us, set his end of the ARCC kit up to record and store all of that information,' Kieron went on.

Bex looked at Sam. 'What did they do?' she asked. 'Tell me the truth.'

'Well,' he said nervously, 'even though Bradley had rescued us, we knew that it was only a temporary thing. Avalon Richardson would still be after you, and us. So –'

'So while we had an operational ARCC window,' Kieron continued, 'we sent out the recording. To everyone in the MI6 contact book, everyone in the MI5 contact book, everyone at the Ministry of Defence and every MP. They all received a recording of her explaining how she was going to torture two boys for information.'

'She was arrested ten hours ago,' Bradley went on. 'She's in custody now. Obviously nobody can work out *our* identities from the recording, and I don't think Avalon will be saying very much, but I've managed to scrub all references to us from her system. We are whiter than white.'

Bex stared into the distance for a while. Kieron, Sam

and Bradley shifted nervously, wondering what she was going to say.

'OK,' she said eventually. 'We may just be in the clear. Good work.'

'Team effort,' Bradley said. 'I couldn't have done it without you guys.'

'Oh,' Bex said suddenly, 'that reminds me. I did some work on the plane, and managed to send some emails and splash some money around. You guys can finally go professional.'

Kieron felt a warm glow sweep through his body. 'As agents?' he asked hopefully.

'Absolutely not,' Bex said. 'As computer-repair technicians. I've set up a company for you, a website and a payroll, and I've rented office space near where you live. Congratulations, guys. You are now the proud co-directors of K&S Computer Repairs.'

'K&S?' Sam queried. 'Not S&K?'

'No,' Bex said. 'K&S.'

Kieron glanced at Sam, and smiled. Sam smiled back. They may not have been agents, but at least they had their own company.

'We need to get advertising,' he said. 'We need to get customers.'

'Oh,' Bex said casually, 'I've got you your first contract.'

'You have?' Sam sounded cautious.

'Yes.' Bex looked from Sam to Kieron, and then at Bradley. 'You are now the official tech support for Bradley and me.'

'We're staying in Newcastle, then?' Bradley asked, smiling.

'For the foreseeable future,' Bex replied. 'After all, we have friends here.'

ANDREW LANE

Andrew Lane is a popular and much-loved writer for teens and young adults. He is the author of the Young Sherlock Holmes series, which has been published in forty-four countries. He has also worked extensively in the extended universe of BBC TV's *Doctor Who*, and has written three adult crime novels under a pseudonym.

Before becoming a writer, Andrew spent twenty-seven years working for the Ministry of Defence on the fringes of the Intelligence and Counter-terrorism communities. He has been inside several classified intelligence headquarters in the UK and US (and not as a tourist).

Piccadilly

P R E S S

Thank you for choosing a Piccadilly Press book.

If you would like to know more about our
authors, our books or if you'd just like to know
what we're up to, you can find us online.

www.piccadillypress.co.uk

And you can also find us on:

We hope to see you soon!